W9-BNG-084

BOOK SOLD
NO LONGER R H P.L.
PROPERTY

RICHMOND HILL
PUBLIC LIBRARY

APR 22 2015

CENTRAL LIBRARY
905-884-9288

THE GIVEN WORLD

MARIAN PALAIA

SIMON & SCHUSTER

NEW YORK   LONDON   TORONTO   SYDNEY   NEW DELHI

Simon & Schuster
1230 Avenue of the Americas
New York, NY 10020

RICHMOND HILL
PUBLIC LIBRARY

APR 22 2015

CENTRAL LIBRARY
905 884 9288

This book is a work of fiction. Any references to historical events, real people, or real places are used fictitiously. Other names, characters, places, and events are products of the author's imagination, and any resemblance to actual events or places or persons, living or dead, is entirely coincidental.

Copyright © 2015 by Marian Palaia

Portions of this novel were first published in slightly different form: "Prologue" and "Two Days, Then the Bus to Cambodia" were published as "Cu Chi" in *Virginia Quarterly Review*, Fall 2012. "Take You Back Broken" was published in *TriQuarterly* as "The Last Place She Stood" in Spring 2013. "Girl, Three Speeds, Pretty Good Brakes" was published in *Passages North*, Spring, 2003.

Jane Hirshfield, "At Night," from *Of Gravity & Angels*, © 1988 by Jane Hirshfield, reprinted by permission of Wesleyan University Press.

Excerpt from "I-Feel-Like-I'm-Fixin'-to-Die Rag," by Country Joe and the Fish, words and music by Joe McDonald, © 1965, renewed 1993 by Alcatraz Corner Music Co. BMI, reprinted by permission.

All rights reserved, including the right to reproduce this book or portions thereof in any form whatsoever. For information, address Simon & Schuster Subsidiary Rights Department, 1230 Avenue of the Americas, New York, NY 10020.

First Simon & Schuster hardcover edition April 2015

SIMON & SCHUSTER and colophon are registered trademarks of Simon & Schuster, Inc.

For information about special discounts for bulk purchases, please contact Simon & Schuster Special Sales at 1-866-506-1949 or business@simonandschuster.com.

The Simon & Schuster Speakers Bureau can bring authors to your live event. For more information or to book an event, contact the Simon & Schuster Speakers Bureau at 1-866-248-3049 or visit our website at www.simonspeakers.com.

Interior design by Akasha Archer

Manufactured in the United States of America

10   9   8   7   6   5   4   3   2   1

Library of Congress Cataloging-in-Publication Data
Palaia, Marian.
   The given world / Marian Palaia.—First Simon & Schuster hardcover edition.
      pages   cm
   1. Young women—Fiction.   2. Brothers and sisters—Fiction.   3. Missing persons—Fiction.   4. Vietnam War, 1961–1975—Veterans—Fiction.   I. Title.
   PS3616.A33865G58   2015
   813'.6—dc23

ISBN   978-1-4767-7793-1
ISBN   978-1-4767-7805-1 (ebook)

For my mother, Dusty, without whose grace, generosity, and tenacity no one in this family would have gotten very far.

In memory of my father, Joe, for first chances, and Mom's Jack for second ones.

For Carl. We are so grateful to you.

And for my uncle, Jim, for going and for coming back.

At Night

it is best
to focus your eyes
a little off to one side;
it is better to know things
drained of their color, to fathom
the black horses cropping
at winter grass,
their white jaws that move
in steady rotation, a sweet sound.

And when they file off to shelter
under the trees
you will find the pale circles of snow
pushed aside, earth opening
its single, steadfast gaze:
towards stars ticking by, one by one, overhead,
the given world flaming precisely out of its frame.

—Jane Hirshfield

CONTENTS

THE GIVEN
WORLD

PROLOGUE

Jasper says this is the kind of heat that makes people in Australia shoot each other. Or stab. Strangle. Run over. Whatever. But we are not in Australia. We are in a once-infamous city whose inhabitants still call it Saigon. It has not rained in months, but tonight it will, and the rain will go more or less unmentioned but not unnoticed. It will still be hot, but the relief will be palpable. In Australia, they will stop killing each other, but only if they get some rain there too.

We have been waiting—playing pool and drinking beer and sometimes, when we can't take it anymore, finding air-conditioned places that will let us in. In those places, you pay the usual dollar for a 333 beer; two more dollars for the air. The Caravelle is one of those places, and the Rex, and now these fancy new restaurants appearing block by block, almost overnight. There is a swimming pool on the roof of the Rex, and it is often full of corpulent Russian tourists, suntanned like scraped cowhide. They are loud, and they never come to the Lotus. This is our bar. No air-con. Rats the size of puppies, but they stay in the dark corners, usually, until closing time.

The government here is renting Jasper from Australia so he can teach young Vietnamese pilots how to fly passenger planes. He is part of a contingent of Qantas boys—another of whom has managed to woo me into bed, which really didn't require all that much effort. This other one looks vaguely like Jim Morrison and has a room at the Rex, with air-con and a bathtub. We are not in love; not by a long shot. If he were one of the French boys, maybe I would be in love. The Aussie is mainly in love with himself, but the bathtub is nice. It slows down the process of going crazy.

Back in February, during Tet, Jasper drank so much it almost killed him and they had to send him home. The day after the hospital set him loose, I waited on the steps of the Rex with him while they put his gear in a cab. He didn't want to go. He'd found his place. He was almost in tears; big, broad-shouldered, rowdy Cairns bruiser, barely able to get the words out.

"Nothing for me there," he said. "I shouldn't have done it."

"It was in the air," I said. "Couldn't be helped." He patted my shoulder. The street was still littered with mounds of pink paper from the millions of firecrackers that had gone off nonstop for three days.

They let him come back last week; he promised to behave. If he fucks up this time, he goes home for good. A little while ago he headed across the street to the Apocalypse Now, a serious bar where people go to get seriously drunk.

He was shaky, even after three beers. I won't see him come
out. I won't see him ever again.

It's slow tonight, and since she is not needed to flirt and
serve drinks, Phượng and I are hanging out at the front
window. It is octagonal and quite large—maybe six or eight
feet across—and contains not a bit of glass. The sill is fairly
wide, meaning a person could sit on it if she were so inclined, and often I can be found perched there, gecko-like,
trying to blend in. At last call, Tho, the bartender, will close
the rusted aluminum accordion shutters and latch them
with a heavy round padlock the diameter of a dessert plate.
I wonder if the shutters are made, like so much is here, of
metal salvaged from crashed American warplanes. I wonder about a lot of things at this window. Last call is still
hours away.

It is April. In a few short years, Bill Clinton will mark
the middle of his first term by reestablishing diplomatic
relations with Vietnam, and Americans will turn up in
droves; some for the first time, some not. For now, we are
few and far between, and except for one in particular, I
have not yet missed us very much.

This American (the one telling this story) is almost,
but not quite, old enough to have been here the first time
around. I don't know where the years have gone. If I didn't
have to count the ones I don't entirely remember, I would
actually be a lot younger. This is not all that funny. I know.
But it was not deliberate, either. Some things just happen.
Shit happens. Everyone says so.

"Gone to Củ Chi already?" Phượng asks. "Visit brother?" By which she means have I gone by now. She says this without looking directly at me, because she knows. I have not gone. One of these days, though, maybe I will surprise her.

Mick has been away more than half my life, but this is the first time I have set out to look for him, as I have been very busy denying the undeniable. When I was a kid he would take me into the foothills of the Little Rockies on his motorcycle. He knew where to look for fossils; knew what they were when he found them. I can still see, set on the palm of his hand, a chunk of quartz etched with tiny filaments, like hairs. He tells me the etchings are the imprint of dinosaur feathers. We are in a cave, and I am holding the flashlight. I search his face to see if he is making it up, but think maybe this time he is telling the truth.

Remember this, Riley, I tell myself. *Hang on to this.*

To Phượng I say, "Not yet."

She looks at me and rolls her eyes. Just up, over to one side and back again, not all the way around. Her eyebrows are pencil-line thin and perfectly arched. I would look ridiculous in those eyebrows. I tell her she looks like Madame Nhu.

"Điên cái đầu," she says. Crazy in the head. I agree: I have seen photos of the madame soon after her husband and his brother, South Vietnam's president, were assassinated in 1963. She is holding court in L.A., accusing Kennedy, not a hair out of place. The woman had some nerve; you have to give her that.

It dawns on me that Phượng might not be talking about

the Dragon Lady. If she isn't, I can't argue. Crazy is clearly my comfort zone, my DMZ. And as for visiting ghosts, the Vietnamese are used to that; it is no cause for commotion.

My brother, if I am being honest, is only one of the ghosts I have come here to visit. By which I mean the shadows in my head and not necessarily dead people, because I still don't know. Show me a body; maybe I'll believe.

The dive we are in, this flimsy but cozy excuse for a glitzy rock 'n' roll nightclub, is fairly quiet at the moment—five or so regulars take turns playing pool, a few strangers and a small flock of taxi girls look on. On a suitcase-size and decoratively beat-up boom box he keeps behind the bar, Tho plays the homemade cassette tapes we give him. Tonight Prince rules the airwaves, along with The Pretenders and a little Culture Club. Some nights Tho's box delivers the same stuff American soldiers would have listened to here: Country Joe, Sly, The Youngbloods, Three Dog Night, Aretha. Occasionally we get the soundtrack for *Good Morning, Vietnam*. We especially love the part where Robin Williams says, "It's hot. It's damn hot." Because it is.

When the conversation about my brother hits the wall that is my refusal to acknowledge any reasonable probability, Phượng and I talk about something easier: in this case, the rain. "*Trời mưa*," she says, a simple statement even I can understand: it is raining.

I nod. "*Rất mưa*." A lot of rain. During our nightly conversations we roam haltingly into each other's languages, my excursions considerably more hesitant than hers, but

I am learning, and Phượng has had far more practice with English.

"Wet rat," she says, and giggles at the play on words. "Wet rat bastard." She is not really giggling anymore, but she doesn't sound pissed either, which makes it difficult to know for sure if she has really pegged anyone in particular for a rat bastard, or if she has been watching more old American movies on Star TV and this is just another practice persona. Probably a little of each, knowing Phượng. She sounds like Humphrey Bogart in Vietnamese drag. I do not ask, and imagine she is just messing around. I am too dreamy with beer and the heat to work it out anyway, watching my own movie, the scenes dim and sputtery as a hand-cranked newsreel.

Outside, cyclo drivers on the watch for passengers pedal their three-wheelers through fitful patches of brightness. They drift strong and stork legged, all sinew and bone skinny. Dangling from their lips or fingers are cigarettes somehow still smoldering in the rain. The way they smoke, so casually oblivious, reminds me of my father—on the porch, maybe, or out in the yard at night, looking up at the sky, for weather, but it's not as if he could miss the stars. I hear my name in his voice: "Riley . . ." Never loud or angry, just gentle reminders: try to grow up with some degree of intentionality and grace; try to believe the world is more benevolent than not. I wonder if he knows I did hear him. I'm sure I never said. Here I am, though, working on it. Working on something.

Firelight emanates from small blazes kept alive with jet fuel and tended on the fractured sidewalks by itinerant bicycle mechanics; these men once repaired jeeps and tanks for the Americans and now keep their tools in battered, surplus, army-green ammo boxes. They have long ago forgiven us for leaving them behind. Buddhists, they say there is nothing to forgive.

My fake-French bicycle is locked up out front where I can keep an eye on it. It is how I get around in this city of five million, to my various English-teaching jobs, to the street kids' center where I try to offer something of relative value, and into which we try to coax them from the stoops, the rain, the robbers. But the kids are so wild—wilder than wild red pandas—and they find their protection in each other, mostly coming only to eat and then disappearing again into the night.

I try to formulate in my pidgin Vietnamese an explanation for Phượng of how the cyclo guys look like those mythological birds to me, and how some kids in America are told that storks bring babies, tied up in bandanas dangling from their beaks. It sounds even more ridiculous in Vietnamese than it does in English, and it also occurs to me how many birds there are already in this story: Phượng, the phoenix, cyclo-storks, the girls at the bar, a scrawny pidgin that is my grasp of the language, a language I am learning to love, for translations like this one, for barbed wire: "steel string with thorns."

Phượng tells me the stork story is so much baloney; she actually says, "Stork babies baloney, Chi." Chi is what they call me here. It means big sister. Hardly anyone calls me by my actual name, but I'm used to that; I'll answer to just about anything.

Phượng has recently been knocked up by one of our local British boys. She tells me this as we stand at the window. Ian, the father, is an old Saigon hand, having been here for three years already, captaining some kind of bamboo furniture enterprise. He is tall, blond, dubiously handsome, and wears his jaded weariness like a badge. I hear the first few years it was all he could do to stay in the country and out of prison, for uncommitted crimes.

This town is full of romantically hazardous men: Brits, Aussies, Froggies. Especially, maybe, the Froggies, with their *Ça va*s, their Gitanes, their sleepy eyes and sexy accents that require of a girl perpetual vigilance. Luc could be a poster child for these Froggies. He looks like Jean-Paul Belmondo in *Breathless*, and rumor has it that he is indeed here to make a movie, though I have never seen him with a camera or a lighting crew, and suspect he is really here (like me) on account of a movie he keeps in his head.

Phượng tells me he has his eye on me. "Luc like you style, Chi. Think Chi beaucoup sweetie pie."

Luc has never said more than two words in a row to me. If he thinks I am beaucoup sweetie pie, he has a funny way of showing it. Phượng says this is because he is shy. Shy and adorable. A little young. A hazard, like I said. Besides, there is that Jim Morrison Aussie, the one I became entangled with almost as soon as I arrived, and who will very soon, and surgically, break my heart—able to do that because this is Saigon, not because the reasons I am sleeping with him have anything to do with love. Love would require a part of me that I have not been able to precisely locate or properly identify the remains of for a long time now.

So that is the romantic inventory—the pertinent bits.

At least I am not pregnant. This time. I look over at Phượng, who leans her elbows on the windowsill, her chin on her interlocked fingers. I say I am sorry for bringing up the storks.

"No worries," she says. Then, "Shit." Softly, infinitely sweetly. She picked that up from me, I think—the word, not the delicate delivery of it. I never heard her say it before we started hanging out together at the window.

"Don't say 'shit,' " I say. "It's not ladylike."

"What is ladylike?"

"Like a lady."

"Woman?" she asks. She looks puzzled, those fine eyebrows drawn together to meet above the bridge of her delicate nose. Her delicate nose that matches the rest of her delicate self. I feel like an Amazon next to her, all five and a half feet of me.

"Different," I say. "More feminine. Ladies don't swear."

"Merde," she says. She's not buying it, in any language.

I swear all the time, though my favorite swearword is not "shit," it is "fuck." Mick taught me how to cuss when I was nine or ten, but that is not one of the words he taught me. It is one I picked up out of necessity a few years later. I try not to say it around Phượng. I do have some manners.

"What are you going to do, Phượng?"

"Don't know. Maybe will go away," she says.

"What? Where?" I am alarmed. For me. I don't want her to go anywhere. She is the only truly sane person I know in this town—besides my students, for whom I must keep up some sense of decorum, meaning I cannot go out drinking with them, and Tho. But I have learned it is not healthy to become too attached to the bartender.

"Not me, silly," she says. "*Nó.*" *Nó* means It. I still don't know what she's saying. "*Em bé,*" she says, and smacks my forehead lightly with her fingertips for emphasis.

"Oh." The baby. I get it; that part I get. Maybe it's the beer, but I don't know what else to say; not sure if she means what I think she means. I realize I don't have any idea what can happen here, what's legal or accepted. I don't know either if Phượng is Catholic or Buddhist, animist or Cao Đài; if she has family in the delta or the highlands; if her father fought with the ARVN or the Vietcong or the Montagnards. I am just an interloper, still uninitiated and incurably dopey, traits Phượng patiently abides.

She straightens her back and casually taps her long, perfect, pink-shellacked fingernails on the sill like she's playing a piano. "Maybe keep," she says, as if it has just occurred to her, but I am not fooled.

"Does Ian know?"

She nods. "Knows. Not happy." She hesitates, stops tapping. "Very," she says.

"Very not happy? Or not very happy?" I ask, even though I'm not sure the distinction will be clear to her. As usual, she's tracking me just fine.

"Not very happy," she says. "But so-so happy."

"Really?" I am shocked. I would not have expected him to be any kind of happy; he has always seemed so content, so immutably rooted in bachelorhood.

"Why surprise?"

"I don't know. I just—"

"I know," she says, and turns to me. "*Người Mỹ.*" American. She leans her forehead into mine, locks eyes, kisses my cheek and floats swan-like away in her silky white *áo dài* to go back to work.

I get another semicold Tiger beer from Tho, watch the cyclos a bit longer as the rain lets up, and eventually return to the pool table, where I sometimes belong. It's getting late, but I am not ready to go back to my place yet, out on *Cách Mạng Tháng Tám*, Boulevard of the August Revolution, needing something closer to pure exhaustion to sleep in this heat, and the noise that almost never stops. I could probably go to the Rex and sleep with the Aussie, listen to his cherished CD collection on his fancy stereo in his hermetically sealed room, but the beers are closer—and warmer by a long shot. Besides, I hate just showing up; I like at least to be invited.

More people wander in—not regulars, tourists—trying, I would guess, to make some sense of this awkward and bewildering city they had surely envisioned differently. Maybe with real sidewalks, traffic signals that people actually abide, or white sand beaches and cabana boys, full-time electricity, food you can eat with impunity. I always say, *Where the hell did they think they were going?* But I didn't have any idea either, so I guess that's not entirely fair. I was, however, not expecting cabana boys or a Gray Line tour. I have been here six months now, and finally what is here is just what belongs. Meaning some part of me has acclimated, planted a little flag, and I can barely imagine—at least when I am awake—going back.

Last week one of the kids, hunkered down on the floor at the shelter, paused while scooping rice from his bowl to his mouth and looked up at me as if he were seeing me for the first time. "Where you town?"

At first, I always said California, as that is the place they have all heard about, seen pictures of, imagine America to be, if they imagine America at all. I haven't tried yet to explain Montana—the perpetual expanse and frigid beauty of it. "*Sài Gòn*," I said. "*Người Vietnam*."

He looked back down at his bowl, dismissing me. "*Nói dối*." Liar. He finished the rice, picked the last grains out of the bowl with fingers that seemed to move independently of the rest of him. "*Người Canada*."

"Nope." I shake my head. Not Canadian.

"*Ở đâu, rồi?*" Where, then? "Say true."

"*Không biết*." I don't know.

"You crazy. Maybe American. American crazy. America number one." He set his bowl down hard on the floor and left me then, without even a fleeting glance back, to wonder if I should even attempt to process either of his pronouncements, or any of mine.

Tonight my pool partner is Clive, of June's, another ratty expat bar between here and the river, a few blocks away.

He is another Brit, always barefoot, and, at fifty-something, fairly old as local gringos go. June is his Thai wife, a fading beauty, all business and hard as bone. Rumor has it that the taxi-girl trade at June's is its main concern, not a sideline like it is here, and June the presumptive madam. Clive is also rumored to move a lot of drugs through the country by paying off the cops and the customs, and partnering with the right guys from Cholon, a less risky trade here so far than in Bangkok. Back in Manchester he worked the steel mills, and when they shut down went looking for something better than the dole.

"Shite work," he told me the first time we talked. "Bollocks and shite not having any."

"I imagine," I said, though I couldn't.

"Bloke I knew in Thailand sent me a postcard. Said the birds were everywhere. And easy. And it was warm. They had this thing called a sun."

He found June in Chiang Mai, conducted a courtship of sorts, and married her in a little beachside ceremony.

"Was she one of the easy ones?"

He turned his head side to side two or three times, slowly, as far as it would go. "Nowt easy about her."

"So why'd you marry her?"

He chalked up, bent down to take a couple of shots, and, after missing the last one, leaned back against the edge of the pool table, tossed his cue stick between his hands and looked up at the grotty ceiling. "The way she said no. Like she'd never been asked such a stupid question. I knew she was the girl for me."

"What was the question?"

"I believe it was 'Would you care to dance?'" He grasped the cue with both hands, waist-to-shoulder-width apart, and commenced a spin, his bare feet executing a remarkable pirouette.

"Your shot," he said when he stopped revolving. "Though ya don't have one."

He was right. He'd snookered me good.

Clive seems to like me, despite my refusal to snooker him or our opponents when I don't have a shot. It drove him crazy for a while, but now I get a little grudging respect for trying to hit something of my own, no matter how hopeless it may look or how many rails I'll need to carom perfectly off of to get there. We are a good team, in any event, and win far more often than we lose. The taxi girls root for us, applaud when we pull out a victory in the final lap.

Tonight we are playing an American from Texas and a chubby Taiwanese businessman who are apparently involved in some sort of rare-monkey export concern that I don't really care to think too much about. About what they do with the monkeys once they get them out of the country. The Chinese guy insists on yelping "Lucky!" every time I make a shot, no matter how simple or how complicated it might be, or how many shots I make in a row.

The Texan responds each time with a lively, drawled "Damn straight, podner."

I would like more than anything to slap them both with one clean swipe.

Clive knows I go off my game when I let myself get rattled by the opposition. He keeps reminding me to focus on the table. "He's blinkered, mate. And that Texas twat is just trying to wind you up. Ignore them."

"I'm trying, but that is so fucking annoying. You notice they don't do that to you."

"*Cor*," he says, "Flippin' gormless. Keep your pecker up."

"No pecker," I say. "That's the problem." But I do get the gist.

"Shoot," Clive says. I make two respectably difficult ones and then miss a dead-easy four ball in the side. Clive says, "Quit pissing around."

"I made two."

"My two," he says.

Between shots, I lean sweaty and slick against the wall, and the temptation to unlock my knees, just give in and slide down to the floor, is almost overwhelming. In spite of the rain, it is at least ninety degrees in here, and the humidity might be even higher, if that's even possible. I resist the inclination to perch on my haunches and instead focus on Clive's feet as he pads around the table. No one has ever asked, at least within my earshot, why he never wears shoes, but I suspect it is because he can't find any here that fit. His feet are not big, in the usual sense, but extremely wide. They look like hairless bear paws.

In the end we win on an amazing cutback Clive slices into the corner. He misses scratching by a centimeter. "Brave," I say.

He pats me on the head. "No. Just good."

"Another?"

"Not tonight, kiddo. I'm knackered. Going home to the missus."

"Sounds lovely." He just smiles and shuffles out barefoot into the dark.

It's midnight, and the place is getting crowded, filling up with overflow from the Apocalypse. Phượng is delivering drinks, so there will be no window time before closing. Ian comes in, takes his usual place at a corner table, and nods at me. I nod back. I know I should get on my bicycle and go home, but the idea is too depressing. I don't want to be lonely any night, but for some reason—maybe the twisted clarity of too many beers, or Phượng's situation, or the music, or the rain, or my brother—I especially don't want to be lonely this night. I wonder where James Taylor was when he wrote that song. Not Saigon, I bet. I bet it was someplace he knew and unquestionably belonged, and that he wasn't even all that lonely.

Phượng takes Ian his beer, and I watch as he puts his hands around her tiny waist and pulls her close for a quick kiss when no one else is looking. I don't count. I am a collaborator. And all of a sudden I want what they have, even if I don't get to know exactly what it is, or even if I've been telling myself for years there is no future in it. I suspect it is something along the lines of love.

Phượng leaves for the bar and Ian waves me over to come sit with him. I am caught off guard by how grateful I feel but mostly am relieved to have at least a semilegitimate reason to stay awhile longer. On the way, I pick up a beer for him and a bottle of water for me. I already know I am going to feel like hell in the morning, but I don't have to hammer in the last nail. Since tomorrow is Saturday, I have only one class—a sweet and ragtag band of earnest college students I will meet at the park in the afternoon—and then the eight-to-midnight shift at the shelter. I'll survive.

Ian takes note of the water, my unfocused eyes, and says, "How many?"

"How many what?" I know what he's asking but don't want to admit to more than I have to right away.

"Sandwiches."

"I was working on my second."

"Thought better of that?"

"I did."

A Tiger sandwich is three beers: one Tiger beer between two other Tiger beers. Two or more sandwiches is tilt. Not pretty. He gives me a thumbs-up. Which is nice. We try to guess the tourists' nationalities and watch them flirt with the taxi girls. Eventually I go home.

Ian was one of the first people I met here, the night I found the Lotus, the first time I was brave enough to leave the one square block containing the eight-dollar-a-night hotel I stayed in for a few weeks after I landed. The block I had confined myself to, terrified of venturing any farther, of crossing the street. I had been in town only four days, but they had been long ones, spent mostly sleeping, dreaming of mountains and highways and home, fox dens and snow caves, waking to wonder what I had done. My room was enormous and timeworn; painted, with what looked like watercolor, a peeling and mottled blue: walls, floor, ceiling, doors, and window frames. The filmy curtains were also blue, and the holey mosquito net. It was like being un-

derwater, and finally I had to get out, before I couldn't anymore. In those four days I memorized the entry for "blue"
in my dictionary. It said:

> of a color intermediate between green and violet, as of the
> sky or sea on a sunny day: the clear blue sky / blue
> jeans / deep blue eyes.
> *(of a person's skin)* having or turning such a color, esp. with
> cold or breathing difficulties: The boy went blue, and I
> panicked.
> *(of a bird or other animal)* having blue markings: a blue jay.
> *(of cats, foxes, or rabbits)* having fur of a smoky gray color:
> the blue fox.
> *(physics)* denoting one of three colors of quark.

It was Ian's table that first Lotus night, and I watched
him win for a long time before I had the nerve to put my
name on the board. I was too unsteady to shoot well but
made a few decent shots and earned myself a beer and
some conversation, in English, which was a lot like being
let out on my own recognizance. But after so much time
and silence, it was hard to get used to talking again.

He asked what part of Canada I was from. Later I would
find out the locals did that to avoid insulting anyone by
guessing they were American. At the time, though, I just
said no part, but close.

"Yank, then?"

"Yank." I laughed. I'd never been called one of those
before.

"What brings you to our fair city?"

"Curiosity, I guess."

"You know about the cat, right?"

"What cat?" He waited for me to figure it out, which took me longer than it should have. "Oh, the curious one."

"Right."

"I do. We have that cat in America too."

"*Con mèo*," he said. My first Vietnamese lesson. I knew then that I could easily come to love a language in which the word for an animal was the sound it made.

He asked me how long I planned to stay, and I said I didn't know. My ticket was open-ended and my purpose was clear as mud.

"Good luck with that," he said, but not in a way that would make me feel ridiculous. More than, in some unnamable way, I already did.

After a few months I constructed something of a purpose: living, getting from place to place, not crashing my bicycle, teaching idioms and street slang, feeding feral orphans. A few months more, and Saigon's incessant din and treacly grime and sleepless lunacy have taken me over. The city carries me along like a wave. Or an avalanche.

Which leaves little time to think about the reasons I came here: most of all to locate Mick, or his bones; or if not his actual bones, then his spirit, and anything else he could have left behind. Something I can see, or touch, or at least find a place in me that will accept this: MIA, after all these years, means gone, gone, gone, really gone. This will mean bucking up long enough to go to Củ Chi—so close it is practically a suburb—getting down on all fours and crawling into the tunnels where the army mislaid my brother.

1. Hawks

They say our early memories are really memories of what we think we remember—stories we tell ourselves—and as we grow older, we re-remember, and often get it wrong along the way. I'm willing to believe that, but I still trust some of my memories, the most vivid, like this one: there was a newspaper, and a headline, bigger than the everyday ones. It was morning and I was alone at the kitchen table, sleepy, my feet resting on the dog—he was a cow dog, speckled black and white, name of Cash—on the floor underneath. I had a spoon in my hand and was waving it around; drops of milk splashed on the paper.

The headline said, "Johnson Doubles Draft to 35,000." It was summer and I was nine. I knew who Johnson was. He was the president. He was tall and talked funny, and his nose took up half his face. The reason he got to be president was on account of the last one getting shot in Texas, by Lee Harvey Oswald, who got shot by Jack Ruby, who did not get shot by anyone. JFK was the president when I first started school. John-John and Caroline were his kids and his wife looked like a movie star. When they buried him, she wore a black veil over her face so no one could see if she cried. John-John held her hand.

President Johnson, in the paper, said Vietnam was a different kind of war. I knew I could ask Mick about that: about how many kinds of war there were, or how there could even be different kinds, but he was outside. My parents were out there too—Mom probably in the garden already, digging up potatoes before the sun got so high and hot it would turn them green, and Dad fixing fences or tractoring or scaring up dopey runaway calves. The usual. Our life.

I collected the bowl of apples and the peeler Mom had left on the counter for me and went out to the front porch. I balanced the bowl on the railing and slid my feet between two spindles to stand on the bottom rail, so I could lean over and get a better look at my brother. Mick was crouched in the driveway next to a black Triumph motorcycle, his high school graduation present to himself. He was hoping to catch a girl with it, I knew, or to go away on it, or both. I was not in favor of either, but he was over the moon. The bike was magnificent.

His toolbox lay open in the dust, and a greasy rag dangled like a cockeyed tail from the back pocket of his coveralls. Most of his blond hair was tucked up under a train engineer's cap, but a few wayward strands crept down his neck and caught the poplar-filtered morning light like filaments of some shiny spun metal. No one else in the family had hair like that. Not even close. I thought about sneaking up behind him with a pair of scissors and snipping off a piece, but it seemed like a lot of work and probably not worth the repercussions. Instead, I looked around for something small to throw at him, as it was my habit to be annoying. I did know better than to hit him with an entire apple.

Without looking at me, he said, "Don't even think about it," and gave one of the screws on the engine an infinitesimal turn.

"I wasn't thinking about anything," I said. I was still searching, but there was nothing. I'm sure I sighed. I was a great sigher in those days. I picked up the bowl and sat down with my back to the wall, scissored my legs open, and set the bowl between them. The peeler was still on the porch railing.

"Crap."

"What's wrong? Can't find a weapon?"

"I left the peeler. It's on the rail."

"Bummer."

"Get it for me?"

"Nope."

"Thanks."

"My pleasure, Cupcake."

I didn't move. I sniffed the air and it smelled like cow farts. I said so.

Mick said, "What smells like cow farts?"

"The world."

"Probably not," he said. "Probably just Montana."

"Oh." I pondered my entire range of geographic and zoologic knowledge, not coming up with a whole lot. "So, does that mean Africa smells like hippo farts?"

"I doubt it. Hippos fart underwater."

"So what other animals are there?"

"Anywhere? Or just in Africa?"

"There. In Africa."

"You have an encyclopedia, Riley. Why don't you look it up?"

"I have to peel these." I took an apple out of the bowl and balanced it on the top of my head. "Plus, it wouldn't hurt you to just tell me."

I heard him sigh. I think he must have taught me how. "All right. Then will you be quiet?" No promises. I made a noise, like *hrrmm*.

He pulled the rag out of his pocket, dipped it in a tin of rubbing compound, and began to buff a tiny scratch on the gas tank. "Elephants. Don't even tell me if you didn't know that already. Antelope, zebras, giraffes, wildebeests, warthogs . . ."

"Warthogs?" I sat up straighter. "You made that up."

"No," he said, "I did not."

I tilted my head forward to drop the apple into my hand, put it back in the bowl, and slitted my eyes like a snake. I considered my options. My tendency to doubt was well earned, but I still believed most of what Mick said, unless the bullshit was totally obvious. He was ridiculously smart. He read tons of books and remembered what was in them. Not like some people.

"What do they look like?" I said, still not sure which way this was going to go.

"Like bristly little pigs. Their tails stand straight up."

I was eyeing the peeler, and even went so far as to set the bowl next to me so I could get up to retrieve it.

"What else?"

Mick said, "I'll draw you a picture later."

"When later?"

"After now."

We were almost done. I could tell.

"Where do these guys live?"

"At the beach."

"The ocean?" To me, the ocean was the most magical place in the world, even though I'd never seen one, never been farther outside Montana than the North Dakota Badlands. But even the Badlands had once been underwater, or so I'd been told.

"Yes. At the beach at the ocean. Where beaches are." Mick popped off the spark plug wire, reached into his toolbox for the ratchet, and loosened the plug. The noise the ratchet made was a bit cricket-like. I wondered if I could tie that in somehow to make the conversation go further. Gave up.

Mick looked over his shoulder at me. I wasn't moving. I could have been dead. "Are you going to peel those apples or what?"

"What," I said, but that was it. I knew it was going to be.

I got the peeler and began skinning apples, imagining for a short time they were small rabbits and me a wily trapper collecting pelts, but it didn't make me feel very good; it made me feel a little sick, in fact, so I tried to take it back, in my head, but couldn't. By the time I finished, Mick had disappeared into the garage. I took the apples inside and set them on the counter. "Here are your rabbits," I said—whispered—to no one.

I whistled Cash from his refuge under the table, and together we padded the two flights up to my room, which had once been the attic. It was small, because the whole house wasn't very big—just a tallish box, perfectly square with the exception of a two-story addition off the back. I could get to the roof of it from my window but had to be careful on account of the steep pitch, for snow. The walls were blue, with tiny green and yellow fish trailing like ivy around the windows. Mick had painted them when he and Dad fixed the space up the summer before.

I was nearly asleep on the floor, one hand buried deep in the fur around Cash's neck, when I heard the bike start up. I bolted down the stairs, banked off the bannisters, miscalculated, and slammed my shoulder hard into the wall at the bottom. I hesitated just long enough to straighten a framed picture there, which was long enough to miss Mick's turn from the long driveway onto the frontage road. I stood on the porch, tracking his progress beyond the hedgerow by the rooster tail of fine Montana silt he kicked up. I watched until all evidence of my brother and his bike disappeared from sight, a mile or more away. Cash leaned against my leg, and I reached down to scratch behind his ears.

"Shit," I said. I did not realize my mother was standing at the screen door until I heard my name.

"Riley," she said, "I really wish you wouldn't swear so often." Mick was teaching me. He was doing a good job.

"Sorry, Mom. But damn . . ."

"Riley. I know." She pushed the door open and held it with her hip, laid her hands on my shoulders, rubbing the one that hurt. I wondered how she knew. "Maybe I'd like to go with him too."

I snorted. "You would not." I tilted my head straight back so I could see her expression, but it was upside down and I couldn't tell anything from that angle. Not that my mother was all that decipherable anyway. We never knew from day to day, sometimes from hour to hour, which mom we were going to get. There was quiet mom, silly mom, fierce-but-not-mean mom, and mom with the faraway look in her eyes. That mom was almost but not quite the same as quiet mom, who still knitted and cooked and made us do our homework. Faraway mom just stood at the window, looking out at what I would remember later, after I'd gone away: the distant mountains, the buff-colored wheat fields, red-tailed hawks drifting with the thermals, poised to drop out of the sky, like missiles, onto errant field mice.

"Mick's leaving, Mom. Isn't he?"

She leaned down and kissed the top of my head. "Looks that way."

"Where's he going?"

"I don't know. I don't think he does either. Hopefully to college."

"When?"

"Soon, I imagine. He hasn't told us yet." She did not sound particularly unhappy at the prospect of Mick going off to school, and that confused me, since I could see nothing good coming of it. At all.

I went to his room that night after dinner to ask him about hawks. Dozens of drawings were pinned to the walls, of everything, seemingly, he'd ever seen when he went outside, or the pieces of outside he brought in: wildflowers, rocks, sticks, bones, trees, birds, reptiles, mammals big and small, mountains, clouds, planets.

He finished the song he was playing on his guitar, set it down, pulled a dog-eared book from the shelf and read: "'Krider's Red-tailed Hawk is a very pale race found in the Great Plains. These are light mottled brown above and nearly pure white below. The belly band is often indistinct or absent, and the tail is usually light rust above and creamy below with faint barring.'"

"'A very pale race,'" I said, or mumbled. I was lying on the floor with a stuffed animal draped across my forehead like some bizarre woolly headdress. "Aren't we a very pale race?"

"We are," Mick said. "Paler than most."

A minute passed. Then two. "Most what?" I didn't even know what I was asking.

"Go to bed, Riley."

Mick played for a while. Bob Dylan. Peter, Paul and Mary. I loved the dragon Puff. Hated it when he had to go. Finally, Mick laid his guitar on the bed, scooped me up off the floor and carried me to my room. I tried to not be entirely deadweight, but I wasn't so easy to carry anymore.

"You're going to be too big for this pretty soon, you know."

"I know. But you'll be gone anyway. So it won't matter."

I waited. I kept my eyes closed.

Mick said, "Good night, Punk."

"Night, Bozo," I said. I think.

I heard him leave on his bike again, sometime in the deep middle of the night. Cash woofed in my ear.

"Forget it, dog. He's not taking either one of us."

When I rolled over I heard something rustle. I pulled a piece of notebook paper from underneath me and held it up to the light coming through the window. I could tell what it was by the straight-up tail and the bristles. It was standing under a palm tree on a beach, gazing out at the waves.

I traced it with my finger. "Hey, little buddy."

I fell asleep, still hearing the sound of the motorcycle long after it had faded, and dreamt of rabbits, hairless and round, like little moons.

At breakfast the next morning Mick didn't even look tired. I searched his face for some clue as to where he might have been, or what he might have seen, or what he was thinking about. He looked exactly the same as he had every morning of my life.

He said, "Quit, Riley."

"Quit what?" I stared at my bowl, at the cornflake crumbs floating there. Like I was an astronomer and they were a newly discovered constellation. Discovered by me.

"Looking at me like that."

"I'm not looking at you. Obviously."

"Riley," Mom said. She didn't finish, but I knew.

Arguing wasn't going to get me where I wanted to go, especially since I didn't know where that was. I sneaked a look at my father, on his second cup of coffee and getting ready to light a cigarette, to see if any help might be coming from that quarter. He tapped the cigarette on the table and a few strands of tobacco fell out. I could smell it, sharp and bitter. Mom stood up and started clearing dishes, raising an eyebrow at Dad when he looked at her. There was a new no-smoking policy in the house, and sometimes he forgot. He put the cigarette behind his ear.

"Was there something you wanted to ask your brother, Miss Riley?"

"No, sir."

"I think there is, and you're probably not going to get your answer by staring a hole through his head."

"I wasn't—"

"What," Mick said, "do you want to know?"

He said it gently enough, but it didn't matter anymore. I knew if I asked, whatever it was, and got an answer, I wouldn't like it, unless he said he was staying put, and I knew that wasn't even a distant possibility. Mick didn't want to be a farmer. He wanted to see the world. He'd been telling me that since I could remember, but I had never realized it meant he'd be leaving *me*. I'd always imagined us somewhere together; somewhere that looked a lot like home.

I said, "Never mind." I excused myself, put my bowl in the sink, and left by the back door. Cash came with me, wagging his tail hopefully.

When the college catalogues came, Mick pored over them at the kitchen table. I helped by tearing the corners off the pages, piling the bits of paper together, and blowing on them so they scattered. Havre and Great Falls were okay, close enough that he could come visit. Missoula was too far away, on the other side of the mountains. Mick had that catalogue open.

"You aren't thinking about going there, are you?"

"Yes, nosy. I am thinking about it."

"But it's so far."

"Not so far, really. Not nearly as far as some places."

"So far really." I started another pile of corners. When it reached a decent size, I blew on it. Hard. Some fell on the floor.

Mick looked at me like he might be angry this time, but wasn't. "This is what people do, Riley. They get out of high school and go away to college. Or some do."

"What about the other ones?"

"They do other stuff."

"Other stuff around here?"

"Some of them."

I waited.

"That's not going to be me, kiddo."

I sat down hard on the chair next to his and flipped through the pages of the Havre catalogue. "This looks nice," I said after a while, even though I wasn't really seeing it.

Mick laughed. "Relax. I haven't decided anything yet." He turned my chair around and tilted my chin up so I had to look at him. My eyes kept blinking, and I swallowed so hard my throat hurt. Mick pushed back from the table and pulled me onto his lap. "I was never going to stay here forever, Riley. I thought you knew that."

I leaned into him, lowering my head to bite one of the buttons on his shirt. "I didn't," I said, sort of, because I had a button in my mouth. "You should have told me."

"I should have," he said. And we left it at that. For a little while it felt okay.

Then he brought a girl home. There had been others, but I hated this one the most. She and Mick disappeared behind his bedroom door, and with my ear pressed to the wood I could hear them murmuring. Whispering. I hated her, and I hated it. He was telling a stranger his plans.

I went down to the creek with Cash, to escape the house and the heat and the terrible tightness in my chest. We lay in the shallow water and I watched the cottonwood leaves turn in the sun, even though there wasn't any breeze. I groped for stones in the sandy bottom and threw them at the far bank. After a while Cash started to retrieve them. "Silly dog," I said, and hugged his wet fur.

I wondered what they were doing in Mick's room—if he was reading to her or playing songs for her on his guitar. I turned over and put my face in the water, to see if I could leave it there long enough to drown. He'd be sorry. He'd hate her too because she was there when it happened, distracting him. I held my breath as long as I could, staring at small, current-smoothed rocks, water plants and tiny fish. It wasn't going to work. I raised my head and took a deep breath.

"Crap."

Mick's bike was still parked in the driveway when Cash and I got back to the house, and I didn't want to go in there. I draped myself over the porch rail and watched the water from my hair puddle on the wooden planks under me. I was dizzy, and my face felt fat and bruised. When my stomach started to hurt from the pressure, I slid toward the edge, until my hands were flat on the porch and my legs stretched out behind me. My mom called, but I couldn't answer. I tried to slide back to where I'd started, but instead I crept forward even farther, until my feet went up and over my head, and I did a handstand into the garden, landing on my back instead of my feet. I never was much of an acrobat.

It might have been funny if it didn't hurt so much. My right arm was twisted under me, and even though I'd never broken a bone before, I knew I'd broken one this time. Cash was crazy barking at the front door, and my mom and Mick and that girl came out. When Mick picked me up, the girl stood off to one side. She was crying. *She* was.

At the clinic in town they set my arm and put my shoulder back where it was supposed to be. The shot they gave me knocked me loopy, but it drove the pain away, or at least deep enough I didn't care about it.

Back at home, Mick carried me up to my room and put me in my bed under the covers. I groped around for the stuffed animal I always slept with and sometimes still dragged around with me. When I found it, I laid it on my chest.

Mick said, "What is that thing, anyway?"

"It's a rabbit. See?" I held it up by its one remaining ear.

"Damndest rabbit I ever saw."

"Still a rabbit."

I slept for a few hours, and when I woke up saw that Mick and that girl had both signed my cast. I tried to rub out her name. It was Gail. Stupid name. Stupid girl.

A few days later we met, officially. She said, "Well aren't you a cutie pie?"

"No," I said. "I'm not."

Mick said, "You think she's cute? Better get your eyes checked." I wanted to hit him with something hard and heavy. They both laughed and walked away across the yard, her hand in the back pocket of his jeans. I sat on the porch steps and banged my cast against the handrail while Cash watched, looking worried. It hurt a lot. My dad found me doing it and made me stop. He sat with me and tried to tell me it's natural for things to change, and for us to not like it much, but then we get used to it, and after a while it's as if things are the way they were always meant to be.

"You're going to survive this, Riley."

"I don't think so."

"I do think so, and I'm the dad. Got it?"

"Sure." I didn't want to make him feel bad, but I didn't believe him for a second. I leaned my head against his arm, and we sat there until my mom came out.

"What are you two up to?"

"Just sitting here." He scooted me and him over a few inches, to make room.

She sat down and smoothed her skirt over her knees. "Grass could use a mowing," she said.

"Thought I'd get to it tomorrow. That be okay?"

"Sure. Or the next day."

"Fair enough," he said.

We all heard the bike but no one moved except Cash, and he only moved his head, and just a little. Mick and Gail waved as they headed down the driveway. We waved back, but they didn't see.

She came almost every day for a while. Sometimes she stayed for dinner. I don't remember what she talked about, if she talked at all. She was pretty, and her hair was blond, but not as blond as Mick's. She liked him a lot. It was kind of sickening to see.

But then she stopped coming. I asked my mom why, and she said I should ask Mick. Because she didn't know.

"She wanted to go steady."

"And you didn't?"

"Seems sort of pointless."

"Because you're going away?"

"Yes."

"Oh."

We were in the driveway. He reached into his toolbox, came out with a screwdriver and held it in his hand, looking at it like he'd never seen one before—like it was a new specimen; a previously undiscovered species.

"Did you break her heart?"

"She says I did."

"Are you sorry?"

He put the screwdriver back and picked up a crescent wrench; tapped it on the hard-packed dirt.

"Yes. I am. Is that okay with you?"

"Sure." I didn't want him to feel so bad. Not about that. I knew he didn't mean to break anyone's heart. Not even mine.

"That's the way the cookie crumbles, isn't it."

"It is," he said. And he tried not to smile, but I saw.

Eventually he took pity on me, bored out of my skull and not able to do very much. He let me help with the bike: hold and hand him tools, turn screws, tighten bolts, polish; especially polish.

"Jeez, Mick, It's shiny already."

"So's your face, punkin' head. Keep rubbing. You missed a spot."

"Ha-ha."

And he took me riding. I didn't even have to ask. I couldn't believe it. He showed up one day with a new red helmet and we took off for the Little Rockies, a small mountain range thirty or so miles away, completely surrounded by the pancake flatness of the plain.

I held on with my good arm, the mending one tucked between us like an injured animal, while we drove through a narrow canyon that began on the rez, just past a small white church and the picket-fenced graveyard behind it. I had to get off and wade while Mick coaxed the bike through a sandy creekbed to solid ground. We rode slowly through sunlight and shadow, between the craggy limestone canyon walls where windblown conifers and ferns improbably, and probably ill-advisedly, tried to grow. On the ridgetops I could see lines of stunted trees, like crouching soldiers waiting for their orders. Charge. Take cover. Retreat.

Mick told me about some animals that lived in the Montana mountains not so long ago, like ten thousand years. Saber-toothed cats with canine teeth seven inches long; dire wolves; short-faced bears; a lion with long, long legs, bigger than a Bengal tiger.

I asked him where they went.

"Probably somewhere they thought people would stop trying to kill them all the time."

"Are there any left?"

"Not the same ones. Newer ones."

"Like what?"

"Like timber wolves. Elk. Bears."

"*Regular* animals," I said.

Mick laughed. "Exactly."

The day he started packing for Missoula, I was ready on the roof outside my window. I had an old Easter basket full of rocks—bigger than pebbles, but nothing too lethal. I waited for him to come out of the house, to head out to the garage for a trunk or a duffel bag. I could see Cash in the yard, watching, with his head resting on his crossed front paws. Dad's tractor was kicking up great clouds of dust along the far fence line; it hadn't rained in months, and the grass-hoppers were eating everything in sight. The forecast said soon, though, and I'd heard my parents talking about how they thought they could smell it coming, even though there wasn't a cloud in the sky you couldn't see clear through.

My cast had finally come off, almost on its own, so we hadn't had to go back to the clinic and pay a doctor to do something, as Dad put it, you didn't need to go to medical school to figure out. My arm from wrist to shoulder was as pale as it had probably ever been. I remembered talk-

ing with Mick about a "pale race," but couldn't remember
what we'd been talking about. I thought it might have been
something about birds.

I heard the screen door slam and scooted to the edge of
the roof, braced my feet against the rain gutter, and waited.
When Mick appeared I leaned over the edge and threw the
first rock. It went wide, but he heard it and looked up.

"Damn it, Riley. If you hit me, I swear—"

He stood in the yard, waiting, daring me to throw another one. I did. I missed again and grabbed the biggest
one in the basket. I held it for a minute while we stared at
each other, and then threw it as hard as I could. Mick didn't
duck or try to get out of the way. The rock glanced off his
forehead, and it began to bleed. A lot. He disappeared and I
heard his feet thump the porch steps.

I pushed on the gutter with my heels, in a hurry to get
up and away, but the gutter came loose, and then bent, and
came looser, and instead of sliding up the roof backward,
I was sliding down. I tried to hold on to the shingles, but
there was nothing to grab.

"Crap," I said to myself. And just like that, I was air-
borne again.

It was nothing like flying, even from that height. I
landed on my back, again, but with my arms straight out
this time like scrawny, useless wings, and all the wind
knocked out of me. It hurt a lot worse than the first time,
all on one side, and as soon as I started to breathe again, I
tried to stop. Mick was kneeling over me, blood from the
cut on his forehead dripping onto my neck and chest, and

he was telling me I had to do it, had to breathe, had to stay still. He kept wiping the blood off, saying, "It's going to be okay."

I wanted to say I was sorry, but couldn't get the words out. He pushed the bangs off my forehead. He said, "Hang on, Riley. Hang on. I've got you."

A helicopter came, and they strapped me to a canvas stretcher to lift me up and into it; I held on and didn't make any noise. They flew me to the hospital in Glasgow and my mom came along. Dad and Mick drove over.

I remember a bright, cold light, and starting to count backward from a hundred. Then a thick bandage, wrapped completely around my middle. They were all standing around my bed.

I said, "Hi," and tried to think back. I pressed on the bandage, to see if I could figure out where the pain was coming from. "What happened?"

Mick told me. Twenty-five feet. Three broken ribs and a punctured lung. I thought he was making it up. "I fell? Again?"

"Yup." He nodded. He looked proud. "And this time you bounced."

A few fuzzy seconds went by. "You didn't know I could do that, did you?"

"Nope. I sure didn't. You're a clever girl." There was a small piece of gauze taped to his forehead. I reached for it, and he leaned down so I could touch it.

"I'm sorry," I said. "I didn't mean to hit you."

He said, "Sure you did." And if he smiled, it meant that

he forgave me. It meant there was no way he'd move away from home because his kid sister was rotten, not very bright, and a pain in the ass. No way.

Mom looked tired, and something else I couldn't read. Trapped, maybe. Ready to run. But I knew that couldn't be right. They all kept going in and out of focus. Dad stood at the end of the bed and held both my feet under the covers in his warm, rough hands.

I closed my eyes. I didn't have a choice.

No one had to teach me to love the morphine, the way it dropped me into a warm pool of amber-colored light and forgetting. For a long time there was no clear boundary between what was real and where the shots took me. Mick and my folks came to visit as often as they could, and Mom stayed over sometimes, and sometimes I knew who was actually there.

After Mick came to say he was leaving, it was easy to believe it was a dream, that he'd changed his mind and wasn't going anywhere. I could believe I'd grown hawk wings and could fly, so falling wouldn't be a problem anymore. With the shots, I could believe all of it. I could believe whatever I wanted to.

2. Bluer and Bigger, with No Mountains

She had a real name, but Darrell didn't know it yet. Not that it mattered. He'd looked for her a few times—trying to stay inconspicuous, which wasn't necessarily easy if you were so obviously rez-bred—and finally there she was, sort of like he remembered, sort of like someone he'd never laid eyes on.

It had rained, and stopped, and now a flimsy rainbow arced over the small town just south, more stretch of the imagination (the rainbow, although the same could be said for the town) than something you'd believe could harbor a flock of happy little bluebirds. And she wasn't anywhere near the end of it. He couldn't picture her in a fairy tale of any sort anyway—little hippie white girl with crazy green eyes, a pocketful of peyote, and a secret. Untamed and intangible. He wanted to know if he'd made her up, or if maybe the whole thing wasn't just some sort of contact high.

Classes were over, the school yard was empty and she

was alone, pacing around the buckled asphalt basketball court with her head down, chin almost touching her chest, setting one foot in front of the other heel-to-toe through the puddles, barefoot. The slight breeze fanned a broken swing to barely perceptible motion; it dangled by a single chain. Another had been wrapped around the high bar a few times and now hung looped there like a rusty snake with a broken back. The slide tilted to one side, its original red paint barely visible amid all the corroded metal. He stood outside the chain-link fence, which was eight feet high for some old and expired reason he'd bet no one would remember now, but he was so tall and long armed that he could easily rest his hands on the top of it. It couldn't have been that high to keep anybody in, since it gapped in places and didn't even have a proper gate. Maybe, he thought, it was there to keep dumb wild things out.

His dark hair kept blowing across his face. He tried a few times to tuck it behind his ear, but the wind would just catch it again, until finally he pulled a rubber band out of his pocket and bound it in a quick braid.

"Hey," he said, not loud, almost a croak, but she heard. She had just taken a corner and was moving away from where he stood; she stopped but didn't turn. He wondered if she knew it was him; thought there was a chance she'd remember.

He'd come from his uncle's house on the reservation, thirty miles away, and the rain he'd hitchhiked through was welcome but early. He knew and everyone else knew it would turn to snow at least once more before the alfalfa and the wheat, the wildflowers and the grass came up again. Before long—and way too soon—the summer dust would cake over the aching green, a color that appeared and disappeared so quickly it was a new revelation every year. Even at three in the afternoon in late April, he was conscious of the sun's arc in the sky. In what passed for warmth after a six-month-long winter of twenty-belows, he could begin to imagine those full summer days that stayed light until ten; shapes, outlines still discernible 'til midnight this far north on the Montana Hi-Line.

He'd seen her the first time the year before, 1971, in the summer, when her dad's pickup had broken down taking a shortcut through the rez, coming back from a trip to Great Falls. Darrell knew how the shadows of the fence posts angled across the road on that stretch at that time of day; dead animals stuck fast and flat to the pavement, paws reaching for the borrow pits, caught in a run. The tow truck had taken the girl and her father to a service station just outside the boundary, where she'd sat at the corner of the building in a patch of sun, watching her father as he leaned against the pickup's fender and smoked cigarettes, quietly shooting the breeze with the mechanic.

Darrell showed up with the new tie-rod from the parts store where he worked, handed it over to the mechanic and had him sign the invoice. He was getting back into his truck when he saw her sitting there, legs akimbo off the sidewalk, shirttail out, jeans cuffed and torn at the knee, ratty beaded moccasins tromped down at the back, long, unruly auburn hair covering half her face or more, sunglasses with blue lenses. By then, she was looking out at the prairie, like she was waiting for someone she knew would be coming along from that direction, not his. He left the truck door open and walked across the lot to where she sat, and then stood a little off to the side and looked where she was looking.

"Not much out there," he said.

She turned her face up to him. "I guess." She was clearly confused by his sudden appearance. Something else too. "Wait. No. That's not right." She sounded a little frantic, like his cousin Leonard, with the stutter, when he knew he was coming up on something hard and unavoidable, like an m-word, like "ma'am"; a word he and Darrell both used a lot, because they had been raised to be gentlemen.

"There *is* something out there. Animals. Rabbits, antelope, paint ponies." Her voice deepened. "Gold in them thar hills." She laughed as she said the last part, but still it had all come out headlong, a little precipitous; "paint" and "ponies" mashed together, so what he heard, even if it was not what she'd meant to say, was "pain ponies." And she was right. He knew that land, those animals. He knew something about paint ponies. Knew about the pain ones too.

"Bones," she whispered, or didn't quite. She formed the word precisely, but not enough sound came out to actually hear. He was watching her mouth, though, so he knew what she'd said.

"What kind of bones?" He pictured human bones. Cow skulls. He wondered what she was on.

"All kinds. Jawbones, finger bones, ham bones." Again the laugh that caught, and skipped, like a scratch on a record. "Bones no one is ever going to find." She looked up again, pulled her sunglasses down lower on her nose. Her pupils were so dilated he could barely see the gold-specked green around them, but he could see it enough. "You just gonna stand there?"

"I guess not," he said, and crouched down in front of her. "What's your name?"

"Ginger Rogers," she said.

He laughed. "Yeah, and I'm Fred Astaire."

"You can't be," she said. "You're an Indian."

"And you can't be Ginger Rogers. You're too young, and I bet you can't even dance."

"Bet I can," she said. She was going to be sixteen pretty soon. He was older. Almost twenty.

"My brother's twenty-one," she said, and picked up a small, sharp, white stone from the pavement and put it in her mouth. "He always will be." For a quicksilver second, panic cut across her eyes again, but then it was gone, and she nearly smiled.

"What does that mean?"

She moved her face close to his, moved the stone into her cheek with her tongue. "It means I'm wasted." She giggled, not exactly like a young girl would; the sound was a little bit raw, edgy, but had some lightness to it even still. He wanted to hear it again. "I can't even see straight," she said.

"I got that. What's your poison?"

"Mescaline. You want some?" She reached into her pocket and held out a clear capsule filled with what looked like chocolate powder.

"Nah. I gotta drive."

"Next time," she said, like there would be a next time.

He had thought it would be easy to find her. The plates on her dad's truck told him which county, and there was only one school. But it was almost a year later by the time he tracked her down, and so much had happened, and was happening, so fast—he was going away soon, and Leonard was already gone—it seemed either longer than the nine or ten months it had been, or like no time had passed at all. It didn't matter. Time was inscrutable like that; he knew better than try to make it correspond to the calendar's notion of days and weeks and years. He wondered if it would act the same in Vietnam. Slow one day, full tilt the next. He'd heard it did something like that.

"Hey," he said again, louder this time. He liked the skirt she was wearing—a denim one reconfigured from a pair of bell-bottoms—the way she had the tail of her red-and-black-checked flannel shirt tied in the front, the bandanna around her wrist. She had to have heard him, but she still didn't turn around. He tried once more. "Hey, Ginger. Where are your dancing shoes?"

She hesitated for a split second more and dipped forward, her hair covering her face and brushing the ground. From there she pushed off with one foot and spun on the ball of the other, lifted her head and flung her body upright in one motion. She looked surprised to be facing him when she stopped, not sure how she'd gotten there, but when she spoke, it was like she had known exactly what she was doing all along. "Why, Mr. Astaire," she said. "To what do I owe this pleasure?"

He walked casually to where the fence opened, trailing his hand behind him along the cold and wet twisted wire.

When he got close to her, he put his hands in his pockets and she looked up at him, same as she had at the gas station, except this time without the sunglasses. Her eyes were that treacherous green—the one, like new grass, that never stayed. "You're late," she told him.

"Late?" He tried to sound indignant, falsely accused, but he couldn't help smiling. This was the girl. "Late for what? How late am I?"

"I had a dream you were coming. But that was months ago. You. Are. Late."

He couldn't tell if she was serious. He'd be surprised if she had really dreamt of him; even more surprised that she would tell him she had. "What were we going to do when I got here?"

"I didn't get that far." She freed a strand of her hair from the mass of it and pulled it across her top lip to make a mustache. "I woke up."

Out at Cherry Gulch, she let him kiss her, let him put his hand inside her shirt. She was flat as a boy, almost, and barely responded with her body, though her mouth was soft and seemed not unwilling, and when he went to sit up she held him tight against her. She smelled of rain and dog and hay. He felt as if some peculiar magic had turned him into an overgrown stuffed animal; a carnival midway bear or tiger. Something benign to hang on to. He didn't know why she made him feel like that, or if her trust was something sensed but not entirely present. He wasn't even sure what he was supposed to be doing, why he had even come, but the pull had been too great to resist. Something about her that first day, tripping her brains out in broad daylight, missing a fragment, obviously, of whatever it is that centers us.

He could feel the bumpy keloid of a long scar slanting along her rib cage; wondered what they had taken out.

"What's the scar?"

"I fell." She didn't say any more then, and he didn't ask. He already figured she didn't tell things on demand.

If she were another girl, he would probably have tried to have sex with her, but this one felt breakable, and he didn't want to break her like that. There were plenty of girls on the reservation he could sleep with, and white girls in town who thought Native boys were sexy, or fucked them to make their boyfriends jealous. There were fights, but they hardly ever amounted to anything. One guy had died a few years earlier, beaten with a crowbar and buried in a shallow grave out on the plain, where the coyotes dug him up and brought body parts to town. They never caught who did it, because they didn't really look. He was an Indian. Insignificant in the scope of things. White people marching around. War. The price of cattle. The weather.

She rolled him over onto his back and sat up straddling his thighs. "I don't understand," she said, "all the excitement about sex."

He laughed. He had a good laugh, and he thought maybe she liked it. "I don't really either. But it's fun sometimes. Sometimes it's a pain in the ass."

"Sounds complicated," she said. She unbuttoned her shirt then, to show him the scar. It ran from her breastbone around her right side to a place in back where he couldn't

see the end of it. He traced it with his index finger. Instead
of a bra, she was wearing a cutoff boys' undershirt.

"Did it hurt?"

"I don't remember that much. I was on the roof, and
next thing I knew I was waking up in the hospital with a
bandage wrapped all around me. I guess it hurt then. There
were drugs. I was just a kid."

"What were you doing on the roof?"

"Throwing rocks at my brother. I deserved to fall."

"No one deserves that."

"I did."

Her voice did a little flip, and he saw a look in her eye
that said, *We are done talking about this,* so he rolled up his
shirtsleeve to show her his own ragged scar, in the meaty
part of his arm just below the crease of his elbow. She
touched it lightly and pulled her hand away.

"Did you stitch that up yourself?"

"Nah, my cousin Leonard did it. After he stabbed me
with a bread knife."

"What did he stab you for?"

"He was drunk. We both were. It was an accident. We
were playing Trailer Trash White Folks."

"Sounds like a terrible version of a bad idea."

"Oh, it was."

He waited a few weeks to come back, partly because it
wasn't so easy to get there, but mostly because he didn't
want to push. She reminded him of a deer who knew you
weren't out to shoot it. Like she'd let you get just so close,
and then bolt to the edge of the clearing; the forest nearly

impenetrable behind her where she knew you couldn't easily follow. Even if you were a wily, woods-smart Apsáalooke bastard. A wily bastard who lived on the wrong reservation and didn't have his own car, who usually got around by hitchhiking but could occasionally sneak the work truck out.

They walked the railroad tracks. Talked about places they'd been and other places they'd never seen but wanted to.

"I've been to the Badlands," she said. "I went to Missoula once."

"How was that?"

"Okay."

"Just okay?"

"Yeah." She shrugged, bit her lip, ducked her head. "Where have you been?"

"Wyoming. Washington, DC, when I was a freshman. Some kind of Indian-kid award ceremony."

"For what?"

"Good grades. Citizenship, whatever that means."

"Means you'd have made a great Eagle Scout, I bet."

"Right."

"Did you go on a plane?" Like she was asking if he'd gone on a rocket ship.

"Nope. Four days on the train. It was cool."

"All by yourself?"

"Me, myself, and I."

"Oh." She nodded. "The three of you."

"Yup."

He remembered how lonely it was, how he wished

Leonard could have come along. Everyone else seemed to be in groups, families, eating in the dining car, hanging out playing cards, kids running up and down the aisles. He'd watched out the window as the landscape changed, the lush green of Minnesota and Illinois, the thunderstorms, acre upon acre of corn and beans and flat land; he'd never been anyplace that didn't have mountains on at least one horizon. Chicago blew his mind: more buildings, and taller ones, than he'd ever imagined. In DC, he'd wandered dizzily through the museums and the art galleries, knowing it would cost a lifetime to take it all in, and he didn't have a lifetime to spend. He had three days. On one of them he met the president, LBJ.

"Did he say anything to you?"

"He asked me if I played basketball."

"What did you say?"

Darrell took an imaginary jump shot. It went in. "I said yes, silly."

"Not yes, *sir*?"

"Probably."

"Is his nose as big as it looks on TV?"

"Bigger."

"Wow," she said. "That's big."

The next time he came, no one would pick him up on the way home. He walked all night—six hours—along the highway to get back in time for work. All the way there he thought about telling her he was going away. He imagined the conversation they would have. Maybe there would be promises. Maybe she wouldn't care.

He taught her about real paint ponies, how the conquistadores had brought them to North America, and the natives had stolen them to ride. "They came with their own camouflage," he said. "And it behooved them injuns to blend in."

She laughed when he said "behooved." Which was why he said it. She didn't laugh often or easily, but when she did, the sound flashed through his brain like a comet, scorching a trail.

One day he told her about the ducks who'd made the continents by pulling up mud and plants from the bottom of a great sea. Before that, he said, the only creatures who survived were the ones that could swim. She said how she had always wanted to see an ocean—the Pacific especially—and how she imagined it was the same as Montana, only bluer and bigger, with no mountains.

"In which case," he said, "not exactly the same." He was kidding, but apparently the humor escaped her. She stood up from where they were sitting on someone's abandoned sofa behind the abandoned theater, out of the hot sun. Walked away from him about fifteen paces, like Jesse James getting ready to draw, and then turned to face him, took off her blue sunglasses, and pointed her finger at him.

"Have you ever seen the ocean?"

"No. I've never seen the ocean. But I've seen pictures of it."

"Pictures lie," she said. "Everything does."

"Everything lies?"

"Yes." She stared him down—a dare to tell her she was wrong.

"Come here." He patted the seat next to him. "Crazy

girl." He saw in her eyes, as soon as he said it, what could only be identified as tears, if she had let them fall. He got up and grabbed her hand. "Come here." She let him lead her back to the sofa. "You gonna tell me?" She shook her head. "You want to hit me?"

"No."

"Sure you do." She made a fist and punched him in the arm. Hard enough. It stung for a second. "Better?"

"I'll be better when you stop."

"Stop what?"

"Just stop."

He didn't know what he'd run up against, but he knew to quit messing with it.

Out past the railroad tracks, a stretch of still and dusty plain lay unbroken except for the skeleton of an old railway spur and a couple of ancient and almost unrecognizable farm implements. Forty miles on was Alberta. He'd heard Canada was an option, but he'd never say it out loud; had never even formed the idea completely in his own mind. She put her hand back in his and with the other closed his fingers, one by one, around it. Dry bunchgrass grew up through the railroad tracks, and the spikes were working their way out in places. A train hadn't been through in years, as there was no good reason to come this way anymore.

"Canada," she said.

"It sure is, eh?" He tried to laugh, hoping she would help him do it. But she just looked at him—he could see himself reflected in her eyes—and then back out at what was there. Not much, was what.

In June, on his birthday, they broke into the clinic and
gave each other tattoos with a hypodermic needle and ink
leaked out of the doctor's fountain pen. Hers was a tiny *M*
on the back of her right shoulder, where she couldn't see it,
and under it the words "Rave On." Darrell didn't ask what
the *M* stood for, and she didn't say, but he had an idea. His
was the outline of a black bird with a big, curved beak.
He drew it on a piece of paper and she copied it onto his
forearm.

"Crow?" she asked.

"Not exactly. More sparrow hawk." She was incredibly
gentle with the needle, biting her bottom lip the whole
time, looking up at him every two minutes to see if she was
hurting him. "It doesn't hurt," he said, "I promise."

"I wish we had some other colors of ink except black."

"We'll fix them later. I know how to make some plant
and bark dyes and stuff."

She smiled, and it dazzled him. "You're the real deal,
aren't you?"

"You betcha, sister."

She bent her head down and went back to work. When
she was finished, she laid the needle aside and grabbed
the hem of her T-shirt to pull it off over her head. She
shrugged out of the boy's undershirt she still wore for
a bra and used it to blot the blood and the ink. When
she put it back on, the bird was clearly visible in red
and black—a repeat pattern, like an avian pileup on the
prairie. Her scar, a wild vine, wrapped around her body.
Darrell pulled her toward him, and she did not resist. He
picked her up and carried her to the examining table, laid

her down, and leaned in to kiss the scar where it began, just under her heart. He held onto the far side of the table, bent low with his arms stretched over her and turned his head to place his cheek in the hollow below her rib cage. She put her hands in his hair and sighed, blowing the air out soft and slow, until her lungs were empty, filled them again and held her breath. He couldn't move. He didn't want to.

Summer started to fade in August, with snow already falling on the Front Range. They watched from the couch behind the theater, where in the sun it was still warm, but wouldn't be for long.

"We should go camping," she said, "before it's too late."

"Like Lewis and Clark."

"Sort of. Only someone needs to be Sacajawea."

"Want to flip for it?"

"Nah. You be her. You'd be better at it. I'll watch and learn. For later."

"Deal," he said, wishing there was just one thing he could change: that everything hadn't gone and got all fucked up. By him. That he wasn't such a coward.

They packed sleeping bags and food out to a cottonwood-shaded beach by the river, a few miles east of town; cooked corn and potatoes over a fire, gnawed on too-rare elk, and sipped on a pint of Southern Comfort Darrell had brought because he thought she might like it. She liked it okay, and it made her less shy. She asked about his family; why he didn't live with his parents.

"Parents," he repeated, like it was a word in an unfamiliar language. "Mom and Dad." He poked at a smoldering chunk of wood until it reluctantly caught fire again, and tossed the stick aside. "I don't know a lot about my father, except he was a mix—a mutt Indian—and a wanderer. They say he was a pretty smart guy, a good businessman, like. I don't know if I ever even met him. If I did, I don't remember. I'm not even sure he's still alive, but I guess someone would tell me if he wasn't."

He looked down at his hands, spread his fingers wide, and put his fingertips together like he was fixing to play here's the church and here's the steeple. But he didn't even know that rhyme. "My mom came from Browning, and she ran off with the carnival. She actually did that. She stands on a stage and lets a guy throw knives at her."

"At her?"

"Around her. It's an act."

"Wow. That's kind of cool."

"Yeah, unless you're her kid."

"Oh, right."

"It's okay." He picked up the stick again and dug a trough in the dirt. "I guess I don't blame her. There's not much here, is there?"

"There's stuff," Riley said, and shrugged. "Did you ever live with her?"

"Once when I was little and she stayed put for a few months, down in Wyoming. But I've lived with my uncle and my cousin Leonard since I was four or five. That's home."

"So Leonard's your brother, pretty much, right?"

He thought about not saying anything, or making something up, but there was no good reason to do either of those things, so he told her how Leonard had fallen through the river ice the past winter, trying to free a goose whose foot was frozen to it. "I tried to get out to him, to pull him back, but the current got him before I could. I could see him under the ice for a few minutes, and then he was gone. We still haven't found him."

He remembered what Leonard was trying to say as he headed out onto the ice. "Geese muhmuhmuhmuh-mate for life," he'd said. "She needs to go back to her muhmuhmuhmuh— Oh fuck it."

Darrell leaned his forehead into hers and made her look into his eyes. "If you're going to go through the ice, do it on a lake. Or better yet, a pond. Preferably a shallow one."

"Then wait for you?"

"That's right."

"What happened to the goose?"

"Went back to her mate, I guess. Leonard got her foot unstuck before the river opened up."

She leaned into him, hard, and he had to lean back into her, or fall over.

When it got dark, they zipped their sleeping bags together against the cold and slid in, lying on their backs while Darrell pointed out constellations and told her their Indian names. One was called "Seven Dancing Girls."

"You made that up," she said.

"I did not. Otherwise there'd only be one dancing girl."

They fell asleep side by side, but woke fully tangled front to front as the sun cleared the canyon wall. Darrell tried to pull away even before he had to, but her legs locked him in and her hips anticipated every move. A rodeo cowboy, he thought, trying to make eight seconds on a saddle bronc. Positions somehow reversed, but he was past the point of no return. When she finally let him go, he pushed himself up so he could see her face, blew out a long, uneven breath, and said, "God you're strong."

He could tell she was trying really hard not to smile with her mouth, but her eyes gave her away. "Now I know," she said.

"Know what, exactly?"

"What all the excitement's about."

"Does that mean you liked it?"

She put her hands flat on the sides of his face and stared at him. She looked briefly insane. "Liked what?" He laughed. His hair curtained both their faces. She grabbed a handful and pulled, but it didn't hurt.

Later, walking back, she nonchalantly aimed her chin at the Little Rockies range and said, "That's where I'm going to spread my share of Mick's ashes when they find him."

He was not surprised by what she said, or that she didn't attempt any kind of foreword to the statement. *M* for Mick. He saw her reach over her shoulder to touch the tattoo, like she was making sure it hadn't disappeared in the night.

"You want to tell me?"

"He went missing in a tunnel or something. They

haven't said very much about it. He was only about two months away from getting out."

"How long ago?"

"Three years. Four months. Nine days." She stopped, picked up a rock, inspected it and threw it toward the mountains. "A long time." She walked on. "If he was here right now, he'd tell us what that rock is made of. Its whole entire history."

"I'm sorry."

"Yeah. Me too." She slowed down and let him walk beside her. "That's why my parents don't really care what I do, so long as I do it around here."

"I bet they care."

"Yeah, I just meant they don't track me or tell me."

"Do you want them to?"

"Sometimes."

"I know what you mean."

"I know you do. That's why I told you."

He'd meant to tell her some things too: about how his lottery number was too low, about how he'd agreed to enlist if they'd let him wait for a while, on account of Leonard and his uncle. Since that first day, he'd meant to.

A few days after the camping trip he borrowed the work truck and came back, sooner than he usually would. He held her against the wall behind the theater, tipped her chin up, and kissed her. He locked her in with his long arms, and told her. For a few endless seconds she didn't move. Then she pushed him away. Her eyes were crazy.

"I hate you."

He grabbed her wrist and tried to pull her to him.
"Don't—"

"Shut up shut up shut up." She twisted out of his grip,
backed up and closed her eyes. She shook her head so hard
her face and hair were a blur.

He knew there was nothing he could say to make it
right; that anything he said would only make it worse.

She stopped shaking her head and tilted it backward,
opened her eyes toward the cloud-covered sun, as if she
were waiting for it to show and blind her. She was holding
herself so tightly he thought she might crack a bone inside
with just skin and muscle. He took a step forward, and
when she didn't move reached out and put his hands on her
shoulders. She put the heels of her hands over her eyes for
a few seconds and then dragged her fingers down the sides
of her face and her neck until they reached his. She whispered, "Don't go."

"I have to. I made a deal. I'm already in."

"No you aren't. Stay. The rez will hide you."

"Not forever. They'll find me. They'll put me in jail."

She looked down at their feet, almost touching in the
dust, raised herself up on her toes, spun, and walked away.

"Hey, Ginger," he said, and she stopped. Her back was
to him, and she held her arms up in front of her, elbows
bent, like she was waiting for someone to put the handcuffs
on. He stood behind her and wrapped his hands around
her wrists. He had to tuck his fingers into his palms to get
a grip. When she tugged, he loosened up and she slipped
away. Just like that.

He left in late September. They'd found what was left of Leonard's body washed up under a pile of deadfall on the riverbank—some bones gnawed or missing—and buried him a few days before Darrell took the bus to the induction center in Butte and then on to basic training in Oklahoma.

He sent her letters, but she wrote back only once. She said, *Someday I will learn to not get attached. Maybe that's what this was all about. Don't think you can come back here and marry me or anything, because I won't be here. I am not going to wait for you too.* There was a long space; he could picture her thinking, pen poised over the page, biting her lip. Then she wrote, *But I am glad I found you. Or you found me. That's the way it went, isn't it? God I was high that day.* Another space. *I don't know if I would have been more mad if you didn't go. I can't get to the place in me that knows that.* Another space and *Don't get killed please.* She signed off, finally, at the very bottom of the page: *Love, whatever that means, Riley, whoever that is.*

Even though she never wrote again, he kept writing to her, mostly about what they were trying to teach him: how to shine his boots, make his bed, shoot and clean an M16, throw hand grenades, eat C rations, perform first aid. He was introduced to the practices of land navigation, or how to read a map and operate a compass. ("No celestial navigation," he said. "The army, she doesn't trust the stars.") He learned the rules of war ("Slightly more complicated, but basically the same as checkers") and the proper way to salute, stand at attention, and march, in ranks inspection, parade, and graduation. They dressed him in camouflage, but the pony requisition never came through.

After basic, they sent him to medic school in San Antonio for a few months, one night near the end of which he beat a redheaded white boy at pool and earned a mauling for it. It was in a honky-tonk he'd been to before, a few miles from the base, and usually he just kept to himself in a dark corner or at the end of the bar. But this night he was feeling good, like maybe he'd finally notched a chink in the armor of the pale world. He'd passed all the tests; everyone had started calling him Doc.

The first blow came from behind him, a pool cue at the knees, swung low like a cricket bat. He grabbed the edge of the table on the way down, came back up with the nine ball in his hand, turned to see who'd hit him. Four guys were standing there, three of them holding cues by the skinny ends, the fourth with a quarter-full vodka bottle he commissioned to smash in one of Darrell's cheekbones.

Someone said, "How does that feel, you fuckin' Cherokee?"

He slid to the floor, one leg tucked under him and the other stretched to the side in some ill-conceived Twister position. He felt but didn't really see until it was walking away the boot that came down on his shin and his ankle, three times, maybe four. He heard it, though—the cracking. On the jukebox, Tammy Wynette was singing "Stand by Your Man."

Darrell laughed, closed his eyes, and in the darkness conjured up an image of that dancing girl, the one he'd heard had left for Missoula. The big city. He'd never gotten a new address, and letters he sent to her parents' house had started coming back. Still, he hoped she'd find what she was looking for; that someday he might see her again and could tell her about the ocean. He figured he'd let her know, somehow, if it was anything like Montana at all.

3. Girl, Three Speeds, Pretty Good Brakes

So that was me, going on eighteen. Not too tall, no tits to speak of, brown hair to my ass, parted in the middle and brushed intermittently, worn just far enough out of my eyes so I could see, but my peripheral vision was not what it could have been. I'd graduated from high school, and left my family and our home in the rearview mirror of a Greyhound bus. Moved to the city—or what, in Montana, passes for one—and stayed awhile. I left a few things behind, but no one came looking to return them to me or to fetch me back. I didn't expect them to. They had enough to deal with.

What I did take along was a whole lot of questions for the world—oh yeah—beginning with *"Why why why why why?"* I often said it out loud, I guess because I was lonely enough to talk to myself. Bewildered too, but I knew enough to go. When I wasn't asking why, I was giving myself orders: *Just keep moving. Hit it, Riley. Get the lead out.* So there was me, keeping myself company, and after I got my job in Missoula, there was my Mustang—my parachute, my escape. I took up driving like some people take up smoking or poker, and set about prowling the roads of a different part of the state—a different planet, almost—than the one I'd come from, a hundred miles north and two fifty east. The one where I'd left my mother and father, their grandson, and their own mess of memories and regrets. I didn't know if they were still reaching, like I was, into empty space, looking to grab onto something no longer there, but it was likely enough.

One of my half-assed dreams, when I was still young, had been to become a diesel mechanic, work on huge things—equipment that could move mountains. It was not something girls normally wanted, but I was not a normal girl, and I had plans for that equipment. I guessed that given the right machinery, my little corner of the world—including all of Montana, parts of western North Dakota and southern Alberta, maybe just a small corner of Wyoming—could be arranged a little more to my liking. I even thought about joining the army. I knew they had some big machines, and I knew if you joined, they took you away. Maybe to somewhere warm, maybe near an actual ocean, where if it was the right time of year, there would be whales. As it was, I was already imagining them in the endless wheat fields, their big humped backs rising up out of all those amber waves of grain. I had a pair of blue-tinted sunglasses that nearly took care of the color discrepancy. Hits of mescaline or the occasional tab of acid took care of the rest.

Sometimes I'd lie out there on my back, and the world

would turn over on itself, so all that big sky—all that inexhaustible sky I knew for some people who weren't me was full of possibilities—instead became a big milk-glass bowl containing my life and all the reasons for me even having one. It would fill slowly with water, and I could feel fish swimming through me, through all my arteries and veins. And then I would start to drown in it, because it was all wrong and it was too big, and I would close my eyes and grab onto the dirt or the grass or the rocks or whatever was there and make the world go back the way it had been, and then sometimes I'd feel myself drowning in that too.

Despite all that, I was a picture, even if it was only in my mind, in my uniform. There was, however, the problem of being too much of a fuckup for even the army to want me. That, and I had not yet figured out a way to forgive them for losing my brother and taking my boyfriend. Or either of them, for letting it happen.

My parents, I knew, saw me orbiting a little too close to the sun, but they didn't try to talk me down, probably because they knew they couldn't, or were afraid of pushing me even further away. I learned how to drive at fourteen and spent a lot of time in my dad's pickup. On the back roads, on the straight stretches, some voice in my head would tell me to floor it. I noticed the same voice never told me to stop if the road ended or turn if it turned. I wondered a few times about the significance of that, and it took a special effort on my part to stay out of the wheat fields.

• • •

In Missoula I found a job at a gas station where the mechanic, Leo, offered to teach me how to work on cars. I worked on other people's, and found my own—bought it off a guy who came by on his way to the train station, needing the fare for San Diego, as he allowed that he did not intend to spend one more goddamn winter in goddamn Montana freezing his fucking ass off. It was September. The car needed the kind of work I could do. I gave him a hundred thirty dollars, two weeks' pay.

After about a month at the station, Leo caught me talking to myself and I realized I wasn't always aware I was doing it. I told him I felt a little crazy. I didn't tell him about my brother or Darrell or the kid, because at the time a connection had not occurred to me, but I told him about the drugs, as blaming those seemed logical—and probably, at least partially, was.

Leo started watching me around the office and in the service bays where we worked and out at the pumps. He squinted at me. "I don't see anything the matter with you."

"It doesn't show," I said. "It's up here." I thumped myself on the side of the head with the heel of my hand, hard; so hard my head rocked.

He took a step back. "Man, did that hurt?"

"Yeah." And it did, a little. "But pain doesn't bother me. It's weird."

"You're weird," he said.

"I told you."

My car was seven years old and looked like it had been through a war. It was about five different shades of black, and there was a hole in the floor behind the driver's seat

couldn't take him because I was too afraid of what I might do, like lose him; set him down somewhere and forget. I was not so out of it as to believe I was even remotely steady enough to take care of a baby. Both my parents, by some miracle I was sure I'd never fully comprehend, seemed to understand.

When I got stoned I would think about my childhood, which always came back to me in black and white and a barely distinguishable range of gray. We had dogs, and farm animals of the regular kind: chickens, cows, once in a while a few goats. I had a big brother who tried against some pretty ferocious odds to teach me about the world and what was in it. A mother who, against similar odds, kept me steady as long as she could, kept me from becoming a human rocket-propelled grenade and launching myself into the atmosphere, where I'd explode into tiny pieces and rain down on the house and the yard while she watched from behind the screen door: another one gone—the last one, except . . .

And my dad, who, no matter what, seemed always on the verge of smiling, like he was telling himself jokes, and if you were lucky—if you asked with the right words—he'd tell them to you too.

Our days: Getting up before the sun every morning and going to bed halfway through *Bonanza* at night. 4-H. The bus to school, the bus back. A long way between us and everyone else. A lot of alone time. And a war on TV, brought to you by Nabisco.

I didn't know—because I never thought it through—that American boys had not been fighting in Vietnam since the beginning of time, or that no one had ever watched a war on TV before. I would watch and look for a face I recognized among the living, but then came the ones they were loading onto the helicopters: the ones that didn't move no matter how long the camera stayed on them; the ones I maybe should have known better than to think about as hard as I did. But I didn't know not to do that. You could tell under the tarps and the blankets that some of them had been blown clear apart.

Boys my age were too young for the war, but older brothers had been going and coming back in shifts, quietly over the years, and no one said very much about it. When they came home, they went back out to work the ranches, and I'd see them on the street or at the feed store and try to match their faces to the ones I'd seen on television. There was a sameness to those faces—something I was too young to identify, but it was etched there, and no one else had it.

I was thirteen when they let us know they couldn't find Mick. When the letter came in the mail, my mother wandered around the house for weeks carrying it and talking to herself, saying pretty much the same thing over and over. For a long time, among all the other voices, hers was the one I heard most distinctly, at the most random times, saying, "I thought they were supposed to come and tell you in person."

It was as if our house were a birdcage someone had thrown a sheet over and forgotten, in the morning—every morning—to take off. I don't remember any talking, let alone laughing, or making anyone feel better about anything, though I know there must have been trying. The quiet was blinding and deafening. Even the barn cats stopped freaking out when anyone came close. They perched in the windows at the top of the barn and watched us come and go, as though they knew those were our final days, and anytime now we'd pack up and leave. But I was the only one who did.

I made it through school, barely, knowing that once it was over, I'd be gone. I left my parents in a parking lot in Havre: my mom waving, some hidden force pulling her away from the bus steps; Dad awkward and incongruous with the baby's carriage, in the background, where he liked to stay. I wanted to put my bag down and go back for another hug, tell him not to worry, I'd figure it out. Like he said. Mom had that distant look, as if she were the one leaving. And the baby, well. I couldn't see him. Dad could have had a mess of those boney cats in that carriage. With their eyes closed, meowing and growling like they do. Bye kittens. Good night moon.

In Missoula, I got my job and rented a little apartment over the Laundromat, where when winter came the steam would rise into my room, and the sweet smell of the soap would cover over the stink of the pulp mill down the road. Still, there was nothing to be done about the smoke from its stacks, which would combine with the smoke from people's woodstoves and the fog that was a natural consequence of the inversion layer in that valley, and sometimes we wouldn't see the sun for weeks at a time. I'd drive out of town then, in any direction.

For a while that one winter I had company: another car I came up on one hazy day outside of Frenchtown, and it looked a lot like mine. There had been approximately no other traffic on the road in either direction since I'd gone by the Flathead cutoff, aside from a few log trucks and one kamikaze U-Haul pilot who was having a tough time staying off the median. I got around him as fast as I could, swerving at the last second while he played *What's My Lane?*, and my imagination previewed for me what might happen if I didn't swerve—if I hit him and lost control; or cut the wheel and cut back too sharply and spun out. I saw the marks my tires would leave in a spiral as me and my car left the road.

The other Mustang might have been doctored up at the same body shop as mine. It had a similar paint job, holes in the top, duct tape. It wasn't an exact match, but close enough I thought I ought to get up alongside for a look. The guy driving had long, straight brown hair in a pony-tail; a mustache; and aviator shades he was wearing even at dusk, with yellow lenses.

The first time we drove together for a while, west on the interstate, north and south of the river, crossing it every now and again like you do on that stretch. On the straightaways we were doing ninety, ninety-five. After a bit, though, I slowed up to let him get ahead, feeling silly out there in the fast lane, not passing anything. I had my radio tuned to static from Missoula, breaking every once in a while to let through snatches of country music—about love, about broken hearts. I'd always figured if I could hear a whole song all at once it might make sense, but the an-tenna on my car was broken at the base, splinted with Pop-sicle sticks and electrical tape, and I had not gotten around

to replacing it yet. So I filled in the blanks myself, with
words I could understand, about cars, motors, carburetors,
timing chains.

At Tarkio I turned around, using my signal to say, *See
you later*, before I got off the highway. He flashed his brake
lights and then he was gone, leaving me and my car, in
some unbidden, imaginary outcome, to bump down the
embankment, over the riprap and into the river, to float all
the way to Lake Pend Oreille and the Columbia or sink and
give the fish a place to hide. Or to drive straight up the slope
on the other side, to a point too vertical, where the weight
of the engine would pull us backward, and we'd tumble end
over end to the bottom—possibly across the road and into
the river anyway. I let my mind have its fun and its carnage, but I was seeing that other black car too, flying along
toward the coast in the darkness, with a radio that probably
worked. I kept my car on the highway. I headed toward
home and bed and tumbling dryers; the smothering smell
of other people's sheets and towels and shirts and jeans.

I stopped at the bar where I knew Leo would be nurs-
ing a beer and playing the poker machine, in a vapor mist
of cigarette smoke and deep-fried chicken. I ordered my
own beer and sat on a bar stool next to him, watching him
draw electric cards, always keeping jacks, eights, and aces
when they came up. We sat quiet except for the beeping of
the machine: the excited noises it made whether he chose
right or didn't, whether the hand turned out a full house or
a pair of deuces, or all but the last card of a straight flush.
After a while I said good night to him and the bartender,
walked down the street and up to my room, where I took

off my clothes and curled around myself in the exact center of the bed, my head under the covers, and slept in one position all night. In the morning, for a few long waking seconds, I had no idea where I was.

I saw that other car fairly often the next few months: up the Bitterroot, in the Mission Valley, west of Beavertail. We were all over the place. I'd come up on him, or he'd appear in my rearview mirror and get up beside me, wave, give me a slightly lopsided smile, and I'd drift back and follow until my internal compass swung me around and guided me home.

Mornings I was generally up at five, at the station by six, in my uniform: dark blue pants and pale blue shirt with my name embroidered in orange over the pocket—that over a layer of long johns, my brother's old horse-blanket-lined jean jacket on top of it all. Leo would already be there, with the propane stove in the garage fired up to take the edge off the chill. The edge was about all it ever took off, and I'd wonder what it might be like to be warm more than four months a year. I'd conjure up a palm tree. A beach. Add the ocean: a body of water without any discernible other side, deep and full of all kinds of slippery things, and whales. It appeared in my mind like a child's drawing: the waves a series of inverted V's across the middle of the page; the whales just below and ready to breach; the sun a yellow ball in the top left-hand corner; two distinct white clouds to break up all that monotonously blue sky.

Most days I'd be off work by two or three, and one freezing and particularly socked-in day in early March I went looking for sunshine. I knew I could find it on the other side of town, east where the inversion (depending on which way you were going) began or ended, like a wall of fog, like a magic trick of the gods, a wall you could drive through and disappear.

I drove out of the murk into a sharp light that nearly blinded me. It felt even colder than it had in the fog, and the air coming through the gap above my windshield blew across my face and practically froze a section solid, from the bridge of my nose to the middle of my forehead. I had the heater blasting, which did not do much but keep my feet, in pac boots and wool socks, from turning into little blocks of ice.

My eyes finally adjusted to the light at Bonner, where the Champion mill on my left was spewing smoke and sawdust straight into the air, and it seemed to stay, motionless, caught in time or an invisible element that defied gravity or dispersion. I drove as far as Rock Creek, circling down off the highway to the north side of the river, and along the frontage road to where it dead-ended at a woods of scrappy pine and brush.

I pulled a tiny roach out of my pocket, smoked it and listened to the radio: an oldies station coming in clear as a bell from Rock Springs, Wyoming. They played songs I'd heard from behind my brother's bedroom door as a child, and sometimes, if he didn't have a girl in there, he'd let me in, take me by the hands and dance with me, spin me around the room to "Rave On," "Jailhouse Rock," "Shout," until I was so dizzy and laughing so hard I thought I was going to pass out. Then he'd let me down easy to sit on the floor, and he'd sit down there next to me, and we'd read or draw or talk about stuff until Mom called us downstairs for dinner.

After he dropped out of college and enlisted, before he went away, he boxed up all his things, taped and labeled the boxes. He wrote his name on them with a fat felt marker, and on some my name or an alias in smaller letters below. I didn't open them when he went missing, because there was no way I could convince myself he wouldn't be coming home. Not in a box. Not in a coffee can. Not a bunch of bones tied together like kindling. Not coming back. Not ever.

His records were in some of those boxes, books in others. He left me his model cars and the dinosaurs and the rock collection. Afternoons during his last few weeks at home, he'd go to one bar or another in town, and get drunk with his buddies who were going to Vietnam with him and a few who had deferments and were staying home. He'd come back an hour or so before dinner and sit out on the porch, not doing anything, just trying to get straight enough to come in and eat with us. He said he was sobering up the sunset, and he'd calculate the number of hours since the sun had risen over the South China Sea. I'd sit at his feet, repeating those words: *South, China, Sea.* He'd laugh while I did it, and all the while I was willing him back home. Asking God, I suppose. It wasn't until much later I realized I should have been more specific about what condition he'd be in when he came back. Just in case.

I drove out of the woods and went to the Stage Station for a beer. I was very stoned and a little shaky, so in order to avoid looking at anyone I got a newspaper off the bar and sat at a table in the one corner still in a patch of daylight. It was earlyish, about four, but you could feel night coming on already, and the lights over the pool table outshone the late-winter sun, struggling, seemed like, just to stay lit.

On the front page of the paper was a story about a guy who'd gone off the road down south of Drummond, and a picture of his car lying on its top by the creek running through there, the old railroad tracks with weeds growing up through the ties, cattails undisturbed in uneven rows along the water. It was too easy for me to imagine how it must have felt as his car left the pavement, all four wheels suddenly in midair, no sound but the wind roaring by, or maybe no sound at all. I looked again, to be sure it really was that guy, and read the rest of the story. It said they didn't know yet how he wound up down there, but he was still alive, in critical condition at St. Pat's in Missoula. They'd reached a brother in Kentucky who said he'd done two tours in the Air Force, spent them mostly in the central highlands at Pleiku, and come home with no medals but did have a little shrapnel lodged in his head.

When I started feeling less wasted, I went up to get another beer and took the paper with me; I showed the picture to the bartender. Told him I'd seen that guy around some, driving a car that sort of matched mine.

"Doesn't look good," is what the bartender said.

"Nope."

He read the story, nodded, scratched above his ear. "A lot of those guys came back a little crazy. Think maybe he just drove off the road on purpose or something?"

"I don't know," I said. "I guess he could have." I looked out the window at the parking lot, the dusky woods beyond, and tried to imagine what animals might be wandering through, just out of sight. "My brother went over there, and he didn't come back crazy."

"Some didn't." The way the words came out sounded like what I'd said proved some opinion he already had on the subject. He was an old guy. He wouldn't have gone.

I stayed to drink my beer, me and the bartender talking about what little we knew about the world. How much water was in it. What kinds of things and people we imagined were on the other side of the ocean. Turns out we didn't really know very much.

When I got back home, Leo was at our bar playing the poker machine. Without looking at me he said, "Where have you been?" He discarded a two of clubs and a queen of diamonds, aiming for an inside straight. "I was starting to get worried."

"I was out at Rock Creek."

He glanced over. "You look strange."

I reckoned I did. I *felt* strange. "You're never gonna hit that straight," I said.

But I wasn't thinking about the cards. I was trying to figure out how anything could be so big it could be more than one thing: the Pacific on one side and the South China Sea on the other. I could not properly imagine the immensity of it, the possibility of all that water and what it could hold. I thought about that guy in the hospital and wondered if he was still alive, if they'd managed to get his car up out of that draw. Decided to go see some things for myself.

I told Leo I'd be leaving in the summer, after I'd saved some money. Together we put a new clutch in my car, a new distributor, brakes all around. We fixed the antenna for real. Laid down some actual carpet in the back.

I went to the hospital and talked them into letting me into the ICU to see my friend. He was in a coma. "Don't expect much," they said. As if.

I sat on a chair next to his bed and watched his eyes move under his eyelids. I whispered, "Hey," and then again, a little louder, "Hey, buddy," but he just stayed in there, in that other world. I couldn't know a thing about it.

It was almost September by the time I'd got all ready to go, and Leo followed me in his truck as far as the Idaho border, to make sure I at least got to the top of the pass okay. Maybe he thought if something happened I could just coast from there, as clearly it would be all downhill from the top of that pass to the ocean. We pulled over among all the semis—cooling off from the climb and checking their brakes for the descent—to say good-bye. Leo kissed my forehead and told me he still didn't think I was crazy. He gave me a new toolbox and a socket set for a going-away present, got in his truck and drove back the way we'd come. Halfway down the mountain I felt something snap inside me, like a shredded fan belt when it finally lets go. It felt strange but didn't hurt like you might think it would.

I sailed across the panhandle and turned left at Coeur d'Alene, figuring I'd drive all night and be in Nevada in the morning. I'd never seen a real desert. I started a list of things I'd never seen. A tornado. Mountain lion up close.

The Southern Cross. Saturn, that I knew of. Penguins. Palm trees. My list got longer as I drove, though I figured soon I'd be able to simultaneously put something on it—an iguana, for example, or a tide pool—and take it right back off again.

I practiced, on that road, keeping the people lost to me at bay. Aside from Mick, a tiny baby conceived just in time, maybe, to live, and named after a barn cat; and his father, who tried to hold me steady, though he couldn't, as he had no way of knowing how. Even if he had, I didn't know how to let him. On that road I was practicing something I would never perfect but knew I was going to need. Maybe not forever. Certainly for a while.

I headed south through Idaho and west through Nevada, collecting images of jackrabbits, casinos, tumbleweeds and dust spiraling across empty fields. I saw a black horse with a white mane. A five-gallon oil can on the side of the road with a bald eagle dead on top of it. A claw-foot bathtub with no feet. An army boot. A coonskin cap hanging on the branch of an old apple tree, rotten apples piled deep around it. California was just ahead of me when it started to get dark again. I drove through the mountains with the top down, even though it was almost Montana cold up there. I needed something like cold to keep me awake.

When I finally found the ocean I couldn't see it, couldn't see anything beyond the edge of the cliff where I parked my car, on account of the fog. I had not expected fog. But I could hear the water, and smell it. I could feel it. I could barely stand not being able to look at it, but figured I'd already waited so long, and the sky had to clear eventually. I moved over to the passenger seat, put my feet up on the dashboard, and fell asleep.

When I woke up, the fog had backed off to the horizon and I saw the ocean, as big and blue as anything.

I got out and sat on the hood of my car to watch how this unlikely element moved; watched the tide come in and the waves break, until I had memorized the patterns of each one. I let in some of what I'd seen along the miles of road between me and home, and what I was seeing now, in shades of something other than gray I knew I could use later on to remember my life. I sat there the whole day. I didn't have any idea which way I'd go when it got dark, but it wasn't a terrible worry. Something would tell me.

I watched the sun get set to drop into the water and couldn't take my eyes off it. The lower it fell, the bigger it got, until finally it was a huge orange ball balancing on its edge, millions of miles from me and my car there on the cliff, but it looked so close—close enough I figured I could throw stuff at it. I got my brother's records out of a box in the trunk, sorted through them. He got into my head easily, despite my best efforts; enough that I could hear him holler in some fake pathetic voice, *No, not that one!* while I tossed some of those records—the ones I never liked; sappy ones he played for girls and the "Stay out" order (for me) was not negotiable. I flung them off the cliff, laughing, *Ha ha ha ha.*

For all I knew, there was no bottom and no end to the ocean, and some of those records sailed a long time before they fell into it. They caught the sun and threw it back at me until it wasn't there anymore, until the last little curve of it flattened out and disappeared, slipping into all that water like the bald head of God reflecting its own image, painted on the twilight sky.

4. Slim

A young woman. Okay, maybe not so young. Maybe forty-two and already a grandmother. Believe me: no one finds this harder to believe than she does. Her name is Rose and she is a little ashamed, on this particular errand, to admit (to herself? to her small passenger?) that she has only ever skirted this reservation. It lies adjacent to a road she has driven many times—the shortest cut between Great Falls and home—but there has never been any reason to actually go in, to stop, until now. That, or she has always sensed she would be unwelcome, or guilty of trespassing, or simply did not belong.

In any event, it is late spring now, and wildflowers— mostly purple lupine, but some red Paintbrush, some dirty-white Queen Anne's lace—flourish in yards and in the many vacant lots, making the otherwise dust-colored neighborhood a little brighter, almost radiant. She takes that as a good sign. From whom? God does not have a place in all this. That would be the kind of wishful thinking she cannot afford.

She carries a red and black wool blanket, wrapped around some small, obviously alive, thing. It is not a puppy or a newborn calf. It is a baby. Her grandson. She has come to offer him to someone she has never met. Not the boy's father. His father is in Vietnam, if he has not had the good sense to go AWOL and head for another country; one simultaneously very close and very far away.

She can't speak for anyone else but imagines they all thought about that passage when the lottery numbers were picked, matched to birthdays, fired like flaming fucking arrows into the hearts of mothers everywhere. But she is not thinking about that now. This is someone else's child (her daughter's, but still), and she doesn't even know if the father—this child's father, who is possibly already a dust cloud floating on the breeze over the South China Sea— even had a mother. Anything, at this point, seems possible. Maybe because there is this baby, who, created a few months later, might now have been . . . nothing. A memory. Carried regret. When the decision came down from the court, they didn't talk about it. It was too late. And this boy's mother was mostly beyond talking by then anyway.

Rose knows a family name and approximate location because of letters sent to her daughter when she still lived with them, and a handful after she left. Early postmarks said Oklahoma, later ones Texas, but the last one came from Montana.

A man answers the door. He is tall and dark and reminds her of the young man she has met only the one time. She says hello, and folds the blanket away from the baby's face. "I believe," she says, holding the boy out awkwardly so the man can see him better, "this is your grandson."

"My grandson," the man says, as if trying to decide if the word could have more than one meaning. "And he came to you by way of—"

"My daughter."

He raises one eyebrow. "I see."

Rose nods. The words are not a challenge but an acknowledgment. That, at least, is how she hears them. "Yes."

"And your daughter?"

"Is in Missoula, I think. She left him with us. To find a family for him."

"Leonard can not be this baby's father."

"Leonard? I don't know who that is. The boy I know is called Darrell."

The man nods. He does not look surprised or wary, as she had thought he might. "Darrell is my nephew."

"Oh," Rose says, knowing she still has to say what she came for, even if she doesn't know how to say it, especially now. The man waits, not impatiently, and she steels herself, slowly blowing out a bellyful of air before she speaks again. "Do you think— Can you take him? I mean, would you? My husband and I, we can't keep him. I'm afraid—" She wants to explain, about her missing son, her already lost daughter, her inability to function some days, to keep track of days at all, let alone keep track of this tiny person. But she can't explain. It would be too much.

The man laughs softly. To Rose, the laugh sounds sad,

or resigned, or both, but she doesn't trust herself to judge what anyone else is feeling. Since she doesn't even know what she is feeling, it would hardly be fair.

"Yes," the man says. "I can take him. I can take care of him."

Is it the answer she wants? God—him again—knows. Simple enough, she thinks. Simple as that. Done.

She looks at the baby, and back at the man. The resemblance is more than dark skin and eyes and hair. "I know this is a terrible thing to ask," she says. "But do you want him? Or do you—"

"Not so terrible," he says. "I understand why you would ask." He looks past her, across the road, up into the seemingly empty hills. "I would like to have him here with me. My boy died two years ago. He was seventeen. And now my nephew is gone too. This house is pretty damn empty." He looks down at the baby in Rose's arms. "Seems right," he says. "I think I know myself well enough by now to trust that."

Rose finds she is jealous but doesn't say.

"Don't worry." He touches her shoulder. "He'll be okay. Tell your daughter. He'll be fine here."

"I'll tell her." It does make sense. As much as anything else does. She hands him the blanket, the baby. The boy looks at him, out of pale eyes that don't really go with the rest of him. He looks quite serious, like a little old man; aside from the eyes, almost like a miniature of the man holding him.

"His name?"

Rose says they call him Slim.

The man smiles as he repeats it. "How old is he?"

"Sixteen weeks."

"Small."

"Yes. He was premature, but the doctor says he's healthy now." She reaches out a hand and the boy wraps his tiny fingers around one of hers. She waits for him to let go, and begins to turn away.

"Would you like a cup of coffee," the man asks, "before you leave?"

She realizes her legs feel like they might not hold her up much longer. "I'd like that," she says. "Thank you. I'd like that very much." She sits on the front step. He crouches to give the baby back to her.

"While I make coffee," he says.

"Of course." She looks into Slim's eyes. She sees they are changing color. She thinks they may be turning green. Or maybe it is a reflection, a trick of the light. He holds a tiny hand up for her hair. She leans her head down so he can reach it. So he can hold on.

5. Not-So-Secret Life

truly believed I was flying under the radar—figured I was inconspicuous or at least camouflaged—but Primo told me that was ridiculous: I was impossible to miss. It was the car, he said, beat up in its massively original way. He said he dug the duct-taped slashes in the rag top, the dope Bondo work around the wheel wells, and what was probably the most fucked-up paint job he had ever seen on a vehicle a person could actually drive. He said it looked like something some Mission *cholo* might be commandeering. A Mission *cholo* like him.

"Yeah, okay, so what." His response when I pointed that small detail out, later, when I knew what the word meant. Even so, he said, even he would not have thought that many different shades of black were possible.

"I knew it ran though," he said, "because you kept moving it."

It's true. I did, but I always stayed within a few blocks of the ocean, because the ocean was why I had gone to California in the first place. Primo said he noticed the Montana plates right away, but not me, the girl sleeping in the backseat.

"If I had, I would have checked on you sooner, to see if you was okay."

"I was okay," I said.

He said, "Sure you was."

Once he found me, it didn't take too long for me to start imagining how we'd tell the story later on, together, to whoever asked how we'd met, as surely people would want to know. I knew, even before anything like that happened, what I would say: I'd say everything was just peachy in my world; that it was Primo who was the lucky one, the one who needed finding.

I was awake, still wearing my pajamas, when he rolled up in his navy-blue *San Francisco Chronicle* truck, got out, and tapped on my window. It was about four, and I was in my sleeping bag in the back, reading *The Old Man and the Sea* by flashlight. I turned it off, but with the streetlamps we could still, if just, see each other. I didn't think he looked at all dangerous or deranged, and was obviously working, unless he had stolen the truck, which seemed unlikely. I trusted, at any rate, that he wasn't skulking around at that hour in search of young girls to prey on, because other than me, I figured no one else was out. After he tapped on the window, he stood waiting, as if he had all day and nowhere in particular to be. I saw him checking out the peeling duct tape that more or less held the top of the car together and, also more or less, kept the rain out, which was good, since there had been quite a lot of it since I'd gotten to town.

It was September, and I was about to turn nineteen. I was almost a grown-up. A nearly broke one. Also really hungry, alone, and beginning to wonder how long I could live in my car. And if the sun was ever going to come up or out again. Because even when it wasn't raining, the fog made it feel like it was. I had thought California was supposed to be a sunny place. Seemed like that's what all the fuss was about. *Come visit. Come see the ocean and the palm trees and the SUN.* Ha.

I leaned forward and rolled down the back window a few inches. Primo crouched slightly to peer in, filling the window and then some. He was not very tall, but he was plenty wide, like he was wearing shoulder pads, and not just on his shoulders. He didn't appear to be fat, though, just solid, like a wall of Mexican. His dark hair was a little long, and messy, as if he'd brushed it with his pillow. Of course mine looked pretty much the same, though it was brown and not black, and there was a lot more of it.

"Hey there," he said, awfully chipper for four in the morning. "How's tricks?"

"Pardon?"

"How's life? You okay in there?"

I glanced around the car, thinking what was obvious to some might not be so obvious to some others. "Could be worse," I said.

"That's good." He nodded approvingly, as if that was the answer he'd been expecting. "I'm Primo," he said. "Usually." He brought his hand up, but the window was in the way, so he dropped it back down to his side again, reluctantly, or so it seemed.

"Hi," I said. I didn't know what sort of etiquette was called for, or what he meant by "usually," or whether Primo was a name or a condition or what. He rescued me, for a minute, from having to work it out.

"What do they call you?" he asked.

"What does who call me?"

"Whoever. Friends? Family? I mean what's your name?"

"Tinker Bell." I didn't know why. It just appeared, like all the other names I'd been given or had made up, Tinker Bell not among them. Mick had called me Cupcake, or Smartass, or Punk, and Darrell had called me Ginger, after Ginger Rogers, but that was different. That was the past.

I could see him thinking hard, squinching up his forehead. "Peter Pan," he said, as if someone had asked him a really hard question and he had, against all odds, come up with the answer. "Right? Never-never land?"

"Right."

He was clearly relieved. "Well, hey there, then, Tinker Bell. Me, I'm still Primo. Almost always."

"Nice to meet you." I was intrigued, at the very least, to meet someone else whose identity might not be carved in stone.

He looked about thirty, maybe thirty-five; it was hard to tell. He asked if anyone ever called me T.B. Because sometimes people called him T.C. Because his given name was Tony, and his last name was Castaneda.

"I don't think so," I said. "T.B. stands for tuberculosis."

A baffled expression came and went. "Oh, right. That wouldn't be so good. Would it?"

"No. Not really."

"Do they even have that anymore?"

"Tuberculosis?"

"Yeah. That."

"I'm pretty sure they do. In some places, anyway." I thought about the rez; thought I remembered hearing something about TB there. But it was hazy, just a flicker. Something Darrell had said? Something from a history book? Maybe cholera or yellow fever. The plague. Whatever it was, I was sure it was something special. Some lovely keepsake to remember white people by. Darrell hadn't held any of it against me, though, not like some. He'd actually loved me, in a way; I could see that, from this distance, even though he'd never said it in so many words. Maybe because I wouldn't let him.

One of Primo's eyes looked strange, and it didn't follow the other one as he took in the arrangement of my living quarters. What little there was to take in. A small cooler in the front passenger seat. Six or seven books stacked on the floor in back. My day clothes—jeans and a red sweatshirt with a wolf design—folded on top of the cooler. A jug of water and a thermos. Remnants of last night's dinner: cheese and peanut butter crackers. An open Buck knife on top of the books. The rest of my life, what there was of it, was in the trunk.

I'd been dining on 7-Eleven fare, bathing in gas station restrooms, couldn't remember the last time I'd properly washed my hair, but there was a dim memory of a shower at a truck stop in Nevada. I hoped I didn't appear as animal-like as I was starting to feel.

"Home sweet home?" Primo asked.

"Yeah, pretty much."

"Nice," he said. I didn't think he was being sarcastic. He sounded, truly, as if he liked what he saw, as if he could see living there, or in a place just like it.

He glanced again at the cooler. "You got plenty of food in there?" My stomach growled, and I wondered if he heard.

"Yeah. Lots." There had been easier lies.

The last bag of ice I'd bought had finally finished melting; a hunk of cheese floated in the water, wrapped in plastic but wet and slimy anyway, accompanied by a hard-boiled egg and a few mealy apples. I had been thinking about dumping out the water and throwing away anything irretrievably rotten as soon as the sun came up, or at least when it got light, somewhere out by the beach, where no one would see and maybe yell at me. Other than what was drowning in the cooler, I owned a half jar of peanut butter, some saltines, and a bag of jerky I'd been working on since Missoula. I had about sixty-five dollars left to my name.

"I don't know," Primo said. "You look hungry. I bet you're hungry, aren't you?"

Ravenous. Eat-a-whole-pig hungry. Hungry for food even more than for someone to talk to, though there was that too. "A little bit," I said, and swallowed.

"You like donuts?"

"I like bacon and eggs." Like my new name, it came out of nowhere.

He nodded slowly. "Knowing what you like is half the battle."

"I've just been dreaming about bacon and eggs," I said. And home, but I didn't say that part. At home it was breakfast time. My mother's kitchen, right then, smelled like bacon and eggs. Dad was eating, dragging a piece of toast through yellow yolk, telling her what a good cook she is.

Dreamt about but not missed. Not allowed to be missed. None of them.

Primo said he knew a place. Open early. Right by the beach.

I said, "Aren't you working?"

"Yeah, but this is the quiet part of my shift. It'll be a while before people start calling in."

"Calling in where? For what?"

"The office. For their papers. If the kids don't deliver them on time, or if they get stolen or wet or something." And there was always something, he said, but to him it was job security. He was out here to fix these things, and he liked it. He was good at it. Talking to people and working with the kids. He liked to work. This work. And he'd been one of those kids once. He told me all of this without taking a breath. It made me happy, him liking his life like that.

I tried to picture him as a kid, and he looked exactly the same, only in miniature. Like a third the size he was now, but with exactly the same proportions and features: same shoulders, same hair, same scruffy mustache, same husky voice.

Primo smiled when I did. "Well, can I buy you breakfast? Or you want me to bring it to you in bed?"

It took about two seconds to weigh the possibilities.

Maybe he was a serial killer or a Bible salesman, but I thought I'd have caught on by then, and truly, I was way too hungry to care.

"Yes, please," I said.

The newspaper truck was really a huge van, all metal on the inside, with the engine cover in the middle next to the driver's seat. There was no passenger seat. Primo told me he'd always thought the engine cover looked like a doghouse, with no door and a flat top. A doghouse for an aluminum dog. One who could walk through walls, who didn't need a door. He had a cup of coffee sitting there, surrounded by an impressive array of donut crumbs. There was a metal divider, like a chain-link fence, between the front and the back, but it was open on the passenger side. Primo set a bundle of newspapers in the opening for me to sit on.

I asked what time he went to work in the morning.

"Two thirty. Except on Saturdays. I get to sleep in all the way till three on Saturdays." He had a low, growly laugh.

"Wow. That's early."

"Yeah, it is. But it's not so bad once you're up."

He loved being out there most mornings, he said, with the quiet, the occasional cop or taxi or garbage truck. There were the bums too, mostly on Geary, but not nearly so many out in the Richmond district as he'd see passing through the Tenderloin on his way from the plant. In the Tenderloin were those guys, and the pushers down on Golden Gate Avenue with their little glassine bags of white powder. The prostitutes stayed downtown too, he said, chilling around their claimed corners, all fishnet-

stockinged and stoned. There had been a bunch of kidnap-
pings and killings the past year or so, but they'd caught the
guys who were doing it, they thought; at least the worst of it
had stopped for now. He warned me about all the different
kinds of trouble a person could get into in the city, told me
which neighborhoods were best avoided, especially after
dark, and congratulated me on picking a relatively safe one
to pitch my encampment in.

I tried to process it all, to not look startled like some
hick straight out of the backwoods, to act like I'd at least
heard of some of these things. I did wonder how much getting used to San Francisco was going to take, and figured it
was a lot. Maybe someone—like maybe Primo—could be
my guide for a little while, until I got it. If, that is, he didn't
turn out to have a machete and a backyard full of bodies,
or Bibles.

I had been waking up early too, out there by the beach
where I could hear the waves crashing, for real and in my
dreams. The sound was comforting but spooky. And there
was that smell: fishy and salty and dark. Since I'd had a
chance to look at the ocean for real, it didn't look the way I'd
always imagined it—a constant blue, with the waves coming
in row after row, steady and predictable. It was a lot wilder
than I'd been expecting, and not always blue. I'd taken off
my shoes and waded in a few times, but it was too cold to go
any farther than about knee-deep. I wondered if it was cold
on the other side too, where it was no longer the Pacific, but
the South China Sea. The three words echoed in my head, in
Mick's voice. I wanted to hear them as much as I didn't.

On our way to the restaurant, Primo made maybe a

dozen stops, pulling up to corners to check on his crew of teenage paperboys. They were huddled in apartment-building entryways, folding newspapers and doubling rubber bands around them, or slipping them into plastic bags. I was amazed at how fast they worked, how quickly their fingers moved.

Primo orchestrated: "Make sure you get that one at Forty-Third and Balboa through the gate today. Mr. *Puto* is starting to give me heartburn." And: "Just bag that one on Lake from now on. You know the one. I'm tired of hearing her bitch about wet papers." The kids nodded, heads down and intent on their work. They'd heard it all before. "Later," Primo said. "Do good."

The restaurant was a little diner that could have been anywhere; it could have been in Montana, in my town, except that it looked out on an ocean rather than on scattered mountain ranges and open plain. I had imagined a fancy, big-city place, but the tables were plain, worn-yellow Formica threaded with gold; the booths red Naugahyde, patched in places, like the top of my car, with bits of duct tape. Creased and crooked black-and-white photos of old San Francisco lined the walls. We were on a cliff overlooking the water, but it was still too dark and foggy to see it properly. The gulls stood out, though, as they were white, and noisy. I could hear them through the windows, their calls a faint echo of the feral kittens back home, mewling in the barn.

Primo said I could have anything I wanted, and what I wanted was orange juice and bacon and eggs. When the waitress asked what kind of toast, I didn't know what to say, because I hadn't known there were different kinds. Primo said sourdough. He said if I was going to live in San Francisco, I'd have to learn to like it.

"I am going to live here," I said.

Primo nodded. "Best place there is. But you need to get the hell out of the Avenues."

"What do you mean?"

"When was the last time you saw the sun?"

"Yesterday."

"For how long?"

"Maybe fifteen minutes."

"It was out all day in the Mission."

I didn't know what he meant. I thought missions were a kind of church, like the ones they built in Montana and sent the Indian kids to, to change their ways and their religion; make them good, short-haired Catholics. And basketball players. I remembered Darrell telling me that, about the basketball teams the Jesuits commissioned of the boys they spirited away from their families, how good some of them were, and how the white players and their coaches always accused them of cheating. But sometimes they'd get a title anyway, because there was just no question; scores were too lopsided even with the bad calls.

Darrell was his team's point guard in high school. Since we met after he'd already graduated, I never saw him play in an actual game, but I was sure he'd been a star. Sometimes we'd messed around on the court at my school, where he'd found and claimed me that rainy afternoon, and the way he moved and spun and pivoted and shot made me dizzy, made my heart hurt remembering. He was so graceful, so tall, so *good*.

I wondered if our son would grow up to play basketball, but didn't think it was possible, since he'd been born so early and maybe wouldn't grow like a normal kid. But maybe it didn't work that way, and he'd catch up, get big, like his father. Wherever he was now. Wherever they both were. *If* they both were. But I was not thinking about them, or where they were.

A jungle, however imaginary and probably wrong, appeared; I bit my lip, hard—a reminder to stay in the present. Vietnam was supposed to be far away—a lifetime away—someone's life, at any rate. Montana too. It did not occur to me that I might be too young to be thinking in terms of lifetimes.

Now that we were in the light, I could see Primo was blind in his right eye. It had that milky look, bluish white, like frozen pond water in winter. There was some scar tissue around it, and trailing off across the top of his cheek. His ear was a little mangled too.

I touched my own cheek, near the corner of my eye. "What happened?"

" 'Nam," he said.

"What?"

" 'Nam. Vietnam."

Damn. "Oh." I felt sick. Like I had conjured up the place with my stupid daydreaming. I put my fork down next to my plate and sipped some orange juice. I should have been ready, though. It should have been obvious. "How?"

"White phosphorus. Our guys accidentally threw some too close, and my face got in the way."

"What's white phosphorous?"

"It's a chemical thing. It lights shit up. Mostly it burns. Sets a village or the woods or a rice paddy on fire and kills people. You can't put it out with water. It's nasty." He turned toward the window, and the fog. "Like that, at first," he said, pointing with his chin. "Only brighter. They called it Willy Peter, like it was supposed to be your pal or something. It wasn't mine, except I got to come home early, so maybe in a way it was." He lit a cigarette, still looking away. "Fucked up pal, though."

He picked up his coffee cup and set it back down again without drinking from it.

I said, "Sounds like napalm." Mick had told me about it, in one of his letters. He thought whoever invented it was sick in the head.

"More or less," Primo said. "Part of the SOP, actually. Of torching human beings."

"SOP?"

"Standard operating procedure. It was wicked messed up."

"That's what my brother says." I looked down at my pancakes, afraid Primo could see that the present tense was a big, fat lie.

"Well, he's right. I guess he was there. Who with?"

"Twenty-Fifth Infantry. Củ Chi. They made him a tunnel guy."

"A rat, you mean. Little." Compared to Primo, I figured, a lot of them would have qualified as little. But Mick re-

ally was. He never got much taller than I did: like five foot
six and a bit. Five eight, maybe, in his boots. And he was
skinny, wiry.

"I guess so," I said. "A rat." It was hard for me to think of
Mick as a rat, even though he'd seemed kind of proud of it.
He was more canine than rodent. But the tunnel dogs were
real dogs. German shepherds. Mick had one for a while,
but it died.

"Can we talk about something else?" I was mashing
what was left of my breakfast with my fork. I wondered if
Primo could feel how much I wanted to bolt, or blow, or
just melt through the Naugahyde seat and the floor, seep
down the cliff, dissolve into the sea or float off to Asia.

He said, "Sure. How about the sun? How about I
take you to see it in person?" He knew. I could hear him
knowing.

I pushed the heels of my hands into my eyes for a few
seconds. "I think," I said, "that would be really nice." I
looked outside, where it was only now getting light enough
to see the water. The gulls quarreled over fish and the fog
stayed, utterly still and seemingly permanent.

When we got back to the truck, Primo pulled a microphone from its holder on a radio mounted to the dash. He
pushed a button on the side and said, "Eighteen-fifty to
dispatch."

After a minute, a female voice came back through the
speaker. "Nothing for you, Primo. Spot and clear?"

"Spot time five fifteen. So far nothing down or open.
Not clear yet."

"Ten-four, eighteen-fifty."

"Ten-four." He put the microphone back and the truck in drive. "Looking good, so hold on, kiddo. We're going for a ride."

"Okay." I sat down on the bundle of papers and grabbed onto the edge of the grate, not sure what to expect but relieved to be moving in a definite direction with an actual purpose: to see the sun. I'd believe it when I had to put my blue sunglasses on.

Primo detoured briefly to deliver a dozen or so newspapers on one dead-end block just off Geary. He kept the doors of the truck open, and swapping hands every so often pitched papers out both sides with amazing accuracy, landing them on steps, under gates, and one on an upstairs fire escape. I was amazed at how effortless he made it look. I wanted to be able to do that. He said he'd teach me. If I stuck around.

As we headed east, the fog began to dissipate; by Divisadero it was completely gone. The Mission was wide awake, brilliant, and uncontained. It was about six when we hit Twenty-Fourth Street, where shopkeepers were sweeping and hosing down the sidewalks, filling great wooden vegetable bins, setting out five-gallon plastic buckets full of flowers. I could smell the flowers from the truck, and a bunch of other things I couldn't identify but which obviously were things to eat. I was still full from breakfast, but my mouth watered anyway.

Primo took me to a Mexican grocery store, where I bought tortillas, cheese, oranges, bananas and bread. A whole grocery bag full, for three dollars. The tortillas were so fresh the plastic package was fogged up, steamy. I held it

to my face to feel the damp warmth on my skin. I stopped
again in front of the vegetable bin as we were leaving, dazzled by the array of chilies—the sheer number of colors and
shapes—but I didn't buy any because I was a little afraid of
them. Primo showed me, for future reference, which ones
were the hottest: tiny yellow ones he said would burn like
white phosphorous.

"You could use these as a weapon," he said, his gravelly
laugh turning a few heads. I wondered how he could joke
like that, but still it seemed a perfectly natural thing for
him to say.

He appeared to know everyone on the block, or to be
known by everyone, and most of them called him Primo. A
few, like he'd said, called him T.C. or Tony. When I asked if
he lived nearby, he pointed to a set of windows above one
of the shops across the street. "*Mi casa,*" he said. I could see
white lace curtains, tied back with pieces of red ribbon. I
figured that was a woman's touch and asked if his wife was
home.

"Nope. She lives with her sister."

"Why?"

"Long story. Boring, too." He laughed, but it didn't
sound the same as it had before. It was quicker, closer to
choking, really, than laughing. He lifted the grocery bag
out of my hands and headed toward the truck. "Time to get
back to work," he said. "We've probably messed around just
long enough."

"Long enough for what?"

"Hit some traffic. Get some second calls."

"Calls for papers?"

"Exactly." He looked sideways at me out of his good eye. "You're a smart cookie, aren't you?"

"I don't know about that," I said. But it was nice, him saying so.

He set the bag on the floor of the truck and asked me to wait while he ran into his apartment for something. He was gone about ten minutes, and when he got back, we sat while he rubbed his eyes and adjusted the mirrors four or five times.

"Sleepy," he said. "I always get sleepy right about now." I was wide awake, but then, I figured, I was way younger, and there was so much to look at.

When we finally started moving, I asked him, "So how come everyone calls you Primo?"

"It means cousin, kind of, or first, I guess. I was born first. I have another brother named Anthony. Antonio, actually. After my dad."

"Your dad named both of you the same thing?"

"Yeah. He would have named us all that, even the girls, but my mom wouldn't let him."

"She wouldn't?" I said. Primo looked at me, his eyebrows raised. I couldn't help but grin.

"Smartass."

I nodded. "So I've been told. What do they call the other Anthony?"

"Tony."

"Oh." I was disappointed, thinking maybe there was another word like Primo for a second son with the same name.

"Nope," Primo said. "We weren't going to call him

Segundo. That would be as bad as calling someone T.B."
When I laughed, it felt surprising and familiar, like something I'd done when I was young.

"What should I call you?"

"Primo. That's what my posse calls me."

Posse. I waited.

"I'll let you in if you're lucky. Keep your nose clean."

"I'll do that."

I told him my real name. We were at a light. It turned
green but he didn't go right away. I looked, and his eyes
were closed and his head leaned back against the metal
grate behind him. Someone honked. His whole upper body
jerked, and he moved his foot from the brake to the gas
pedal.

"I like it," he mumbled. "But I was sort of getting used to
Tinker Bell." Just as though there had been no break in the
conversation, and he hadn't fallen asleep at an intersection.

"I answer to pretty much anything," I said, wondering if
sleep-driving was a common occurrence among newspaper
drivers, or if it was a special talent only Primo possessed.

I kept sleeping in my car, because I was not ready to give
up the ocean yet, knowing the sun did in fact exist here and
that it wasn't so terribly hard to find. Besides which, I didn't
really have any place else to go. Primo showed me where
the Y was in the Sunset District, and introduced me to a
girl who worked the desk in the evenings and would let me
in so I could shower and wash my hair. He found me most
mornings, picked me up so I could ride around with him.

One of the kids called in sick a week or so after Primo and I met, so we threw his two routes: 170 papers on six or seven blocks. I already knew by then the basic process of folding and banding, and Primo taught me how to wing the papers, sort of like a Frisbee, snapping my wrist so they'd go where I aimed them, and sometimes they did. The buildings with open entryways were the easiest shots, of course, since there was nothing in the way. Gates were harder, but they had their openings too. I began to see the spaces under them, at the very top and between the bars as their weak spots, places to attack. Primo drove both sides of each block, calling off addresses, and I threw. If a gate came all the way to the bottom or the bars were too close together, I jumped out of the truck to fit the paper through one gap or another. When there were several tough ones in a row, Primo drove slowly alongside as I trotted down the fog-damp sidewalks, arms loaded, feeling like a one-girl assault force.

I was concentrating so hard I didn't even notice the sun. Primo had to point it out to me.

"Check it out," he said, motioning with his chin. I stopped dead, screeching to a halt, looking a lot, I bet, like Wile E. Coyote.

"Holy shit," I said, throwing a paper straight up in the air.

Primo shook his head. "You can't swear around me like that. My virgin ears."

"Sure."

When we were done, he gave me five dollars.

"For what? No." I handed it back.

"Yes." He stuffed the bill into the hip pocket of my blue jeans, caught my hand, and held it to keep me from reaching in to get it out. When I gave up and said okay, he let go.

At last call he dropped me off at my car. I thought about taking a nap, but the sun was too bright and tempting, so I went to the beach. I was always surprised at how empty it was. That day only a few people strolled down by the water; one guy throwing sticks for his dog, a big black Lab who bounded into the surf over and over, came out, shook the water off and stood panting and shivering until it was time to rush the waves again.

I sat on a piece of wood that looked a lot like the burnt remains of a railroad tie, wondering how it could have gotten there. I remembered walking on the railroad tracks at home with my brother or with Darrell, or alone, thinking I might walk those tracks all the way to the coast, but when it came time to go, it was the Greyhound that took me. I tried to imagine what it would be like to still be there but couldn't wrap my brain around the baby, or the gone-away boys; anything I imagined about home at all would probably be just another lie I knew better than to tell myself. The only things I could picture clearly were Mick's bedroom, the kitchen, and my dog Cash, who had never chased a stick into the ocean, and never would.

Later, when the fog started to roll in, I drove around until I relocated a library I'd been to once before. I prowled the stacks, feeling thiefish, like I meant to steal something, though I knew I didn't. I asked the librarian if I could check out a book, but she asked for my address and I didn't have the presence of mind to make one up. When I left it was with—inside my wolf sweatshirt—*A Separate Peace*, a book I'd loved in high school and would bring back to the library as soon as I'd read it again. I could still so distinctly see one image from it, of a boy standing on the limb of a tree—a silhouette against the sky—and then falling.

Later that week, Primo invited me over for dinner. His place was small and there wasn't much in it, but it was comfy enough. There was one real bedroom, a living room, and a kitchen with a little closed-in porch behind it. The porch had its own door to the outside: steps leading to a tiny yard full of weeds and ornamental flowers and plants gone wild. I was particular to the bougainvillea and its papery petals that came in so many outlandish pinks and reds and oranges; I'd seen them all over town. "Is that the official plant of San Francisco?" I pointed to a red one near the back, an especially unruly one that had climbed up and over the fence. Like it was trying to escape.

"I don't know. Maybe?"

"I see them everywhere," I said.

"I guess I don't," Primo said. "Maybe I should pay more attention."

"SOP," I said. "Looking at stuff."

"Gotcha." He patted me on the head. "I'll give that a shot."

He cooked rice and beans and pork chops, and we sat at the kitchen table to eat. Primo drank three Tecates with his dinner, and I drank a sweet Mexican soda. A couple of days later I met him at the apartment for lunch, and he ordered from a tamale place down the street. I had never eaten tamales before, and was fascinated by the corn husks and the consistency of the cornmeal, the amount of work that obviously went into the process.

"My wife makes a mean tamale," Primo said. "Quite the production. But I don't get to eat them anymore."

I was digging through the cornmeal, excavating the meat inside. I asked Primo what his wife's name was; how long she'd been gone.

"Rosa," he said. "She's been either going or gone on and off for years. But this time I think she really means it." He sounded resigned, and sad.

I told him my mother's name was Rose.

"Sweet." He raised his beer bottle and clinked it against my soda one. "Here's to the Roses and the Rosas," he said. "To T.B. and T.C."

On my birthday, Primo took me to lunch at a Cuban place on Lucky Alley. After a little bit of stuttering preamble, he offered his little back porch room for me to live in until I got on my feet, got a real job, a place of my own. "Don't think it's weird," he said. "We're compadres, officially, and besides, it's going to get cold soon."

I didn't think it was weird at all but did wonder what he meant by "cold."

"Forty or so." He raised one eyebrow, as if that was some serious weather.

I'm sure I snorted. "That's not cold. Forty *below* is cold."

"You'll be whistling a different tune when it comes, *chica*. Especially if you're still sleeping in that car. Better take this offer while it stands. I might change my mind." He smiled, because he didn't mean the last part, but I said yes anyway, because what I wanted more than anything, all of a sudden, was to live in that little space, with my own door to the outside and a yard wild with red flowers.

Primo said I should find something to do, to come back in a few hours, after he'd had a chance to get my room ready. I drove thirty miles down the coast, stopping at foggy Half Moon Bay to wade in the water, which was even colder than it had been just a few weeks before. I stayed as long as I could, though, because I loved the way the sand felt, melting out from under me when the water receded. I threw stones and watched the shrieking gulls dive after them.

Silly birds.

The room was perfect. Primo had found a trundle bed somewhere, and a little blue dresser with animal and flower decals stuck to it, probably by some little kid all grown up now. Tiny white Christmas lights draped around the windows and looped from corner to corner along one wall. There were fresh flowers in a yellow vase on the windowsill. Propped on the dresser was a framed print of an angel guiding two kids across a rickety bridge over some artist's depiction of a raging river, but the river was too narrow to be scary—like narrow enough for any decently coordinated kid to jump across. I picked up the picture and laughed. "Who's that?"

"You don't know her? What kind of Catholic are you?"

"A not-Catholic."

"Right. I guess I'll have to convert you."

"Fat chance," I said. "And when was the last time you went to church?"

"None of your beeswax," he said. "That is Our Lady of Perpetual Help. She's staying."

"I don't need any help," I said. "I've got you. I'm good."

He took the picture out of my hands and set it back on the dresser. "We all need help, little one. Even fairies."

He was off the next day, so we stayed up late and watched cop shows and movies on TV. I went to bed about midnight but woke up thirsty a few hours later. I could hear sirens in the distance and remembered I had been dreaming about being in the hospital, in the ICU, after I'd flown off the roof at home. I went into the kitchen for a glass of water and could see flickering light from the TV still on in the living room, but the sound was off. I peeked around the corner to see what Primo was watching. At first I thought he was sleeping. He had his shirt off and was sitting up on the couch, but his head hung forward, and his chin was nearly resting on his chest. I saw the rest then: a piece of cloth tied around his arm, the syringe on the carpet in front of him, his hand dangling over it. A lighter. A bent-handled spoon. I must have made a noise, and Primo heard me. He lifted his head and looked. His good eye blinked a couple of times, like he was trying to clear a mist from it.

"Hey," he said, "it's Tinker Bell." He reached over and untied the cloth from his arm, held it out to me like some kind of offering, looked at it like he didn't know what it was or how it had got there, and crumpled it in his hand.

"Are you okay, Primo?"

"Yeah." He nodded slowly and scratched his face where the scar was.

"What are you doing?" There had been a letter from

Mick once, telling me about all the drugs the guys did because it made them feel better about where they were and what was going on around them. Mick smoked pot, but some—a lot, he said—were doing harder stuff. He said it was scary how tempting it was. How logical it seemed.

Primo still hadn't answered me, and both his eyes had closed, though he was still scratching his face, the same spot, up and down.

"Primo," I said again, kind of loud, for me. "What are you doing?"

He reopened his eyes and tried to grin, but it only took on one side of his face. "Killing the pain, sweetie. Don't you worry. It's all just a crazy dream." I saw the rest of the scars, smooth and pink like Barbie-doll plastic, covering half his chest and his whole right shoulder.

I sat down on the floor. "I'm not dreaming, Primo."

Slowly, he picked up the syringe, wrapped the cloth around it, and set it on the sofa next to him. He sighed and started to work his jaw around like it had a mechanical malfunction. He tried to say he was sorry, that he wasn't strung out, really, but I stopped him. "I'm not a kid," I said. "Tell it to somebody else."

"All right, then, big girl." He shook his head, like a person coming out of the ocean with water in his ears. He sat up straighter, but his voice was still molasses thick. "I believe you. So tell me what you're not dreaming about."

I bit my bottom lip hard enough to make it bleed on the inside. I was cold and I started to shiver. I had to let go of my lip so I could clench my teeth against them chattering.

"You do what you have to do, but you are not the only

one—" My voice was shaking so bad it was hard to get the words out, but I kept going. "Goddamn it. I don't care what you do out here. Just fucking come back when you're finished. Satisfied. Fixed. Whatever."

His head began to fall forward again, but he yanked it back up, and his eyes were still open, the good one looking at me.

"Deal," he said. "Consider it done, Tink."

I didn't say good night. It wasn't night. I stood up and went back to my room, plugged in the Christmas lights, and got into my sleeping bag. I stared at the ceiling as the lights flashed on and off against it like a conflagration of fireflies. I listened to Primo gather the remnants of his not-so-secret life, listened to him stumble around in the dark out there and stash it all away.

6. Kid on a Mission

Frank had married young, a ballerina, but that was all over now, left in Dallas where the quarter-Mexican part of his mostly Italian heritage fit in, but not much else. He was dark and rangy, with long arms, long legs, the patience of a saint, and a heart murmur. Once the draft board classified him unfit for service, and the dancer classified him unfit for love, he developed a bad itch to be somewhere other than Texas. San Francisco drew him, along with a million other unraveled souls, but he didn't come to San Francisco for the drugs or the easy sex, he came for the music, slinging a six-string Martin and a voice like Jerry Jeff Walker on ludes. He bypassed the Haight for a studio in the Sunset, where the streets were wide and quiet and the fog felt like a blessing after so many years of no-mercy-for-the-wicked (or the innocent) desert sun.

He played for tips in the coffee shops a time, put together a band good enough to open for some of the bigger acts, played Kezar Stadium and Monterey and quit, at the tail end of '69, at Altamont, when a too-high fan named Meredith Hunter got himself stabbed by a Hells Angel— four deep wounds in his back, one in his head—which may or may not have preserved the lives of a couple of young, petulant and exasperated Rolling Stones, threatening to stop the show, just stop it, if those cats didn't cool their jets. They were wondering what was wrong with America. What had gotten into the kids.

Frank was wondering the same thing. " 'Gimme Shelter' my ass," he said. He was talking to his drummer, who didn't really know he was being talked to, because he was so high on angel dust he thought the stabbing was part of the show.

A friend talked Frank into going down to the union hall to get his Teamster card, and by the time he met Riley, he had five years in, enough to be vested at the newspaper and with a permanent swing shift. It was perfect: two days in his own neighborhood, two in the Marina, and one in Daly City, where the fog was so thick it made the Sunset look like Ensenada. He was happy being single, being off-stage, no real responsibilities except to get the papers off the truck and collect a few delinquent bills. The paper cost five dollars every four weeks, delivered through the gate. When a one-bedroom opened up in his building, he moved into it. Two hundred forty dollars a month. He got a dog at the shelter, an electric guitar and a Pignose amp at the pawnshop, and never turned the amp up past halfway. He messed around and wrote some love songs, put it all down and got to bed by ten. Went to school during the day and got his BA in literature. Wrote some bad poems. Made the dean's list twice. Skipped graduation because he couldn't picture himself in one of those black gowns. He knew he'd look a damn fool.

Spot, a seven-month-old heeler mutt, slept at the foot of the bed, and when Frank tossed and turned, Spot yipped in his sleep, like he was saying "Cut it out." Frank was grateful for the company. He stuck the framed photos of his ballerina wife away in a drawer when he heard she'd remarried, and one day pulled them out and took them down to the sidewalk. He leaned them against a lamppost and watched from his window as a woman pushing a shopping cart toward Geary stopped to add them to her belongings. She lined them up around the perimeter of the cart, on the inside, so it looked like a beautiful and tragic tutu'd lady was waiting (on her tiptoes) for a white knight to come and throw her bail. He started bringing the dog to work with him, figuring someone would eventually tell him to stop, but no one did.

The kid rolled in from Wyoming, or one of those big empty states that wasn't Texas. She got tangled up with Primo; tried, from what Frank could tell, to keep him from going under. That didn't work out so well, but she stuck around after all the party candles went out. She'd been living in Primo's apartment and managed to hold on to it until his wife moved back in, and afterwards lived in a bunch of different studios, mostly in the Mission, moving every year or so. Restless, Frank guessed. After they got to be friends he helped her move a couple of times, in his newspaper truck. The trucks were handy for stuff like that. Moving in. Moving out.

Riley loved Spot. Brought him bones. Scratched his ears and between his shoulder blades until he made noises that sounded like words. Called him "silly dog" and kissed his cold, wet nose.

Primo had gotten her a couple routes of her own in Eureka Valley, and she worked them for a few years— probably made a couple hundred a month. She'd be done by five thirty and then hang around—all the drivers knew where to find her—to help and get paid extra when other kids didn't show up. She was good. She could throw a hundred papers in the straight blocks in about six minutes flat. All business. No time to bullshit. It was like she was on a mission; kind of hard telling, though, what it was.

When she turned twenty-one, she finally got herself hired on as a casual, and Frank would see her working on the dock, loading the panel trucks and the bobtails and the semis with bundles of the daily news. She was still serious as hell when she was working, but sometimes after all the trucks were loaded she'd relax a little, hang out with the transportation guys, smoking cigarettes—sometimes a joint—and yakking. The others were a little in awe of her, tough as she was, first girl ever hired to work the docks, to drive. Maybe they expected her to cry once in a while. The job could be a bitch. They all felt like crying sometimes.

Frank was there one early morning when she got a splinter the size of a toothpick under her fingernail, slamming down a bundle at the side of one of the old-plywood-lined bobtails. She shut down the chute for about thirty seconds, came out into the light where she could see what had stabbed her, pulled it out with her teeth, and went back to work. He was loading his own truck right next to her and watched her pull the splinter out. He knew it hurt; it hurt him to see it. She showed it to him later—that chunk of wood, and it was a chunk—which she'd stuck in her pocket, and the streak of red that ran almost to the cuticle. If you looked at it from the tip of her finger, you could see the hole it made. Fuck. Frank would have gone home. Let someone else load that sucker.

He told her what he was thinking. "You should get out of here. Go home and soak that finger in something."

She looked at him like he'd lost his mind. "Why would I do that?"

"Because you're hurt?"

"Nah. Nothing's broken."

"Nothing has to be broken. They'll let you go. They have to."

"I don't want to," she said, jaw set, eyebrows raised. He got it. He stuck around and helped her load the next truck, half expecting her to tell him to split, but she didn't. She favored her hand when she could, and when the light from the dock crossed her face, he could see brief flashes of pain there.

Later some of the drivers gave him a hard time. "Isn't she a little young for you?"

"I wasn't hitting on her. I was helping her. Any of you assholes could have done the same." They grumbled, walking away. Didn't like being called assholes, but sometimes the truth hurt. And she wasn't that young. And it's not like he was so damn old.

Another time she got jumped in the alley coming to work. Gave up her wallet and still got kicked in the head. She was bleeding like crazy—the way head wounds do— when she got to the plant, but just wadded up a handful of newspaper and held it over the cut 'til it stopped bleeding. It wasn't a really big cut—didn't need stitches or anything, just a butterfly—but the bruise around it was pretty scary looking. This time a few of the drivers tried to talk her into going to the hospital, but she wouldn't. She took some aspirin, and after a while started whistling, because most of the money she had on her was in her boot. She wouldn't even call the cops.

"Five bucks," she said, and shrugged. "He probably needed it more than I do."

There were other incidents: cuts, more bruises, falls off the dock or a slick bumper; Frank thought maybe she was a little accident-prone—some people just were—but she'd always put her head down and go back for more.

Tracking her wasn't easy. It's not like she was either soft or hard, just . . . accepting, or something Frank didn't have a word for. Zen. Maybe. Like a little monk, though he couldn't see her liking the comparison, so he never said it out loud.

He could tell she liked working the dock okay, but what she loved was driving the big trucks, the bobtails. Back then you didn't need your Class C, just a regular driver's license and a right arm strong enough to shift the gears. On Sundays they'd send her out with the overflow: the bundles that wouldn't fit in the small trucks. She'd take the ones for the Avenues to a bank on the corner of Geary and Arguello, stack them against the brick wall all nice and neat, then go trade extras for just-made, still-hot bagels and hand them out when the drivers came to pick up their loads. It was nice, like a little oasis in the middle of the night; a place to stop and catch your breath, to find you weren't totally alone out there.

When Frank worked the Sunset, he'd see her truck sometimes—late, when she was done—at Ocean Beach or somewhere along Great Highway, the girl looking so small in the driver's seat, forehead resting against the steering wheel, staring through it at the ocean while the sun rose behind her. Or not, since out there the sun didn't always rise. Sometimes he'd stop and talk to her, but he learned to recognize a certain look that said probably best to leave her alone.

Not everyone was comfortable around her. They'd always been an all-boys club, and letting a girl in meant something had gone haywire, seriously. She took some grief from a handful of blabbermouths, and mostly rolled with it, but a couple of times she went off. The way it looked to Frank was the ones she went off on had it coming. Even when she wasn't taking down some joker talking about her ass or whatever, she had a mouth on her that would surprise a fellow, for real. He was glad she never got mad at him.

There was one driver she got close to early on: Eddie, who everyone suspected and later found out for sure was gay. A fag, then. A homo. "Gay" wasn't even a word yet, at least not one any of them had ever heard. Anyway, Frank would see them together a lot, and the thing he noticed was how often Eddie could make her laugh. It was nice to see, nice to know she could do that. Some of the guys referred to them as "the girls," but Frank didn't. Because he didn't think it was all that funny.

One morning she and Frank were coming in at the same time after last call, driving side by side on Geary. It was a warm day already and they both had their doors slid open. She had her whole left leg out the driver's side, her foot up on the side mirror bracket—a total gangster lean. A car pulled up next to her in the turn lane, and the guy driving yelled through his passenger window: "Is that a good job?"

"This is a *great* job," she said. And she was smiling wide, bopping her head to some happy song inside it. She threw a paper to the guy through his window and took off waving when the light turned green.

After they got back to the plant and checked in, she and Frank walked out together.

Riley said, "You want to go get a beer? I know it's kind of early, but—"

"Early? We just finished an eight-hour shift."

They walked over to the M&M, drank a pint, ate some fries, and talked about the job, the clueless supervisors, the chance of rain on Sunday (rainy days were a pain in the butt). He asked her about Wyoming, and she looked puzzled for a second.

"Oh. You mean Montana."

"Yeah, right. Montana, sorry."

"It's okay. Easy to confuse those places, I guess, if you're not from there."

She told him about the farm, the dog, her parents. "They're pretty laid-back," she said. "They're really nice people." She hesitated, gnawing at her lower lip. "I should probably write to them or call more often. I bet they worry about me, off in the big city. Especially my dad. You know how dads are." For a second, she looked about twelve.

"Why did you leave?"

"It was time. I wanted to see the ocean something awful. I think I may have been a fish in a past life. Like a flounder. Both eyes on one side of my head."

"That would be interesting," he said. "Make it kind of hard to drive."

She picked up a french fry and put it back down on the plate. Straight-faced, she nodded. "That's true."

It was easy for her to make him laugh.

He asked if she had more family, brothers or sisters. She made a movement with her head, but he couldn't tell if it was a nod or a shake. She took a long drink of beer and said, "Have you ever seen a barn cat?"

"Not that I can recall."

"Really? A guy from Texas?"

"Not a lot of barns in Dallas."

"Oh. I see."

She told him how they jump, springing into the air like grasshoppers, or those tiny African bush babies she'd seen once on TV.

"When you open the barn door," she said, "it's like the

whole place comes alive. All these scrawny little cats climbing the walls or shooting straight in the air like bottle rock-
ets."

"Did they have names?"

"Yeah," she said. "They still do, I bet. My dad names
them all Slick or Slim. Or some variation, like Slick
Britches or Slim Bob."

"He can tell them apart?"

"Mostly. He's like that. Pays attention to things he thinks
need attention paid to." She turned her head toward the
window. Frank looked to see what she was seeing, but
it was just another day on Howard Street: construction,
double-parked cars, a guy passed out at the bus stop, still
holding tight to an empty Colt 45 bottle. He figured she
was probably missing home, which was perfectly natural.
We all miss home sometimes.

She insisted on paying. "A shitload of overtime last
week," she said.

Eventually she had enough seniority to get her own
home-delivery district, where she got to hire her own kids
and teach them all the tricks she'd learned from Primo,
and some new ones she'd taught herself. She ran a tight
ship, and the kids did a good job for her. Later on, when
she started calling in sick, hers was the best district to sub
on, because you knew there wasn't going to be any trouble.
Just get the papers out to the corners, and the kids would
do the rest. No complaints, no hassles, no showing up late
or not at all. It was sweet; she kept it that way by treating
them right, like adults, like human beings. And for a time it

seemed like she'd found her spot, a place she could be contented, a place she felt like she knew what she was about.

She and Frank met regularly for coffee during work, helped each other with down routes, killed time together at random corners waiting for complaints or last call. Sometimes Eddie would join them; sometimes one or two of the other drivers. She said they should form a band, call themselves the Vampires.

Before too long, she was hanging around Frank's apartment like she lived there, lying on the floor using Spot for a pillow; tooling around with the Martin (she knew a few chords, but got frustrated trying to make the changes); pulling books down off the shelf and asking Frank about poems, stories, certain words. She wanted to know what everything meant, and he tried to explain that most of the time there was no single meaning; a lot depended on who was trying to figure it out, and what they brought with them to the show.

"The show?"

"Yeah. The show. Life."

She liked that. "The life show," she said.

One time she asked him if he'd gone to Vietnam. She was playing his guitar, not looking at him; the question came out of nowhere.

"No," he said. "I didn't have to go. And they wouldn't have let me even if I'd wanted to."

She looked up. He read in her expression, *How does that work?*

He tapped his chest. "My ticker. It's a little bit broken."

"Oh," she said. And maybe it sounded like there was something in that small story she doubted, or didn't like, or hadn't wanted to hear, but he was probably hearing things himself, filtered through the unavoidable fact of all those other guys going and him staying behind. Probably.

It was something, in any case, they didn't talk about anymore.

The wheels started coming off slowly at first. Since bad behavior at the paper was more common than not, and people rarely got fired for any of it, those wheels took their time. First Riley became something of a regular at Hanno's, a bar in the alley behind the plant. She had a few new pals by then who were pretty good drinkers, and it didn't take long before her car—this incredibly beat-up Mustang—would be out there from quitting time at eleven o'clock to three or four in the afternoon, and sometimes later. Much later. Like going-back-to-work time.

And there was a lot of coke filtering into and around the city; a lot of the drivers, including Riley, were snorting it pretty regular. Frank tried it, but he didn't really enjoy it, and the hangovers were awful, jump-off-a-bridge depressing. He got some from her a few times before he realized he was trying too hard to like it. She wasn't dealing, just sharing with a select few. Seemed like she bought in bulk, so she always had extra. Not pillowcases full or Colombian cartel lots, but plenty. The thing was, she was making pretty good money, like everyone else, and the only person she had to support was herself. And the hours didn't help. If you wanted to stay up days and pretend you were normal (after a fashion), it helped to have a little bump, and coffee wasn't going to do it. Aside from the illegality of it, and the cost, it could seem like a really good idea—assuming you could handle the aftermath.

Except then it got to be more habit than play, and she thought it would be even better to try balancing one high out with another, like Jim Beam with beer backs, pills, and other kinds of powder, and pretty soon she wasn't coming to work, or she was coming to work still high. They looked the other way for a while because she'd always done such a good job, but then one night some new supervisor, thinking he's going to butter some butts downtown, yanks her off her district at four in the morning and sends her over to S.F. General for a drug test. Game over. Goddamn it.

It's not the seventies anymore, and Eddie's boyfriend Lucas is one of the first to die from a disease they haven't even decided on a name for yet, and Riley's no help at all because she's living out at Haight and Stanyan in a tent (because they towed her car and she can't come up with the scratch to bail it out, to move back into it) with a bunch of vets who can't seem to get their shit together (imagine), and she's their mascot.

Frank knew he wasn't the only one who was a little in love with her, and he was pretty damn sure he had about zero chance of ever being able to do anything about it. He saw how natural it was for her to gravitate toward damaged, and he wasn't nearly enough of that. Not that he wasn't a little wrecked—it sort of came with the territory—but not sufficiently. He never asked her out on a real date, brought her flowers, nothing like that. But he kept an eye on her after she got fired and started living out in Golden Gate Park. He'd go pick her up and take her to breakfast, trade papers for bagels and bring them to her and her crew. Those 'Nam guys didn't like him much—him with his truck, job, clean-cut clothes and combed hair—but she'd give them a sign, some tilt of the head or sly smile at the corner of her mouth, to let them know he didn't mean any harm and that he wasn't going to steal her.

But he did. Not because of them, but just because. Because he couldn't leave her out there.

He knew this bar, the Wild West End. It was up in Bernal Heights, off the beaten track, and he'd go there sometimes when he didn't feel like seeing anyone he was already too familiar with. They had a garden out back and it was a nice place to unwind, to watch a football game, shoot some pool. It was a girl bar, more or less, but they'd let anyone in, and no one bothered him so long as he wasn't an asshole, which he wasn't. He got to know one of the bartenders, and one day she told him they were having a tough time covering all the shifts; she didn't want to work more than she was already working, and did he know anyone who was looking for a job—someone who could put up with a little crap.

He brought Riley in—spent some time talking her into it—and her interview consisted of smoking a joint with the owner and the owner's sidekick, this queen named Andy, in the ladies' room, and after that the job was hers. Pretty soon it was like she'd been born there. They took her in like an Easter chick and it looked like she never looked back, at least not at the part about getting up to go to work just when everyone else was leaving the bars. He knew she had to miss it, though: the independence, the sunrises from the top of Jackson Street, the kids, the ocean, the balling it down the grade toward the Golden Gate Bridge on a deadhead run, scaring the crap out of tourists in their lane-wandering Winnebagos.

So he started picking her up when her late shifts ended, to ride with him, to keep him company, and she'd fold the papers and throw her side of the street, and he'd take her to breakfast when the sun came up, and when she let him kiss her a few times, he thought they were both in love. But they weren't. But he was. And what she offered him in return went like this:

"If I could fall in love I would. But I don't know how." Or, "I don't trust myself. I've made too many bad decisions. But stay close." He didn't mind the "stay close" part, even if it could sound like she was playing him, but what it sounded like didn't matter because he didn't think she was that kind of girl—didn't think she knew how to *be* that kind of girl—and staying close was what he wanted. So he tried.

But their versions of close, and of staying, were different. Frank hung in there, because Frank was good that way. Which, as it turned out, was probably the whole problem. She was barely keeping it together, and she told him—once only—that sometimes he made her feel bad. Just him, a not-fucked-up person. All right, then. He thought maybe someday it would change, and he'd be ready if it did. Ready like spaghetti. Ready like something.

She made enough money at the bar to get another flat, and the cops broke up the encampments at the park, but she still knew where to find those guys, down on Sixth Street or in the alleys, in their refrigerator boxes, or in an SRO for a night or two when the checks came first of the month. Andy, the swamper, had a second job cooking down at Harbor Lights, the only place in town a broke junkie (and weren't they all that?) could go to detox without a seventy to eighty percent chance of dying from the jones. When Riley and Andy got to be friends, Riley would show up sometimes with one or two of her mates and Andy would feed them out the back door. Because they weren't going in. No way. And she wasn't about to try talking them into it, because she wasn't going in either.

7. Old Boots. Local Boys.

Dear Riley,

This is the part I hate most. All the times I've caught myself thinking if I never had him, or had given him up, then I would never have felt that awful pain of him going missing. And of you going missing after him. Sure, all that pain is still alive and well, but now—and it has taken me completely by surprise—it's like something I can carry, and not something that's constantly sitting on my chest. Crushing me. I want the same thing for you. I wonder what it is like to be you, now. I wish you would tell me. I have your last letter here. It's two years old. You were delivering newspapers. You wanted to go to school. Now? I don't know. It's all just echo.

That other letter. What were the words they used? "Presumed dead." Whoever thought that was something tolerable to say to a person should have their heads examined.

*I went missing too, didn't I? Your mom: MIA. And
stayed missing for a long time, probably when you needed
me most. Or maybe I just want to feel like you ever needed
me. Like you ever needed anyone but your brother. But you
did, and I was your mom.*

*Now that I have reached, or can at least imagine I see,
the end of this ten-year-long dark tunnel (exactly what
it feels like), it is time to admit (confess?) some things,
and the first is I barely remember you leaving, sweet girl.
There's just the one glimpse. You with your little blue
suitcase, standing on the bottom step of the bus. I can see
the driver behind you, his hand out for your ticket, but
you've turned back around toward me and the baby, and
you have this funny look on your face. I tried to decipher
that look then, and have been trying to ever since. Seems
it was some combination of defiance (you were not going
to cry), fear, wonder, relief. Gratitude. I know you, and I
believe that about you, that you were grateful. You smiled.
Just one of your quick sideways smiles, and god knows
what it meant, but I held onto it. Slim was still so tiny,
only a couple of months old. But he was getting healthy by
then, so alive—tough as old boots, the doctor told us later.
His lungs were working on their own, almost like nothing
had ever been wrong, like they hadn't been the size of
sparrow wings when he was born, and about as much use
for breathing. He didn't cry much the few weeks we had
him after you left, but he had a holler that would scare the
squirrels out of the trees when he was really mad about
something. He definitely took after you in that way. You
were a very determined child.*

*At the bus station, he was in that old carriage of Mick's
and yours your father had dug out of the attic. Cleaned
it up and rolled it into your bedroom one morning while
you were still asleep. I don't know where he found that
ribbon, or that <u>bow</u>(!). I really don't know what he was
thinking at all. The baby was still in the hospital, and you
were spending most of your time in bed, or lying out in the
wheat fields, still as death, staring up at the sky. Maybe he
thought you'd stay, be a mom, get married to that boy. Or
some local boy if we could find one that would have you. I
knew better. You were never going to be that much like me.*

*Did you ever do the math, Riley? I'm sure you have.
It's not so hard to calculate. At twenty-five, you will be the
same age I was when you were born. Your brother was (is?
what a tempting word "is" is) eight years older than you.
So what were the odds? I know a lot of girls have babies at
seventeen and eighteen, some even on purpose, but (this
is so hard to say) that was not meant to be my life. Did
you know I got all A's in high school? Heck, I got an A in
calculus. I probably never said, because it didn't really
matter anymore, but I was going to go to college, among
other things. I wanted to be an astronomer. Remember
looking at the constellations? You can still see them here. I
wonder if there are any stars at all where you are, in that
big city. All that ambient light.*

*I don't know how you feel about it now, but I'm glad
you didn't stay. I'm glad you didn't stop your life here. Is
that a terrible thing? Maybe you wish now you still had
him, that somehow he could hold you steady, that you
hadn't let him go. I don't know. We've never had those*

conversations, and I don't know how to start, or if I should,
or how it would end. I'm afraid it would be with me
losing another piece of you. And lost as you already are
these days, or as I think you must be, you still probably
understand, maybe better than most, that kids don't
necessarily hold you steady. Even if they do, somehow, hold
you in place.

I wonder where you keep him. Is there some secret
place inside you, like the one where I keep Mick? A
mother's place, even if "mother" is a word you can't quite
make apply. I imagine you rolling your eyes. And biting
your lip. Like you do. Did.

The thing is I never really got used to the idea of being
a mother. With you, maybe, more than with Mick, but
then it was almost like you were his and not mine, and it
was for such a short time before, like I said, we both went
missing. With Mick it was just like having a little brother.
I was so young, and I'd always wanted a brother. I used to
bother my mom about it endlessly, but she always said if I
wanted one, I'd have to go out and get my own. A strange
thing to tell your kid, but I'm pretty sure she didn't mean
it that way. I think if I've realized anything in this life, it's
that no one teaches you how to be a parent. You just do
it, and it works out like it works out. She was just trying,
like every other mom in the world, to do what she thought
was best, or what would get her and her family through
another day without blowing a gasket.

But what I was saying, what I keep trying to say, is I
don't think I ever felt like a MOTHER, like an "M is for
the many things you—" Ha. I don't even know how it goes.

But isn't that what nine months (or seven) of carrying them around is all about? Making sure you get that? I don't know. It's all so very blurry. Our options then were the same as yours. Foster home. Adoption. Keep him and get married, to someone, somehow, or stay single and let the whole town talk. Or leave town, but go where? I didn't even know a place I wanted to go. Florida sounded nice. I liked the idea of the ocean. (We have that in common, you and me. But you went and found it.) And the coat hanger option. Actual coat hangers. I knew a girl in Chinook—her team used to play basketball against ours—who tried that and died at sixteen, or maybe she was seventeen by then (it doesn't really matter, does it? Or maybe it does to someone, like her mother). In some back room, alone except for that limp rag of a little one sliding out of her on a river of blood. So they said. So I remember. There were other stories too. More than you might think, although you surely heard some too. And the memory of them still, after all this time, makes me want to tear my own head off. I didn't want that to be me, even more than I didn't want to marry a man I barely knew. My dad said he was a good one, though, who would take care of us. A widower. A neighbor. His wife died in the car overnight one winter, coming back from town in a blizzard. Slid off the road and ran out of gas. She was still warm when they found her. He told me that on our wedding night, and he cried. I had always thought men never cried. I thought they couldn't. I slept on a cot in the nursery for months, but gradually we became a team, learned how to love each other in a kind of precarious way. Dad was right. Your father is pure good. I never was in love with him, but now I know that's not always for keeps either, and what we have has survived a lot. And I do love him. And I had to realize early I wasn't what he wanted either. Buck up and get on with my life. Mick made that possible. And necessary.

I believe you knew. I have to think Mick would have told you. Or maybe you figured it out for yourself. There was nothing about the two of them that was the same. Nothing. But it worked. It was beautiful. I love them both for that. It could have gone so wrong. It could have been so much harder than it was. I was pretty lucky, after all, in my little unluckiness.

Mick's real father? He was nobody, really, by which I don't mean he wasn't somebody in his own right (we all are at least that, aren't we?). But besides that, he was just a boy who worked on a neighbor's ranch one summer. He was from Fargo, and I think he was some kind of Scandinavian, like they are out there. He had the bluest eyes and the softest blond hair. He looked like James Dean. Of course I had to dig that out of my memory later on. Mick was sleeping in the backseat, and you weren't even walking yet, and we were at the drive-in to see Giant. *I nearly died. But your father was there. Of course I didn't say anything. It was crazy, with Mick there right behind us and all. Just crazy. I felt like I was sitting on the electric fence, or like all my nerves were on the outside of my skin. It took me days to get over it, over wanting to feel like that again. If he'd showed up at the door, I would have taken him out to the barn. No question. Even now, maybe, though it's probably impolite of me to say it. I can't imagine you minding.*

*I told Mick when he was twelve or thirteen. He asked
me because one of the kids at school—the son of one of
my high school friends—called him a bastard. I was so
angry, and I wanted to lie, but I didn't. Mick was so smart
you couldn't lie to him (and I've always been a lousy liar
anyway), and he wasn't really even upset. He just wanted
to know.*

    *What is it I'm even trying to explain to you? I hate to
think I'm making excuses for not being altogether present
all the time, for not always (ever?) being entirely there
even before Mick went off and disappeared. The thing was,
I knew. And sometimes I could drag myself back, from
wishing to be somewhere else, someone else. I remember I
used to practice, actually in the mirror, how to talk to you
the way I imagined I was supposed to. I'd say, "Riley, let me
see your homework." "Mick, does that girl's mother know
she's riding on that motorcycle with you?" Sometimes I'd
make myself laugh. Other times it would just open a hole
in me. Because I didn't know how. I was making it up.
And even though now I recognize that's what all parents
do, when you're in it, and everything you see or hear says
you're supposed to know, it just makes you feel wrong. Add
to that how young I was, and how much I really did want
to be, or at least be able to go, somewhere else, wanted
Mick to really be my little brother, and for you to be his
so I could escape, go off and be what I was meant to be.
Glamorous and smart and educated and alone. Like Jackie
Kennedy. If only for a little while. Then I could come back,
knowing something different and exotic, and settle down.
Be satisfied.*

*I would never have traded either of you for diamonds,
but sometimes I wonder. I can't help it. I can't help but
think of all the children born as that stupid war was
ending who maybe wouldn't have been. Hard to imagine,
once another being enters your universe. But I don't have
to tell you, do I.*

*Or why we couldn't keep him. I was still so cracked
open over Mick. So close to blowing it the first two times.
Your father wanted to keep Slim and raise him. He loved
that baby so much. But he let me give him away. And Slim
is fine. His other "grandpa" still writes. We got a letter just
last week.*

*This probably isn't fair, writing you now with all of
this. Maybe I think if I tell you what I know you can use
it to find your way back. Not here necessarily—I think
you're probably gone from here for good—just back from
wherever you are. There was so much emptiness in your
voice the last time I talked to you. I keep thinking I'm
going to get a call someday. From San Francisco. From
someone other than you.*

*Obviously, this is not where I was meaning to go with
this, or maybe it was. Either way, here we are. I started
out just wanting to explain something, like where I was
when I should have been with you guys. All three of you.
At home, appreciating my family instead of a million
miles away or at the damn window, envying the hawks
their wings, their freedom. Christ. I was, I <u>am</u>,so bad at
so many things.*

*I used to think making love with that boy was my
original sin, like in the Bible, the sin that had already*

started to make the rest of my life tumble over, little by
little, like dominoes. When you fell off the roof and nearly
died, and then when Mick left, even before they lost him, I
felt like I was paying for those afternoons in the hayloft, for
sneaking out at night to meet that boy by the river, shuck
my clothes like a lizard slipping its skin. I couldn't help
myself even if I'd wanted to, and I didn't want to. It's all I
could think about. I wanted to melt into him, melt him,
like butter. Now I wonder if it was the same for you. The
not being able to help it. The feeling like God was going to
make me pay and pay.

I just met that boy, your young man, the one time,
when he came looking for you. It was hard to lie, and I
think he knew. I really am the worst liar, and with you
in the next room, listening, that made it even harder. I
remember he was handsome, though, and tall. What was
his name? Something old-fashioned. Darrell. I think that
was it. And he was a gentleman. Very polite. Shook my
hand when he left. Called me ma'am. He brought a little
bouquet of wildflowers and you tore them apart after he
was gone, a petal or a leaf at a time, taking your time,
and scattered them around the yard. You had a look, girl,
that scared me. Now I know what it was. I wonder if my
mother saw that same look in me. Like an animal bent on
escape. You did it. You were determined.

And is it any wonder you both wanted to go? Not at all.
I know you would not have left Slim if I hadn't talked
you into it. I didn't know I wasn't going to be able to keep
him here. But I was still holding on for dear life, and so
desperately believed if I kept believing, did everything just

*right, one day Mick would walk up that driveway, kick
the dust off his boots, kiss me hello, and go upstairs to
his books and his records and his guitar and draw me a
picture of wherever he'd been. Then you could come home,
and I could have my second chance.*

   *I want so badly to explain all this to you in a way that
makes sense to both of us. This is me, Riley, your mom,
trying to figure out how to do that and not mess it up any
more than I already have.*

   *Your father, on the other hand, just says to tell you
hello. Your father sends his love. He misses you a lot. So do
I. And Cash. He's old now, can't catch a rabbit anymore.
But he still tries.*

   *I hope this finds you. I think I hope that. Maybe it's
too much. I have no idea where you are. Call if you can.
Collect is fine. Happy New Year, sweetie.*

                                        I love you, Mom

8. The Last Thing You Need

"So this orphan walks into a bar," Cole says, to make Riley laugh, although there is no more to it, just the one line. It is not a joke at all. He gives her his best Elvis look: blue eyes narrowed (eyelashes ridiculously long), head cocked slightly right and down, the merest rumor of a smile at one corner of his mouth. She is five, maybe six years older than he is, which is not quite twenty-one, but he has a fake ID she pretends to believe even though it is an obvious hack job.

He watches as she consoles another regular, listens attentively to a story of love gone wrong, the inability to find someone new, the futility of trying.

"You just haven't met the right person," Riley says. "But you will. You have so much to offer."

In one month, Cole has heard these same words come from that beautiful mouth at least ten times before, spoken to at least ten different women with ten different ex-girlfriends. Well, sometimes the ex-girlfriends overlap; it's sort of that kind of a bar.

An hour later, she is pouring a club soda for a repeat wagoneer who is obviously hanging on by a weakening thread. "One day at a time," Riley says, without apparent irony, and the gal repeats it.

"Yes," she says.

Riley says, "Maybe a meeting?" Gently. No judgment. It's that kind of bar too, sometimes. "I think there's a two o'clock at St. Kevin's."

"You're right, there is." She downs her soda, squares her shoulders, and reaches across the bar for Riley's hand. "You're a doll, sweetheart. Thanks for saving my life, again."

Riley pats her hand. "You're going to be fine."

When the woman leaves, Riley sighs. "Whoa," she says, and pours herself a shot.

"Everyone loves the bartender," she tells Cole later. "It doesn't matter who it is."

It does matter, he thinks, but it is just like her to believe it doesn't. It matters that she's nice to people and doesn't act like she's something special just because she can reach the bottles without climbing over the bar. And she's funny. And pretty, sometimes. She has that mouth; he loves watching it—the way it never seems to be able to stay still even when she isn't talking. And he loves how she gives everyone a bunch of second chances, because she knows that human beings are flawed. He knows this because she has told him, but he is not supposed to tell anyone else.

He brings her presents: strawberries, pizza, Valium, flowers he's picked out of someone's yard. When he brings the Valium, she says, "How did you know my favorite color is blue?" She cuts one in half, chases it down with a beer. She picks the toppings off the pizza and feeds the crust to a dog someone's tied to a parking meter out front. The flowers go in a chimney glass, set on the bar by the beer taps. Customers ask where they came from. "My new boyfriend," she says, and laughs. Cole watches her mouth when she does it.

He plays songs on the jukebox for her when he can tell she's starting to wear down. Songs like "Brown Eyed Girl." Even though it is not one of her very favorites, when he plays it he knows that she knows it is for her, even though her eyes are green, like his mother's eyes were, the way he remembers them. The Van Morrison song she really loves is the one about Jackie Wilson, the one about heaven, and smiling. He sings the chorus to her, and often she will smile when he does, and this is what they do: flirt harmlessly, avoiding any complication, any chance of collateral damage.

The orphan joke is on him: he really is an orphan, his parents dead of a car wreck in the California desert east of Barstow, where the Mojave begins, and doesn't end again (as far as his mother was concerned) until Albuquerque. She kept a diary, and in it she hated, with a steadfast determination, the desert; envisioned breaking down and having to walk until their knees buckled, the sun so bright and hot it filled the sky, with only a narrow, pale-blue band of not-sun just at the horizon. She imagined their skulls bleaching alongside cow skulls and scaly armadillo skeletons, and she didn't like it at all. But there was contract work at Los

Alamos, and a couple of times a year they had to go. When the station wagon rolled, Cole was thrown clear. He was six, and still dreams sometimes of sliding face-first through the sand, hands out in front of him, like a runner trying to touch third base before the throw comes wicked hard and fast from the outfield.

"Did I ever tell you," he says, bouncing a quarter, in some trick manner, off the wooden floor and snatching it out of the air on its way back up, "that I was named after John Coltrane?" He knows, since he'd been in the bar last night with her until past closing, that she has a hangover, and he is hoping to maybe distract her from it. He doesn't get hangovers. Not really. She has told him it is because he is young. "Just wait," she says. "You'll get yours too." But he doesn't expect to live long enough to be old enough for that. Does not count on it at any rate.

"Only about a hundred times," she says, smiling with that mouth. She stacks just-washed glasses on the stainless-steel drain board and dries her hands on the white bar towel she pulls from her back pocket. Takes two more aspirin and washes them down with Kahlúa-laced coffee. She'll be cured—or drunk again—by the end of her shift, but she'll keep it together; like always. Almost always. At least more often than not.

"How about the one—"

"Where your heart was turned around backward when you were born?"

"Yes. That one. Did I ever tell you that one?"

"No," she says, coming around the bar to sit next to him and listen. "Tell me the story about your heart."

It is not a long story, but it comes with illustrations: before and after. On a small white bar napkin, he draws with a black felt-tip pen the outline of what is ostensibly a baby boy. He draws it without lifting the pen so it ends up looking like the outline of a chunky adult chalked on the sidewalk, the aftermath of a drive-by down at Army and Folsom. He draws the heart, shaped exactly like a Valentine candy one, and reaches across the bar for another napkin. The second drawing looks almost exactly like the first, except on one he letters a small *B* on the heart, and an *F* on the other one. "See," he says, putting the pen in his back pocket, "that's how they did it. Unhooked it, flipped it over, and hooked it back up again. Good as new." He pats himself on the chest like a Boy Scout in the bleachers, waiting for "The Star-Spangled Banner" to get to the good part.

It isn't good as new, though. His heart isn't. It needs special care, and instead he feeds it pints of Anchor and shots of Beam. Speed sometimes, when he can get it. Riley, unlike the other bartenders, is stingy with the whiskey. He knows it is because she cares about him, and because he tends to get sullen on the brown stuff; it makes him feel sorry for himself. He doesn't want to feel sorry for himself, but he does want the warm numbness, the feeling of invincibility he has heard most young people have until they are at least thirty. He has some years to go yet and would like to feel that way for a few of them anyway.

Spring comes on a Sunday, and they walk to the flea market at the bottom of the hill. Riley lets Cole hold her hand, for a little while. It makes him happy, makes him feel safe, or as if he is taking care of her. He pretends he has a girlfriend; a version of Riley who could be that. The market smells, in turn, like diesel fuel, Mexican food, and the bay, and Cole sees a group of men in animated conversation in another language. They all look very serious, despite the fact that one of them is wearing a foam hat shaped like a wedge of cheese. Cole points the group out to Riley.

"*Très chic*," Riley says. And they laugh, go on to paw through tarnished silverware and cheap jewelry. Riley tries on a ring made from an old silver spoon. Cole wants to buy it for her, but she says, "Don't be silly. I don't need a ring. I'd just lose it." She puts it back in the case and walks away. Looks back to make sure he isn't up to something.

When they are done shopping, they take the bus back up the hill because they are carrying their purchases, not because of Cole's untrustworthy heart. They have both found cowboy boots: Riley's a pair of deep-brown, hand-tooled Tony Lamas and Cole's a gaudy pair of snakeskins with no discernible label. Riley has added to her collection of T-shirts, and Cole has found one as well. It says, "Dip Me in Honey and Throw Me to the Lesbians."

"Oh yeah," Riley says. "The girls are going to love that."

"I know." He is delighted, grinning pork chop to pork chop. Some of the women at the bar are still not smitten with him, but he knows very soon any lingering resistance will be futile.

When they get back, Lu—one of the irregulars, out for the time being on her own recognizance—is the first to weigh in. "Where the fuck did you get that?"

"Flea market," Cole says proudly.

Lu holds her hand out. "Give it to me."

"Sorry, Lu. Not this one."

She narrows her eyes. Turns her back and hunches over her drink. "You little shit."

He laughs. This one loves him for sure. He can tell by how fierce she is. And she is the same with Riley, only different. They have a thing, but Cole hasn't figured out what it is yet. He thinks it might be a simple wish on Riley's part to mend broken objects. Of which he is not one.

When Riley is busy, and it is pointless or at least ill-advised to vie for her attention, Lu and Cole play pool together, or pinball, or wander around the neighborhood collecting stuff people leave out on the sidewalks. They present Riley with treasures to take her mind off her hangovers, her regrets, her drug-addicted boyfriend, and to keep reminding her that they are her best (however damaged) angels. They give her a broken but still beautiful and delicate gold chain; an old green typewriter missing only a few keys; potted succulents for the windowsill, clay pots chipped in places but still perfectly good. Some of the scraggly little suckers are even in bloom. Riley makes room for it all, since neither Cole nor Lu lives anyplace in particular.

"We are campers!" Cole says. Because life is nothing short of a grand adventure.

At the moment he is camping out at a pizza joint just the other side of the panhandle. The man who owns it is an old friend of his mom and dad, and has given Cole something of a job—gopher, really; fill-in prep cook—even though the kid is nothing if not unreliable. He tries really hard. But something keeps wanting to yank him back, to a time when he was someone else's responsibility.

After closing—if Riley has not drunk all the shots people buy for her during her shift, and/or snorted any of the lines of coke they leave for her in the bathroom—and after Cole has helped her clean the bar, Riley drives him to the restaurant, to sleep on his bedroll in the small dining room.

It is usually after three by the time they get on the road, and this night they are still wound up. She leaves the car parked on Stanyan, and they run together into Golden Gate Park, past the tents and sleeping bags scattered at the edge, through the tunnel, onto the soccer fields, and then farther, into the woods. Other nights they've gone all the way to the ocean. They don't care that the grass is wet or that the moon shines down on them only in their minds, hidden as it is by the unrelenting fog. They pretend they are actually *in* the ocean, in a fabulous place only they know about, able to walk around and breathe underwater because they are special.

Sometimes Riley takes her clothes off and dives into some damp thing: Stow Lake, a lily pond, a pile of medicine-scented eucalyptus leaves, the sea. She lies down on the wet grass and tells Cole stories about Montana and its mountains; its dinosaurs, fossils, and preposterously blue sky. She talks about the South China Sea and about a brother she says she invented because she is an only child. He wants to hold her, bury his face in her hair, tell her he knows how she feels. But it is enough—he lets it be enough—to be connected to her by this, by anything.

Before he met Riley, Cole had never gone into the park, had not known of its many wonders or just how big it was, how many places in it a person could conceivably hide, and how unalike all those places were from one another.

"One minute," he tells Lu, back at the bar, "you're in Hawaii. Then Australia. Then the redwoods. Then—"

Lu breaks in. "Before you know it," she says way too brightly, "you're getting a blow job from some guy behind the fence in Queen Wilhelmina's tulip garden. Under a *wind*mill."

"Jesus, Lu," Riley says. "Give the kid a chance."

"Well, it's true," Lu says. "That's what they do out there."

"In a very small part of a very large park. You are such a cynic sometimes."

Lu snorts.

Cole says, "Sometimes?"

"I am not cynical," Lu says. "I am a realist."

Riley shakes her head, does that oh-no-I-won't-smile maneuver with her mouth and her eyes, and goes back to washing glasses. "Don't you two have some trouble to get into somewhere else?"

Lu downs her brandy. "Come on, you little rat fink. We'll find something. Let Glamour Girl here entertain the masses."

It's early afternoon. There's no one else in the place. Cole hates leaving Riley alone, because he thinks it makes her sad. Sadder. But she sounds serious. And they won't be gone long.

"Shot for the road," he says, as if he is just another customer and his money is as good as anyone's.

"Fat chance," Riley says. "Nice try, though."

Cole laughs. "Thanks, Mom."

Riley raises her eyebrows. He tries again. "Thanks, baby."

"You two make me sick," Lu says. "Stop it right now."

She and Cole leave arm in arm.

Lu says they should take the bus downtown, straight down Mission Street, all the way to the end. But first someone has to go back into the bar and get two dollars from Riley for the fare. That someone being Cole. Riley gives him ten bucks.

"Aren't you going to tell me not to spend it all in one place?"

"Nope."

"Cranky."

"I'm not cranky, sweetheart. I'm tired. I'll be better when you get back. Promise."

"Okay." He stands on the rail and leans over the bar, turning his not-quite-clean-shaven cheek toward her.

She kisses it. "Git," she says. Behind the bar smells like limes and bleach and spilled liquor. He wonders if she even notices it anymore.

"Will you miss me?"

"How can I miss you if you won't go away?"

"Ha," he says. "That's *my* line."

"Mine now."

He waits. She sighs, and her eyes are a little squinty. He still sees a light in there, though. "Yes, I will miss you."

Outside, he finds Lu sitting on the curb with her back to

a parking meter, smoking a cigarette with her eyes closed. The sun is out and the wind hasn't begun to blow yet.

"Pretty day," Cole says.

"What do you know about it?" She pushes herself up off the concrete, offering him the crook of her arm.

"Nothin'," Cole says, certain it is the correct answer.

"That's right," Lu says, as they head down the hill to the bus stop.

The 14 arrives and they get on, finding seats together because this far south it is not jam-packed with bodies yet. As the bus crawls through the Mission, stopping at nearly every corner, more and more people board, and nearly all of them, when they speak, are speaking Spanish.

"Do you understand any of that?" Lu says.

"A little." Because he is a California kid, Cole had Spanish in elementary school, and his mother would practice with him. "*¿Cómo se llama?*" she'd say. Some days he would be Roberto. Others, Antonio. Someone new every day. "*¡Me llamo Zorro!*" Leaping onto and then off the couch, into her arms.

He learned more in high school, before he dropped out. "*La luz del porche está prendida,*" he says to Lu. "*Pero nadie es en la casa.*"

"What?"

"The porch light's on, but nobody's home." He cracks himself up. "Pretty good, huh?"

"*La luz,*" Lu says. "*Nadie.*" She looks over at him. "What did I just say?"

You said, "The light. Nobody."

"How do you say blue?"

"*Azul.*"

She repeats it, stretching out the *ooooh* sound. "I like it."

"There are more where that came from."

"More what?"

"Colors." He starts to name them.

"Easy, Buckwheat. Don't overload me."

"Right," he says.

They are at the corner of Nineteenth and Mission. A man with a Detroit Tigers baseball cap and a red halyard around his neck that says "I ♥ Guadalupe" is standing next to the bus, under their window, and talking to himself, waving his scrawny arms around like a drunken orchestra conductor, though he does not look particularly drunk.

Lu says, "I wonder where old Lupe is."

"What?"

"Lupe. Guadalupe."

"I think it's a place," Cole says.

Lu says, "I don't think so. I think Lupe went out to shit and the hogs ate her."

"You're so bad," Cole says. "I don't know what Riley sees in you." He is kidding, but somehow it comes out as if he isn't.

Lu doesn't appear to be fazed either way. "She sees this," she says, pointing to her chest. "She knows I'm all heart."

"Must be nice."

"Oh, buck up." She graze-punches him across the shoulder. "It's a lovely day."

Cole looks out the window. He loves this street. To him it is one big carnival all spilled out onto the sidewalk. Cotton candy is the predominant smell, but also chile *ristras*, oregano, pot smoke, pee. Every single building has a storefront on the ground floor, and they are selling *everything*. Furniture, clothes, animals, produce, flowers, luggage, *chicharrones*, toys, appliances, stereos, Mylar *quinceañera* balloons. He thinks there cannot possibly be enough people in this seven-by-seven-square-mile city to buy all this stuff, but there it all is, and hundreds of people crowd the street, carrying pink plastic bags, pushing shopping carts, lugging chairs and boom boxes to god only knows where.

At Sixteenth Street he sees the junkies nodding out, their backs to the broken-down escalators, and rockheads searching the sidewalks, picking up anything small and white, hoping for a miracle. He turns to ask Lu if they really believe that any of those pebbles or bits of chalk or cigarette filters or scraps of paper are actually going to turn out to be something they can smoke, something that will make their ass-out lives feel worth living awhile longer, but she's gone. He looks out the window again, sees her cross the street. He starts to get up, to follow, but the doors close, and he watches as the bus pulls away; Lu's shoulders are hunched up around her ears—she knows he's watching—and her head is down, but she finds her way to a group of young men, bunched up and slouchy on the corner, and they take her in like a long-lost cousin.

He does not get off at the next stop. A plan is a plan, and he is a little bit angry with Lu for walking out in the middle of their expedition. He knows Riley won't be very happy when he comes back alone, but it's hardly his fault. Lu's a free agent; she can do what she wants.

Riley refers to Lu's wanderings as her "trajectory," as if Lu were a satellite, or a spaceship exiting Earth's atmosphere. "There's never a warning," Riley says. No indication that the spur Lu is traveling on is about to end. Because then there's a chance someone will try to stop her, talk some sense into her thick skull, and she's not having any of it. Which is fine, Cole thinks. Riley's got more than enough to keep her busy, as far as he's concerned. The bar. The boyfriends.

Rumor has it there's a good boyfriend somewhere, sometimes, but he doesn't seem to be a very effective one, so Cole dismisses him. The bad boyfriend doesn't dismiss so easily.

No one ever sees the guy, since he doesn't come into the bar, but Cole is sure he's seen evidence of him. Riley won't cop to it, though. She cops to running into things, like doors, cops to falling down. "I was *so* drunk," she'll say, as if this too is the start of some kind of a joke. Sometimes Cole wishes he had a gun and the backbone to use it, or knew some really badass guys who would rough the fucker up, make him stop, but thinking like that makes him feel out of his league, not to mention ridiculous. His only choice is to be there as much as possible, to take her mind off whatever bad thing happened last.

Riley doesn't seem overly surprised when Cole tells her where Lu got off the bus.

"Her favorite corner," she says, like she's saying "Her favorite burrito place." She bites her lip, taps Cole a big Anchor Steam and herself a little one, and goes outside to smoke a cigarette. Cole goes with her. They sit on the back stairs, from where they can see the bar, see if anyone wants anything, but it's still pretty slow.

"What is it," Cole says, "with you and Lu?"

Riley laughs. "You mean are we an item?"

"I don't think that's what I mean. Are you?"

"No."

"What, then?"

"UFFUs."

"What's a UFFU?"

"Unidentified Flying Fuckup. Want to join the club?" She laughs, and it is not quite the unhappy sound he expects.

"Sure," he says.

She wraps her arms around his neck, submerges her face in his chest. "You can be our mascot." He doesn't know what to do with his hands. He sets his beer down next to him to see if maybe they'll figure something out on their own, find some landing place that maybe won't freak her out, but before any of that can happen, she lets go and stands up, drains her beer, and pours the last drops over the railing into the scruffy garden. As soon as she gets five feet into the dark bar, he can't even see her anymore.

Time passes, but it does not fly. Lu appears. Lu disappears. "Like magic!" Cole says, and Riley rolls her eyes and shakes her head. He doesn't care. He is still alive. She still loves him.

One night in winter, when Lu has called an extended runner, and Riley's boyfriend has taken off with all her cash and left his fingerprints on her arms in purple to match the black eye, and she has given Cole every shot of Beam he's asked for and gone shot for shot with him and the bar closes, somehow, magically, all by itself, they end up on the pool table. Their clothes come off and the next thing Cole knows they are fucking and he is well over the moon, sober almost from the sheer relief of her legs around him, her hands somehow on his hip bones, her mouth her mouth her mouth. "Baby," he says, next to it, into it.

"Don't talk," Riley says. "Shhhhh."

He moans, collapses. Riley bites his shoulder, but not hard. More like an afterthought.

He moves to her side and decorates her with an array of shiny pool balls, placing them strategically on and around her body. He finds her scars. Shows her his. Riley points out constellations on the ceiling, as if the stars are really there. Wearing each other's clothes, they head for the panhandle.

Riley gets pulled over on the way back, blows a 2-something, tells the cop to go fuck himself, and they keep her 'til she sobers up and the boyfriend himself comes down to throw her bail.

"You should have called *me*," Cole says the next day, when she tells him about it, how considerate and attentive the boyfriend was, how sweet, how good the Bloody Marys tasted down at the Ramp.

"Right," Riley says. "You don't have a phone number. Or money."

"I'll get a phone," he says. "I'll get a job, and a place. We can move in together."

Riley looks at him, slowly shakes her head. "Not gonna

happen, kid." She says it as gently (he knows) as she knows how. It still sounds like yelling to him.

He wants to yell back, but it is not in him. "Why not?"

They are sitting at the bar, with one bar stool between them. "For starters, you are too young for me. And you are too nice." She is tracing someone else's initials carved into the wood. "I'm a hot mess, honey. I'm the last thing you need."

For a second, he thinks he hears something in her voice, some chink he can break through, but when he looks her jaw is set, and, if anything, she looks like she's miles away— from this place, from him. Like he's the last thing on her mind.

Finally, she faces him again and smiles. The word he is looking for is "rueful."

"How do you like them apples?" she says.

"I hate them apples."

She stands up and kisses the top of his head. "I do too," she says as she pulls her bar towel from her pocket and starts wiping down already-clean tables.

Cole walks to the pool table to prowl its perimeter. "What about this?" He motions at the felt, never looking at Riley.

"That," she says, "was a whole lot of fun. You're a whole lot of fun, sweetie. You're a doll. You're the best. You're a champ."

"A *champ*?"

"Yup."

"Fuck that," he says. And leaves. Halfway down the

block, he turns to see if she's coming after him, but she's just standing out front looking up at the sky, like she's waiting for something good to fall out of it.

When he gets to Mission Street, Lu is getting off the bus. She says, "I had a dream about you. My cat was in it."

"You have a cat?"

"No. Listen. Shut up."

He leans against the brick wall of the restaurant on the corner. He waits.

"It was weird," Lu says.

All dreams, he thinks, *are weird. Life is fucking weird.* But he doesn't say it. Because it's too obvious.

"You died," Lu says. "They brought the coroner's van, and they took you away. I missed you. I was sad and I forgot what color your eyes were. I had to ask my cat."

He doesn't like anything about this dream so far. "Your cat you don't have," he says.

"Yeah," Lu says. "That one."

"So what did the cat say?"

"*Azul,*" she says. Just like she said it the first time, stretching it until it won't stretch anymore. It sounds like the low howl of a coyote at moonrise. Somewhere in the unbreakable heart of the oblivious desert.

9. Take You Back Broken

"I feel like someone's put a torch to me," Lu sighs, from the floor, as if there's something appealing about that notion. I lie down on the cool, scarred hardwood next to her but don't touch, my toes an inch from her ankle, stretching into her and away at the same time. I suspect she really would like to be on fire, that she would be pissed if I put her out. We are a pair, not a couple, mostly because I am still (stubbornly, she says) straight, still like boys de- spite the improbability of surviving them, and she may be too wild anyway, even for me. We are in Oakland, during a string of rare ninety-degree days, because we are out on a pass of sorts and because it is necessary for us to be here, as opposed to the city across the bay, where in our world people and their lives simply come apart, and we can't seem to do a thing to stop them.

It's August and too hot to touch, skin to skin, too hot to even think about outside. Outside is where you go when you are being punished, at least until dark; then inside is punishment, jungly and fierce. Equatorial, like Papua New Guinea.

She pronounces it *Pa-POO-Ah*. Irian Jaya, she tells me, is its other half. She starts meandering around peninsulas and archipelagoes—Indonesia, Malaysia—comes creeping up on Burma and the Irrawaddy.

I say, "Stay out of Vietnam." Sixteen degrees north of the equator but still scorching, from what Mick's letters said.

She says, "I know."

When she sits up, it will be to smoke a cigarette and work on a drawing of a forest, in deep green, brown, and black, with a few white smudges standing in as rabbits. She will say this forest is in the kingdom of Bengal, though it no longer exists as a kingdom. When I tell her that, she will show me one of her maps, of which she has many, some of them very old. She collects dog-eared . . . things.

"Oh yes it does, Cookie. It's right there." She'll flick that map with her index finger, a sharp, snapping sound. "See?"

It is hard to argue when it is in black and white like that. Black and white, red and blue. She claims, when she is not drawing or painting, to be a geographer. When she is not drawing or painting, dope sick or high, or trying to figure out how to get high. She's never actually been anywhere, except here and southern Indiana, the long black-tar highway in between. She left when she got old enough to fight off the inbred uncles, steal a car. I came later, from the north, and at first she was jealous of my wholesome, perfect family. Of how I led my personal Lewis and Clark expedition to the edge of the continent, obliviously determined to beat the crappy odds and discover the Pacific on my own.

There was an intersection of sorts. A convergence. Or maybe an eclipse. And now it is nighttime. We fall asleep on the floor under the creaky ceiling fan. Even sheets weigh too much. The air trying to come through the windows smells like wild animals. Random gunfire in the distance wakes us up. Gang wars. Little boys with Uzis. Lu growls, but softly.

"You want to bring the outside in, but you can't," I say. "Not even you."

"We could take out a wall."

"What about winter?"

"What about it?" What she means by that, I know, is that winter is not certain, if nothing is. Besides which, these walls, not a one of them belongs to us.

On the subject of fire, she continues to deny ever having set one in the bar. The burned spot in the faded linoleum, burned and melted through to the wood underneath, was someone else's handiwork. She doesn't say whose, but I bet she was there. That happened a long time ago, maybe ten years, way before me.

"I hate that Andy keeps telling that story," she says. I have not mentioned the fire, but she has reminded herself, and I know exactly what she's talking about. It's a sore point with her, being falsely accused. Andy is the swamper at the bar, queer as Liberace but not quite as glamorous, a long-haul regular and witness to years of bad behavior in what he calls the Lesbyterian Church. He tracks all of us, me included now, and although nelly and sweet and generous, he is a terrible gossip and not above making things up. I don't know why the fire story bugs Lu so much; maybe because she has never lied about all the stupid things she actually has done, as she generally doesn't give a rat's ass what people say or think.

When I first saw her, she was loudly berating a blind girl from her usual location, leant James Dean–style against the wall by the jukebox, cigarette perched on her lip, smoke narrowing her possum-brown eyes. She pointed at me and demanded to know what year it was. I thought maybe it was some kind of a test, but I didn't know if there was a trick to passing it, so I just said. She did a little math, turned back to the girl. "I'm thirty-four years old," she announced, poking a finger into her own chest. "Look at me." To a blind girl. I was behind the bar, still new and not a little nervous, and everyone else who was in there at the time was appalled, or acting like it. I thought it was funny. I knew that girl. She was a pain in the ass. Got drunk every afternoon and tripped over the dog. Poor animal had a haunted look, bruised fur. I had to draw the line at rustling a blind girl's dog, but, boy, was I tempted. Lu would have done it, I bet, if she'd thought of it and had someplace to keep it, but she was on the street more often than she was off. Or camping in someone else's living room.

She came back over and over to flirt with me, but could never get my name right.

"Rachel."

"Not even close."

"Bailey."

"Bailey is a dog's name."

She demanded a nickname. I had lots of those.

"My brother used to call me Cupcake," I said, and she promptly forgot that too.

"Cookie," she said, five minutes later. In a way, she invented me. I could not have invented her, as I did not have the experience or the capacity. When I got to know her, the bit that she let me, sometimes I called her Loopy, sometimes Sloopy. Sometimes she answered. She and Mick would have been close to the same age, and something about the way she leaned on that wall wanted to remind me of him, but I didn't let it. I could already see it would be complicated enough without that, and probably hurt.

A few years on, Lu and I are both still alive, for reasons maybe some god knows and maybe doesn't. We are house-sitting in Oakland for one of the regulars, who's gone off to Thailand for a few weeks. "Probably to molest little boys," Lu says.

I shush her. "How come you always think the worst of everyone?" She just looks at me, her mouth pulled off to one side of her face, part of her lower lip between her teeth. I turn away, and she blows softly on my cheek, her breath black licorice-ish—she's been eating it by the pound. Hardly drinking, no drugs for three weeks, the first two at Harbor Lights. Enough time to detox without dying, but not a chance in hell of even that first, let alone twelfth, step. I can't believe she hasn't jumped out the window yet. I hold her in place with my incredible will. She lets me. For now.

We are here because it is unfamiliar territory. Not perfect, but Lu doesn't yet know any of the local kids, the ones on the streets a little farther east, hawking their powdered oblivion. *Special. For you. Today.*

Those first months at the bar, right before Wendy died, she and Lu were crashing at a friend's place in Glen Park, maintaining: Lu still driving a cab sometimes, and Wendy cleaning a few houses, but they were not telling the whole truth. Wendy still looked like she'd just stepped off the porch at Tara—all girl all the time. She smelled exactly like magnolia blossoms, in memory if not in real time. They didn't tell that she'd fallen backward, wrecked on rosé wine and Mexican Quaaludes, off the deck, and ruptured some critical organ. Too high, too scared to take care of business. Terrified of the emergency room at General: the iodine smell, triage. People utterly ass-out, moaning and raging. Because once you went there, you were officially fucked. Wendy finally died of hoping it would all, somehow, sort of, like it always had, work itself out in the end. When she had gone, Lu came to me, and I tried like hell to figure out a way to keep her.

Pinball was one way, and the guy who came to collect the money usually left a bunch of credits for me. For us.

We had totally different styles. She bashed the hell out of the machine, tilting it and swearing at it, as though it had intentionally done her wrong. "Mother*fucker.* I oughta—"

"Oughta what?"

"Cut its legs off."

"Then how would we play?"

"We would sit on the floor, like little children. You could teach me how."

"Ha-ha. Out of the way. My turn."

My action was all in the hips, and mentally coaxing the ball to within reach of the flippers. It was an old one, Spanish Eyes, the score racking up by tens in a little square window behind the back glass, the clacking noise like dominoes falling. The gunshot crack of a win or a match sent us into a minor frenzy. A double match: we were untouchable.

I rarely had many customers before three or four, so when we were all bashed out, we'd move to the pool table. Lu kicked my ass on a regular basis, but she taught me how to sink one or two on the break, how to leave the cue ball where I could make the next shot.

"Hit it low, Cook. Get under it but keep it on the table. Soft now, you're not trying to kill anything."

We never snookered each other, since that would have been cheating. When folks started filtering in, Lu faded out. I hardly ever saw her go.

I had surprised myself by making it to and past twenty-five, and thinking that made me a grown-up making a grown-up decision, fell for a guy who knew how to keep a girl on her toes: a freebasing Cajun bricklayer who wasn't about to let me bring Lu home, or else I probably would have. As it was, I was on call. About the fourth time, I got the hang of it.

"Hey, Cookie. I need a ride."

"Not going to the projects, Lu."

"Cookie."

"No."

I picked her up and drove her across town, our destination the projects at Hayes and Buchanan—the same ones,
as it turned out, the boyfriend frequented, though I never
saw him there. Maybe they had a different entrance for the
high that would fix whatever sickness ailed him.

"You worry too much," Lu told me. "I'm not going to get
you into anything I can't get you out of."

"That's comforting."

She opened the door and leaned out to puke. I pulled
over, and she cussed me. "Goddamn it, Cook." She dragged
her sleeve across her mouth and pulled the door closed.
"Drive like I taught you."

Once she'd copped and eased back into herself, there
was no one I'd rather have been around. When the ghosts
were asleep or off somewhere playing poker, or even the
rare weeks or months she was actually, comparatively,
clean, she'd bust open the front door of the bar, light
streaming in behind her, and wrap her arms around me.
Hold me in a full body clench, drenched in Marlboro and
brandy fumes, and just a tolerable touch of panic. She said
she'd been born with that panic, spent a lifetime stuffing it.
Slept with a .357 under the pillow, when there was a pillow.

Some days—the steadiest ones—she'd go to the zoo,
draw the animals, capture their essence in a few stark lines.
Wildflowers were another favorite, sprouting crazy-legged
from stumpy, misshapen vases, the colors startling and
otherworldly. Later on she did a series of her cat in various
poses, on an assortment of perches around the only room
she had in years she could call her own, and in each one he

looked shocked to see her there, as if they'd never met or maybe only in a dream.

The Cajun also had some charming tendencies, and a peculiar schedule only he could fathom. Day one of the mystery rotation: beat me up, steal my money, disappear. Day two: stay gone. Day three: run out of drugs and money and come home. Expect soup. Homemade. Vegetarian.

In that town in those days, the odds of choosing a loser were pretty good if you were drawn to edgy like I'd turned out to be. I have no idea what I wanted that edge for. Maybe it's just the way I was. Or maybe I thought it would give me a chance to fix something that had only the remotest chance of coming unbroken. Whatever it was, every time I showed up with a fat lip or a black eye or fingertip-shaped bruises on the backs of my arms, Lu would offer to shoot him for me. I always turned her down, out of some sense of irrevocability, or not wanting to have to drive all that way to visit her in San Quentin. "One of these days, Cookie, I'm just going to do it. I don't need your fucking permission." She'd stare me down, waiting for a sign of weakness, a sign I'd had enough, but I wouldn't give it to her, not yet. Thought I could save him, is what I thought. Repair him, damaged as he was.

He was full of ceaseless surprises, but Lu wasn't. She was my stand-up guy, and all her secrets were already out. She wasn't going to come up with some new dark episode or previously disguised, dreadful personality trait; that shit was pretty much already on the table. And we wouldn't be lovers. She just wanted to hold me and look after me, chase

the other girls off. After my tour with the bricklaying coke-
head, that was good enough. And even though our hearts
worked in tandem, I never expected anything resembling
consistency, flat knowing I wasn't going to get it. By the
time Lu infiltrated my life, I'd done enough time with
the shell-shocked and war-wounded, the alcoholics and
the drug addicts to count her showing up clinically alive a
bonus.

"Hey, you. Looking good."

"Don't lie to me, Cookie."

"Really?"

"No. Lie to me. Buy me a drink."

I lent her money and everyone told me I was crazy.
Well, of course I was. The years since I'd left Montana had
fallen well short of a pure, unadulterated, youthful-type
trajectory, and my soul was every iota as snakebit as some
of the worst ones. Climbing out of the ditch was a hit-or-
miss proposition, and even though I was working on it,
down was still a hell of a lot easier way to go than up. Lu
was my reflection some of those days, and sometimes it
scared me half to death.

We get through the weeklong autumn heat wave in Sid's
flat, and whatever atmospheric front brought it in disappears back out to sea. Everyone goes a little crazy when
it gets steamy like that, and Lu's even crazier than normal
with the early arrival of hot flashes, brought on by the
weather—she likes to believe—but more probably by the
whiskey and the drugs. The hot flashes prove she's a girl

too, but she adamantly denies it. That's something she left in the rearview in Indiana, back there with the gropey uncles, the cousins she says stank like sour milk and lighter fluid.

A little fresh fog cat-foots east from the City. Lu hugs herself and shivers when I say the part about the cat's feet. I tell her about the poem Carl Sandburg wrote and she says, "You're so smart, Cookie. How'd you get to be so smart?"

"I'm not," I tell her. "I just read a lot. I have a lot of books."

"Books," she says, the tone of her voice signaling something irrefutable, as if she's just realized a few things are that simple and no one is going to talk her out of it now. I don't tell her that even in my life nothing is that simple; that when we lost Mick I inherited those books, and only barely had the good sense not to throw them into the ocean when I first got to California, when I realized no god had any intention of answering my questions—here, or in a horizon-to-horizon wheat field under the three-hundred-sixty-degree Montana sky, or anywhere else, from what I'd been able to determine.

The end of the week I have to go back to work, but Lu says she's okay, and she has been keeping it together pretty well. Her eyes are clear, and the shakes have subsided to barely noticeable. She's back to dressing like a gentleman. When she's on, Lu is remarkably fastidious about what she wears, mostly tailored men's britches and pressed white shirts. Sometimes a French racing cap, sometimes a derby. She's pretty cute, but that is something I am not allowed to say with my actual voice.

She watches me dress, does a quick pen-and-ink of me standing by the bathtub in my slip, pulling my Friday-night-only stockings on, grimacing at the torture of them, but she doesn't draw that part. The sketch is all black and white, until she colors the windows in red and orange, with crayons gripped in her fist like she's wielding an ice pick. She makes it look like the world outside is burning, and then finds a small strip of brown velvet somewhere and ties it into my hair.

Since I close at two and the subway stops running at twelve, Lu has to come get me after work. We're both driving one car these days, a car I bought but that somehow we both own and she has christened Alice. Alice is a 1969 baby-blue, four-barrel 383 Plymouth Fury that Lu just had to have, and if nothing major goes wrong, I can usually keep her running myself.

After we finish stocking the beer, washing the glasses, and sweeping the floor, we shoot a quiet game of pool and blaze out of town. Looking back from the Bay Bridge, the city behind us is all smoky pink with sodium-vapor light radiating up into the clouds, refracted through the fog. Lu drives, cabbie-fast and maniacally as always, and I lean out the window to shotgun the briny-smelling breeze into my lungs. I look west into the darkness, and see incomprehensible, ceaseless ocean, clear to Asia and back. Miles and miles. Really far and really deep. Lu says, "You ever think about jumping, Cook?"

"Never," I say, and I'm not really lying. I don't think about jumping, but I do think about falling—wonder for how long I could make it feel like flying—but I'm never going to get close enough to the edge to do any of those things. Seems silly to have the conversation at all, in that case.

"I don't believe you," Lu says, downshifting into second to pass a semi on the right, just before the lane ends. He has to brake to let us in and yanks on the air horn. It's really loud.

"It's hardly going to matter if you drive us off a bridge."

"Oh, be quiet, Cookie. Have I ever killed us?"

Oakland is still awake when we get back. Even though we're pretty close to the relative sanity of Berkeley, there are still a few young Turks hanging out, waving come-hither dime bags at us, watching just a little longer than maybe they'd watch a couple of guys driving through. Lu doesn't look anywhere but straight ahead, doesn't blink, smile, cuss, or nod. When we get to the flat, she throws herself through the door and onto the center of the bed like she's just escaped a ravenous tiger.

"Jesus Christ. Maybe you need to blindfold me."

"You'd have to let me drive." I know what is called for here is not a joke, but it's been a long night, and maybe I think I can make her laugh.

She throws the keys at me, hard. I duck and they hit the wall. "Not funny," she says, her voice close to cracking. Hearing it surprises me.

"Sorry. I'm tired." I sit down next to her, pick her hand up, and feel her pulse. It's going about a million miles an hour. "Criminy." I put my head on her chest and listen while her heart slows to a semi-normal speed.

I'm nearly asleep there when she says, "You want to check my teeth too?"

I sit up. "No. I want to go to bed. But you're going to have to give me some more room."

"Were you always this much of a pain in the ass?"

"I reckon."

"It's a wonder your mother didn't drown you in the horse trough."

"My mother loves me." Last time I checked. Which was a while ago.

"So you say." She turns over onto her stomach and spreads her arms wide across the bedspread, her face mashed into the pillow. She says something, but it's impossible to tell what.

"Speak English."

She turns her head to one side. "Don't let me go, Cook."

I take the ribbon out of my hair, tie it twice around her wrist. "There. Now you are in my custody. You can't escape."

At five, it is just beginning to get light. Sirens and dogs howl somewhere not far from here. I crawl under one of Lu's outstretched arms, and when I wake up hours later she's gone. All her shit and some of mine: the car, the cigarettes, gone. It's noon, and the steps and the sidewalk are lined with wilting crimson bougainvillea petals. "What the fuck am I supposed to do with these? Goddamn it, Lu." I am out of words. I pick up a handful of the red petals and hold them until a breeze comes and blows them out of my hand. Inside I press the same hand flat into her side of the bed. I'd swear it's still warm, sweaty in the indent her body left. I pack my little kit bag, put Sid's key under the mat, and head for the subway.

Alice comes back to me because the tow and impound notice is mailed to my address. I go down there and talk the cashier into releasing the car into my custody. Lu surfaces about three months later. I hear what she's doing from Andy, who's still at Harbor Lights, feeding Lu now, and her new girlfriend; smuggling them leftovers out the back door. They're both strung out, flopping in an abandoned building on Sixth Street. The whole neighborhood is being torn down, all the residence hotels emptying out to make way for lofts and condos. Lu and her gal are lucky to have a roof; the alleys between Market and Mission are lined both sides with appliance boxes and shopping carts.

I tell Andy to have Lu call me. "Tell her all is forgiven. Tell her there's nothing to forgive. Tell her something." A few days later she shows up at the bar right at one, when I open. Rode hard and put up wet, as my brother once liked to say. She stares straight down and mumbles into her sweatshirt. I know I couldn't raise her stubborn head with a car jack.

"Don't look at me, Cookie."

I just want to heal her all up. I have medicine. "You want a drink?"

"I want a gun."

"What happened to yours?"

"Some cocksucker stole it."

I sigh, pour her a brandy. Her hands are shaking so bad she has to hold the glass with both of them. I can see fresh track marks on the backs, among the smaller veins and the tiny bones. That piece of brown velvet is still tied around her wrist, hanging on by a few fine threads. She won't meet my eyes, and all I can think to ask is how she is and know what a ridiculous question that would be, so I don't say anything. I go back to setting up the bar, cutting limes, making Bloody Mary mix. The place smells a bit more like bleach than booze still, since Andy was in this morning cleaning. Light prisms through the beer signs overlapped in the front window, illuminates the settling dust. For lack of something more befitting the occasion, I examine the floor and see how scarred it is, not just in the burned spot, but all over. Lu says, "I did not set that fire."

"I believe you."

"You'd better, Cookie. No one else does." I know some people who would call that a burden, a moral obligation, but I am not one of those people. Nina Simone sings softly on the jukebox, about the morning of her life. Lu finishes her drink.

"You got fifty bucks?" she says. Like she's saying, "Can I have a bite of that?" I hand her a wad out of my pocket. "I'll pay you back," she says, crumpling the bills up even more. "I will, goddamn it."

"I don't care about that. Just don't die on my dime." I pick up a lemon, wonder if I can throw it hard enough to break a window. "Just don't." I put it back down, take the big stainless-steel bucket to the alcove where the ice machine is, by the back door that leads to the deck and the garden, where by my count seven trees have been planted for dead people in the five years I've worked here. And those are only the special ones. We don't plant trees for just anybody. That would require a second lot. Probably some new zoning. I don't need ice, but Lu needs space to pull off her ever-astonishing vanishing act.

I say, "I am not planting a tree for you, Lu. You can just forget about that." I don't say it very loud, and she probably wouldn't have heard me even if she wasn't already gone. She's left a cigarette burning in the ashtray. She knows I hate that. I leave it burning, to remember her by. Lu one; Cookie fuck-all.

The new girlfriend lasts until spring and then dies on Lu's birthday in April. Lu calls a few weeks later, and I go pick her up at Fifth and Harrison at three in the morning. It's raining, but she's standing out in the open, no coat, saturated like she's been swimming in the bay. She has a small duffel bag and a pure black kitten in a carrier behind her in a doorway, out of the rain. "I was afraid you wouldn't see me."

"I know how to find you. You glow in the dark. Get in here." I don't ask about the cat right away, and we drive back to my flat in the Mission. My roommate and his girlfriend are out of town, so I can run a bath for Lu, keep her for a day or two. I put the cat in its carrier in the bathroom to keep an eye on Lu and put her clothes in the washing machine. When she's done in the bathtub, I wrap her in a bathrobe and put her to bed. "You sick?"

"Not too terrible. Been doing some home-remedy detox since Chrissy OD'd. Pot and Valium. I got a stash." She doesn't try to hide the abscess scars on the back of her right hand. I hold it and run my thumb over one of them. Smack doesn't burn like that unless it's cut with something really weird.

"What the hell, Lu. Speed?"

"I don't know. Seemed like a good idea at the time. Something new. Chrissy liked it." She looks at the scars like she's seeing them for the first time. "That's what killed her. She was just a kid."

"I'm sorry, honey."

"I didn't know how much, Cook. I think I almost died too. My legs went right out from under me. My heart must have just been stronger than hers."

"You're a pro, Lu."

"You bet I am." She looks away so I can't see her eyes. After a minute, she reaches into her pocket and holds out a handful of little blue pills. "You want some?"

"Not now. I'm pretty sleepy. I'd just waste it."

The cat yowls from the bathroom. I raise an eyebrow at Lu, but she just says, "He came to me in a dream. His name is Mick."

"Mick." At the moment, whatever it means that Lu named her cat after my brother, accidentally or not, doesn't register. Not on any scale. That's how good I am. "Does Mick eat?"

"There's food in my bag."

I get the cat, the bag, a bowl, a towel, a dishpan with some torn-up newspaper in it. I say, "We've got 'til Sunday."

"Time enough," she says. Then, "What's that line? That song? About Valium. That Rickie Lee Jackson song."

"Jones," I say.

"Yeah, sure, whatever, Cook. But what does she say? You know."

"She says you shouldn't let them take you back. Broken."

"Like Valium?"

"Right. And chumps."

"Out in the rain," she says. "I love that. It makes so much sense."

"It doesn't really," I say. But it kind of does.

I could just holler, but I might not ever stop, so I close my eyes and play dead instead. When the Valium kicks in and Lu falls asleep, she's curled around me like a boa constrictor.

Amazingly, she stays cleaned up for a while: two months and a slip, two more, et cetera. It gets so I nearly start trusting her to show up when she says she will, even though a part of me is off in the corner, frantically waving its arms in alarm and asking loudly, "Have you completely lost your mind?" She gets a little room down on Market for her and that cat, a place that's safe and not blow-your-brains-out depressing like most of them. The guys at the front desk are nice and, of course, immediately fall in love with her because she's smart and funny and doesn't take any shit. She gets a steady cab gig with National, driving mostly night shifts, but night is her best side anyway, since she's still really vain and it's so much harder to see in the dark how the years have worked her over—better than the Cajun could ever have done to me and been allowed, by Lu, to live.

I don't see her every day, or even every week, but she stops by the bar when she can, shows me her drawings, the old atlases she picks up secondhand—ones that show Zimbabwe as Rhodesia, Southeast Asia as Indochine. We do normal things, like go down to Divisadero for Philly cheesesteak lunch dates, or Valencia for cheap sushi or Vietnamese.

She sits in the backyard at the bar, sketching the skyline, the haphazard tree cemetery, the wild masses of flowers and vegetation that never seem to die back here, but only hibernate a few weeks in winter. Nothing like Montana, where winter lasts from October to May or longer, and when the spring Chinook starts to blow, you feel like the thaw has been your whole life getting there. (Some dad or some brother takes a little kid outside, and they stand in a brown patch of dirt and dead grass. "This," the dad says, or the brother says. They take their boots off to feel, with their feet, the earth come back to life.)

We're in Saigon Saigon one day when Lu asks about Slim, who he is, and my brother, how old he was when he died. She knows about Mick. Some things but not everything.

I'm pulling splinters off my chopsticks, arranging them in a pile by my plate. "I don't know anyone named Slim." I want to stick one of those splinters in my eye. She's waiting, and I want to surprise her by doing that. But I'm too tired. "Mick was twenty-one when they lost him. Why are you asking me these things?"

"You know you talk to them in your sleep?"

"How the hell would I know that?" I get up, drop ten dollars on the table, walk out to the bus stop. She doesn't try to stop me.

The next week, at the bar, she eyes me out from under the brim of her hat, astonishingly aware that there is a line dividing what we talk about from what we don't, and that she has crossed it. I think I'm more disoriented by her awful cognizance than by her unerring ability to open up places that by all rights should have permanently, or at least officially, healed over.

"Why did you name your cat Mick, Lu?"

"He reminded me of Mickey Mouse. His little crazy ears . . ."

"You are such a fucking awful liar." She doesn't contradict me, but it does occur to me that maybe she isn't lying. We stare each other down for as long as we can stand it. I will not for a second admit I could be wrong, and she knows that I know it's a possibility. This is something new to me, being held to account by someone with her ducks, if not in a straight line, at least in a loose formation, and I am not good at it. I want an out, and this time she doesn't have to give me one.

But she does. "He reminded me of you too. Those crazy little ears."

"Fuck you, Lu. You and your cat." I can barely talk, but screaming is a clear and present option.

She comes behind the bar before I can get away and grabs me by the arms just below my elbows, leans her forehead into mine and says, "It don't mean shit if it doesn't hurt, Cookie. Don't let him go."

"Don't. Tell. Me." I pull away from her and back up against the basement door. "How to remember him. You don't know a fucking thing about it."

She stands there with her hands still open, her eyes bright and wide. "I'm trying to help, Cook."

I laugh, knowing it's the cruelest thing I can do. "Now, that is fucking funny."

She backs away, hands up in front of her now, unconsciously fisted in a boxing stance, almost a crouch, protecting her rib cage, her belly. "Hey," she whispers, "it's me, your stand-up guy. Remember?"

My teeth are clenched. "Fuck you fuck you fuck you so much." My teeth feel like they will always be clenched now. Like this is permanent, this grinding pain.

I watch her go and try to find a way to blame her. Turn Janis up on the jukebox as loud as I can stand it, unhang the beer signs, and wash the filthy windows so actual sunlight can get in. My jaw aches. I don't care. *Take* another little piece of my heart. I don't fucking care.

Lu stays away for a short while and then sashays in one hot September afternoon like she's been showing up at exactly this time every day. She brings me a burrito, with one bite out of it. I shove her quarters for the pool table.

"Rack 'em."

She lets me win, but barely, and does it so slyly I can pretend it was an honest game. Then she slaughters me; takes no time to run the table and banks the eight with six of mine still out there. She lets me break the next one so she can reteach me how.

"Getting sloppy, Cook."

"I didn't have you here to keep me honest."

"Is that what we called it?"

"Maybe."

"What else you got?"

Nothing. I'm all out.

In late October, on a Sunday, I am watching half a block of the Tenderloin go up in flames on the TV. The wind has been blowing hard since yesterday, and now the fire is creating its own small storm. The sky is completely black with smoke, blocking out the sun. It looks like a bomb went off and we can smell it here, four miles away, and a drizzle of cinders is already beginning to fall on this hill. The fire trucks can't get down the alleys, to get the ladders up to the windows and broken fire escapes. For some reason the fire hoses don't fit all the hydrants. Something explodes. A water main breaks. People jump. Others are caught in the hallways and stairwells and their rooms and burn, for real.

Lu calls to tell me she can see it from where she is too, somewhere south of Market, in a bar. She tells me the job is gone and the little cat is gone and the little room is gone, and she just needs a small loan to get a bite to eat and maybe a tiny fix, to get well.

She says, "I didn't set this one either, Cookie." She tries to laugh. I try to laugh with her.

I say, "I know. Stay right there. I'm coming." But when I get downtown, I can't find her anywhere. There's just a small pile of ashes on the sidewalk in front of the bar. I think this must be the last place she stood. I crouch down and rub some of that ash between my fingers, feeling for teeth, pieces of bone.

10. Nothing Like the Other Dogs

finally get that God isn't going to quit taking my people and leave myself wide-open. This time I do not even want Frank to attempt to glue me back together. I want whatever is the opposite and know just where to get it. Go looking for the Cajun (right where I left him) and make him take me down to Buchanan to see what the fucking attraction is. Smoke from a small steel tube until my lips blister. I can't get high enough. Keep the job for a month, maybe two, but then just stop showing up. The owner (I hear) sends Andy to look for me, thinking maybe I'll turn up at the back door at Harbor Lights, but that's the last place I'm gonna go.

I move back into the flat on Capp Street, and every time the Cajun goes to hit me I step into it. The taste of blood is the realest thing I can imagine. I hate the dope—hate the high—but it's cheap and easy, and I don't have to remember anything or anyone.

The house comes down around us, more or less. Holes

knocked through the walls, windows broken by anything handy to throw. We try to keep it down, and to the back of the place, where the neighbors aren't so nosy or so uptight as the ones in front. The guy upstairs is a drunk, only, and minds his own business. Most nights we hear him come home late and an hour later hit the floor when he falls out of bed.

I Ie isn't going to say anything.

The people over the fence complain only when the Cajun gets out his saxophone and plays it in the yard. I don't blame them. He sucks. Couldn't play a scale to save his life, and thinks he's John Coltrane. Sometimes they throw bottles, the neighbors do. The Cajun flips them off, throws the bottles back, and plays louder.

He still works, and I have some money saved, so sometimes we still eat. Sometimes we'll end our binges on a weekend and go up to Potrero Hill to play softball. Someday I'll find photos: both of us smiling, his arm wrapped proprietarily around my shoulders, my ball cap pulled down low. Someday I'll run into people we know, who will say, "We always wondered what you were doing with that guy."

"I wondered myself," I'll say, but I'll be lying. I know exactly what I'm doing.

One bad night's next morning, about two months in, he takes me to the farmers' market, by way of apology. I manage not to think about Cole, watch a hundred people try not to notice the black eye, and when he starts yelling at me for taking too long to pick out an avocado, I walk away and hide in a carport up the hill. If it weren't for the shiner,

I could have stood it, but with it, and all those people knowing, there was no way. I watch from my hiding place as his truck goes by, and don't know what to do next. The bar seems a pretty clear choice, though, once I consider my options.

It all comes to a screeching, non-cartoon halt when I come home later, lit just enough, to find a trail of lingerie in the dining room and a young hooker with a paring knife waiting for me in the bedroom. The girl is scared, and I mouth the words, "Don't fucking talk. Where is he?"

The girl points to the bathroom. I hold my hand out, whisper, "Go." The girl hands me the knife, handle first, and leaves with our bedspread wrapped around her.

When he comes back, he is not the least bit ashamed—he's livid, self-righteous, a prick, as usual. "Where's Angel?"

"Went to poop and the hogs got her, I guess." I can't do Lu's delivery, but I can feel her there, so close behind me there's no space between us at all. Dumb thing to say, regardless.

He hesitates; almost has the good sense to know something's up. I never talk back. But he's too high, too practiced at what he thinks comes next. When his hand goes up, I get him across the belly. I'm not going for the kill, just a semideep flesh wound, one all-encompassing payback.

I call 911. "Send the cops too," I tell the dispatcher. "I'm pretty sure they're going to want to take me to jail."

Before they get here, I grab his saxophone, stand over him, hold it up and say, "You don't know how to *play* this." He moans. I try to feel sympathetic.

The public defender does his job and gets me mostly off

on self-defense, though an argument can be made, and is made, either way. The guy is good, and the jury doesn't really give a shit about the perp or the victim.

I do a couple of months, and when I get out go by to thank the lawyer.

"Plans?" he asks.

"See if they'll let me work at the bar again, I suppose."

"You have a place to live?"

"I know someone who'll let me crash for a while."

"Getting high much?"

"Nah." I tell him what my counselor says. "Jail's a fairly effective intervention program."

"So I hear," he says, and nods. "What ever happened to that guy? By the way."

"I hear he went home and tried to kill his brother."

"Paying it forward?"

"Something like that."

He asks me where I'm from. Originally. I say Montana. He wants to know if I have people there. I say I do.

"You ever think getting out of this city might be a good idea?"

"Nope. Never thought that."

"Really?"

Really. I don't even know if I'm lying. Maybe people will quit asking me impossible questions. Maybe he's right, and I should get out of here. I know the way. I know that highway still goes.

For a while I sleep on Frank's couch, and occasionally crawl into bed with him when I can't get warm. We try making it a few times, but my knees keep slamming shut, like my hip bones are spring-loaded. I know I'm driving him crazy, so I go. He says I don't have to but he's wrong.

I get my job back, tending to the masses. For a long time no one asks where I've been, but when someone finally does, I say, "Was I gone long? Did you miss me?" She cocks her head, gives me a quizzical look and half a smile. I say, "You can't miss me if I won't go away." Still smiling, she shrugs and nods, takes her beer to a table by the front door.

God, I'm funny.

I dig in, maintain, decide I'm going to get my shit together. I see Frank. I don't see him. He lets me do what I want and I don't judge him for it. He says that's good of me, and we laugh. Time, it goes by. It's a process. I remember almost every day that makes up this time. One day a letter comes, from Gail, in Montana. I can't place her and then I can, and it is just a flash: a seventeen-year-old love-stricken girl patting me on the head. Me growling, or something comparable. She says now she is forty, and she feels her life slipping away. She sends newspaper clippings that talk about Senate hearings, POWs, and MIAs.

A mismatched cadre of senators and congressmen are convinced the government has information about soldiers, still alive and held captive in Vietnam. I don't know. For what? She tells me in the letter that they've created an office to collect information, inform families, keep track of these things. There are "family meetings" in different places around the country, where you can go and hear about the progress they're making, the people they've found, all of them dead and in pieces.

There's a meeting in Seattle next month. She wants to

know if I want to meet her there. Yeah, right. Only if they bring Mick to it. Alive and whole.

I write back, say thank you for the information. She's still in Montana, teaching in Great Falls. She sends a bracelet with some other guy's name on it. MIA 1971. I send her a postcard of the Pacific Ocean, say, "This is where I am now. This is where I came to forget. I can't help you. I can't help either one of us." I don't tell her I recently went to jail for stabbing someone, though if I did, it might make her stop writing.

Against my better judgment, I go to the library and do more research. They are compiling a list of missing soldiers with descriptions of where they were last seen, what they were doing, what probably happened to them. Plane and helicopter crashes. Many drownings, which I did not expect. Hardly anyone went missing in the tunnels. Mick was always special that way. *Not like the other dogs.* He used to say that about Cash when Cash did something goofy, like collect rocks or bark at them. He probably didn't think it applied to him, but it did. He was nothing like the other dogs.

I read about the tunnels, how the guys went in with nothing but a pistol, and the blade of a bayonet to check for booby traps. They had miners' lamps, which made them perfect targets. But in Mick's case, no one heard a shot, an explosion, a cry for help or of pain, nothing. He went in and he didn't come out. At least not where they were waiting.

A few years later, when they were done with the Red River Delta and Hanoi, the B-52s headed south to carpet bomb Củ Chi, from where we'd been getting our butts kicked for a long time. Tết and all that. Mick was gone, somewhere, by then. Or he wasn't, and became part of the carpet. Or maybe he's in Saigon playing Russian roulette, waiting for Robert De Niro to come and take him back to the Smokies. Or the Rockies, their long-lost cousins to the west.

In spite of Gail and her letters, I'm being really good, getting a little cocky even, thinking, again, maybe I'll go to college and get out of booze and babysitting. So, of course, some whacked-out patron I've cut off vaults the bar and knocks me down the basement stairs. To remind me not to be so goddamn sure of myself. Frank comes to collect me.

Something in me wants to slap his sweet face and so-nearly-contented loneliness. I don't know if that's what kind of girl I've become, but at least I know I don't want it to be. He puts ice on the bruises and gives me brandy.

"For medicinal purposes," he says. I smile because I know if I do, I can have anything I want. And what I want is to want this, to be here, trying the best I know how, to match love with something like it.

I can cook a few things, and do: spaghetti, tacos, pot roast. Most nights I come home after work. Sometimes I go ride with Frank in his truck and help with the papers. We finally make love in the back of the truck, on a pile of newspapers and a sleeping bag he keeps in there. My tailbone bruises, and the bruise feels like something real. I like it. I like Frank. Mostly I like seeing a single image of the world.

But this goddamn smile. It feels like it's painted on. My skin feels like it's painted on.

Gail won't stop writing. It's like she's throwing bricks.

Something's got to break. I guess when you get right down to it, something already has.

11. Two Days, Then the Bus to Cambodia

hear that now you can fire Kalashnikov rounds for a dollar a shot out at Củ Chi, and they have widened and deepened the tunnels to accommodate Western bodies. Mick had the perfect build for tunneling, and he liked dark, enclosed places. I still can't imagine, though, after the stories I've heard, how he went into those things. I have tried for years to tell myself it was lucky, in some alternative configuration, that he didn't have to come home damaged and try somehow to fit in. I've known some of his compatriots, here and back in the States, and not a one of them is right in the head. They're light-shy and twitchy, still startling at certain sounds, still having the bad dreams after so much time. The suicide rate for the tunnel rats is even higher than it is for the guys who got to shoot at other people, and get shot at, out in the open. Sometimes they take other folks with them when they go. Innocent bystanders, as if any of us is truly that.

Meantime, I drink and shoot pool and pretend that I

am helping somehow, with the kids and with my students, though it really did not take me long to figure out it is not the Vietnamese who need help here.

When I feel myself approaching critical mass, I burrow in at the Rex with the Aussie, who works with the Vietnam Airlines guys out at Tân Sơn Nhất, training pilots and mechanics about airplanes in peacetime. These guys, he's told me, know plenty about planes in wartime: their water buffalo drink from bomb craters turned lotus-choked ponds; their kids are born missing limbs, or with their limbs put on lopsided. By God. Every couple of months he gets a ten-day leave and goes off to Norway—to hike, to "veg out," he says, unwind before he goes *berko*. When he leaves this time, one of his pals finally tells me, in as kind a way as possible, that the Aussie is in Norway because his drop-dead Norwegian model girlfriend has just had his child there, a boy, and he is pulling together the paperwork to get them permanent visas and bring them back to Saigon.

"So," this pal tells me, "maybe you should forget about him now."

"Done," I say, though of course we both know that is a big, fat lie. I have not had time to forget. Give me some time.

"He should have told you."

"Should have. Maybe he was going to when he got back."

"Pigs fly," he says.

I spend twenty precious dollars on a four-minute phone call to San Francisco, to my keeper, my tender, my friend— the one whose heart I took such lousy care of because I still had no business trying to operate mine, and because there was nothing dangerous or particularly fucked up about him. It has been over a year, so clearly he is surprised to hear from me, and he waits for me to tell him why I am calling. I listen to his breathing, watch the seconds go away on the pay phone at the post office. I am standing under a larger-than-life-size portrait of a smiling, radiant Ho Chi Minh, in what is officially, at least in name, his city. I say into the phone, "Do you miss me?" but I have not left enough time for an answer at the pace we are going. I want to be missed. MIA like my brother, but with the prospect of being found. Flags flown and torches carried. APBs out for my arrest. I don't care how.

Finally, I hear, "I don't know what—" The line goes bleep, then dead. I do not call back, though I should, to say I am sorry for what I did, for who I am, for calling, for reminding him, for asking for something I don't deserve: for someone to want me. For a reason to one day, perhaps, in this lifetime even, recross the ocean. Selfish as that reason might be. Crazy as it might be to believe, even for a little while, that it would do.

I think about calling home. My real home. I think about calling.

My pool-playing buddy Clive gets arrested; it is unclear exactly what for, but suddenly his taxi girls have taken up residence in our bar. The cops beat him up and he spends two weeks in jail with a fractured cheekbone, a badly stitched flap of skin covering it, and a dislocated shoulder. When he gets out, he is wearing filthy bandages, a sling made of an old ammo belt, and shoes. June has already been deported back to Thailand. Their bar is shuttered. Clive has no money—as they have searched and taken what they could find, frozen his bank accounts—so we take up a collection and gather 350 US dollars between us. He has two days; then he's on the bus to Cambodia.

When we give him the money, he cries—blubbers, really, like they say.

Ian asks first, "What's the plan, mate?"

"Got none." One-handed, Clive clenches the edge of the bar like it's a high window ledge and he is outside, suspended over a very long drop. He bends his elbow and leans in to put his forehead against the wood, in a motion that could be mistaken for prayer. We wait, grouped in a loose semicircle around the pool table, while he gathers himself. He turns and eyes the felt longingly. Then he looks at me. "Learn to snooker, girl. Can you do that? At least the ones who've got it coming."

"I'll try, Clive."

"Might learn to like it."

"Never know."

Gentleman that he is, he shouts us all a round before he goes. We write our real names on beer coasters so he can send mail to us *poste restante*, knowing it will never happen, knowing in a few months he won't be able to match but a few of the names to faces, but it is what we do: send a piece of ourselves with him. He leaves, his new shoes somehow broken in already, molded to his feet like black wax. His shoes are what we look at as he ambles away, how they carry him off, ungainly and unbelievably gone.

A couple of nights after Clive leaves, Ian and I get a few beers in us and decide to break into his bar. Luc, the Froggy that Phượng has her eye on for me, comes with us. We're presumably going just to check it out, and then Ian says he thinks Clive mentioned a stash somewhere, maybe in the storeroom, but he doesn't know of what or exactly where. Could be money or hash or some other kind of drugs. "Could be girls," Ian says, not sounding like he's kidding.

We hail three cyclos. The young drivers race halfheartedly, figuring out quickly that we are not tourists and don't want anything but a ride. There is no rain tonight and instead just half the moon. The river reflects it, rainbowy with diesel, smelling like exhaustion and fish. We pay the drivers at the corner nearest the bar and wait for them to drive off before we duck into the entryway, where Luc goes to work on the cheap Chinese padlock. It's big, like the one at the Lotus, but Luc demonstrates his wizardry by picking it in about twenty seconds flat. "Voilà," he says, a bit theatrically.

Ian makes it through the door without mishap, but Luc and I sort of fall through it, into a snarl of overturned bar stools and sundry wreckage. "Ô la vache, crap, sheet, merduh," he says as we untangle ourselves. I get a bit of elbow in the ribs—deserved retribution, I suppose, for taking him down with me—but when he gets to his feet, he reaches for me, to help me up. It is dark but for a bit of that half-moon filtering in through a high window. I have a small flashlight with me and switch it on. The bar looks like the Ia Drang Valley after the First Cav got done with it. Nothing that should be standing is; all of the pictures have been torn off the walls; June's collection of porcelain figurines and other knickknacks is smashed and scattered. There is broken glass, like shrapnel, on every horizontal surface. It scrapes beneath our feet as we make our way to the storeroom door. I can't believe Luc and I didn't get cut when we went down, but somehow we hit a clear patch.

"Lucky," I whisper. Neither of them looks at me or asks what on earth I am talking about.

Ian opens the door, and incredibly it appears untouched. It is almost empty, and meticulous, as June would have kept it. There are several bottles, unopened, of the local whiskey; a single case each of 333 and Tiger beer; and, on the top shelf, a few gallon jars of snake wine, complete with snakes, coiled inside as if they are sleeping off a big night. A hammock stretches across the back wall, attached to rebar-fashioned hooks on either side. I picture Clive in here on a hot afternoon, fanning himself with the day's edition of the *Saigon Times*, a beer on the floor within easy reach of an outstretched arm.

Ian starts palming the walls between the shelves, looking for a secret compartment or a trapdoor. I hold the flashlight for him while Luc sits on the floor, smokes a cigarette, and watches us. "You think you will find some dop?"

Ian laughs. "What ees zees dop?"

"You know," Luc says. "Dop. Smok. Hashish."

"Maybe," Ian says.

After he's gone over every inch of wall, he borrows my

flashlight to inspect the wooden floor planks. He finds a
tiny chunk of hash in a crack between two of them, and
another one, and another, like a trail of bread crumbs leading out of a forest. We are stunned to find anything at all
and wonder how it got, and stayed, here. Luc keeps saying
"Incroyable," as if he is saying a prayer. Ian finds maybe two
grams total and divides it up among us.

"Let's get out of here," he says, and Luc gets up from the
floor. They start for the exit, but I hang behind.

"I'll see you guys later."

Ian says, "Share what you find?"

"Sure."

Luc says, "Watch out the gendarmes."

"The gendarmes got nothing on me," I say.

My eyes have adjusted to the darkness, so I assemble the
few bar stools that are still intact and line them up where
they belong. Clear a space around the pool table and find
a broom. It is while I am sweeping up the glass that I see a
large patch of dried blood on the floor. I figure Clive caught
his cheek on the corner of the table somehow in the fray
and lay there for a time while it bled, watching his Vietnam
life pass before his eyes.

I am taking stock of the pool balls caught in the table's
net pockets, seeing if they are all there in case someone
should happen by at three in the morning looking for a
game, when the door opens and Luc slides through it. He
throws the bolt on the inside and makes his way to me
and my broom. "Why you still look? Why you don't stop
looking?" He takes the broom out of my hands and leans
it against the wall. "Now," he says. He sounds exasperated,

a little breathless, like maybe he ran here, but that is highly unlikely. Nobody runs in Saigon.

It is not the most eloquent kiss—not what I would expect from a mouth that offers up words like bites of ripe dragonfruit—but it is a kiss. He actually tastes nothing like fruit of any kind but like cigarettes and cognac and, for some inexplicable reason, butterscotch. I don't know where to put my hands, and after a minute he puts his on the sides of my face and then pulls tenderly away. He has a pipe, and we smoke some hash. It's strong so it doesn't take much to get me stoned. We finish clearing space around the pool table and shoot a couple of games in the near darkness. The smack of the balls as we scatter them across the felt and drop them into the pockets is the only sound, except for an occasional lorry or motorcycle or boat motor in the distance. Saigon is sleeping. So rare.

After a few games, Luc looks at his watch. "Time," he says.

"Time for what?"

He doesn't answer, but goes to the storeroom to fetch a jug of snake wine. While I lean against the wall and watch, he pours it around the room, over the pool table, the bar stools, and the bar.

"Are we going to burn it down?"

"*Oui*," he says, as matter-of-fact as that kiss, and empties the last of the snake wine, and the snake, onto the floor.

"I wonder what kind of snake that is." Despite how stoned I am, I know how stoned I must sound.

"A dead one," he says. "Let's do eet."

Snake wine is basically grain alcohol wrapped around

a serpent, and it goes up like gasoline. Luckily, Luc has made sure that we are all but out the door when he lights it. We take off for the river, and smoke begins to pour from the windows. Flames climb from the inside out and up to the roof. We find a small, uninhabited boat tied up to a bigger boat, and huddle together in the bow, breathing hard, watching Clive's bar disintegrate. The front of the big boat is carved into the shape of a dragon and we are in its shadow. No one comes to put out the fire. A few sleepy cyclos pedal up and sit, backlit by the flames, in a row at the curb. They look like they are watching a movie.

I am reminded, inexplicably, of the Aussie, who will be coming back any day, and I wonder if I will even tell him I know about the girlfriend and the baby, or just go on until they get here as if nothing has changed, seeking refuge in a room that could be anywhere, in any country, at any time. Or maybe I will do the more rational thing and take up with Luc, and we will burn stuff down. I think about Frank and how careless I was, how I never looked back until now, and still don't know why I didn't, or why, now, I have.

I try to remember what Clive looked like, how he moved and the way he spoke. Every time he starts to slip away, I bring back that one quick dance, that pirouette, and begin again. I am glad the bar is gone. All those knick-knacks.

When the sun comes up, we walk along the quay, stop at a *phở* stand, and sit down on low plastic stools under a mesh awning. There is a small, dirty-blond dog asleep next to the table. He has many small scars around his muzzle, and his ears and stubby tail twitch away the flies. The soup is good and hot; we top it off with basil leaves and chili sauce, stir it all together. My lips burn as I eat, but I can't drink the water, so I just let them.

Luc asks if I have ever been to Củ Chi. I say no, not yet. He says how can that be? He says he has a motorcycle. A real one. Russian. Not one of those little 50cc jobs. I nod. When we finish eating, Luc pays the bill and kisses me on both cheeks.

"Saturday?" he says. I do not say anything. I do not say no. He waits a minute and says, "Ten o'clock. *Le matin.*" He goes. I finish my soup. The dog watches.

I teach two classes at the business school, and after they are over ride my bicycle to the zoo. Two of the street kids I know are selling postcards and "shwing" gum to dumbfounded visitors they have helped cross the wide boulevard, where the onrush of bicycles, motorbikes, and the occasional car or lorry never pauses or breaks for even a second. The kids acknowledge me with almost imperceptible nods, and they don't try to sell me anything. In one corner of the zoo, I find a large black bear in a very small cage. He is not moving and his paws are covering his eyes.

I go home at four to shower, change, and eat, arrive at the bar at six, get a beer from Tho, retire to the window with Phượng. The sun sets as it does here, without prelude, and the sky goes from light to dark as if a switch has been thrown. Phượng leans her back into one corner of the window frame, her fingers laced across her middle and her head turned to gaze outside. Her expression tells me nothing, but I have seen her and Ian in deep conversation, laughing sometimes, sometimes not laughing. *They are going to keep the baby,* I think. *Together.* And I am jealous of what they have.

"Will miss Mister Clive," she says.

"*Đó là sự thật.*" It's true.

She looks at me, one eyebrow raised. "Been study?"

"Some," I say.

"Phượng think a lot," she says. "Good on ya." She smiles, makes a small fist, and socks me lightly on the shoulder. "Me too."

I say, "You are such a knucklehead."

"Next week lesson," she says. "Have to go now."

"I-Feel-Like-I'm-Fixin'-to-Die Rag" is playing in the background. The line "Be the first one on your block to have your boy come home in a box" is the one that always makes me flinch. I picture my mother (Dad in a shadow behind her) looking out at the snowy buttes, tracing patterns in the frost on the insides of the windows, trying to imagine a place where there is no winter, where it is always hot, and when the rains come after weeks of threats and dry thunder and lightning in the west, people pour into the streets and squares to soak it up in the most literal sense—to express their gratitude for the one absolute requirement of a country like this one, a place where at one time, not all that long ago, what most of them probably wanted more than anything was to raise their families, farm their land, and be left the fuck alone.

I sit on the windowsill and watch Phượng walk away. Her *áo dài* is blue tonight. (*Of a color intermediate between green and violet, as of the sky or sea on a sunny day. The boy went blue, and I panicked.*) I know it is a special one she wears when she has a date. I expect Ian will show up to get her pretty soon, in his tattered linen sport jacket, and they will go to the roof of the Rex for dinner, stand at the edge of the terrace and watch the city: the young couples on their motor scooters, riding around and around the circle in front of the opera house on Nguyễn Huệ, slowly, hypnotically; the cyclos parked on the side streets, smoking, patiently waiting for passengers—someone, anyone who is prepared, however reluctantly and in whatever condition, to go home.

12. Somewhere in the Real World

The ad says, "Sunny Potrero Hill flat. Share with two 'males.' Straight-friendly. Must like cat." The only cats I've ever really known were the barn kind, wild and prone to grasshoppering at any movement that could possibly be considered untoward. I assume the cat in the ad will be different, will allow petting and behind-the-ear scratches, like Cash would, if he were still around.

I like the idea of an animal, of getting to know something gradually, little by little, with no obligation to converse. I've come home tongue-tied is why. From Saigon. After the equivalent, in time, of a tour of duty there, and then some. I'm shell-shocked, though not in the usual sense. It is no longer Vietnam but America, now, that shocks, with its shiny veneer, its heaps of shrink-wrapped paraphernalia. Besides which, the war has been over for a long time.

At least that war has. But there have been others since, ongoing and everywhere, and maybe they are partially to blame for the fact that something feeling quite like armed conflict still carries on in my head. Armed but deceptively quiet, as if all the combatants are required to use silencers, and the stealth missiles to remain stealthy clear to impact.

I didn't want to come back. I had grown to love being one of the missing, living in a place where no one could find me, no one could just stop by or call me up. I was so far away from my memories, I could almost pretend they were someone else's. I had learned that distance was a force field—so very useful—and my mind was so busy trying to get me through the city and the days, I could forget for long stretches of time I'd ever had another life.

But I had. It had not gone anywhere, maybe temporarily into witness protection.

It took several weeks and a serious effort just to go buy a plane ticket, and it killed me that it had been so easy. To leave Vietnam. In one piece. I did not think it should have been that easy.

When it became apparent that I would never do it by myself, Phượng went with me and coaxed me gently into the EVA Air office. "See? No problem." She put a dainty hand on the small of my back and pushed while I resisted. Phượng is surprisingly strong for a five-foot-tall, ninety-pound girl, and I found myself moving forward, in a swimming-through-tar sort of way, despite my best efforts to stand still or, better yet, back up all the way to and out the door.

"Nice lady help you." The way Phượng said "help," it came out sounding like "hey-oop."

I knew she was making fun of me, however lovingly, because I was acting like an idiot.

"I could do with a little less sarcasm," I said.

"Yes, dear." The tiny girl continued steering me toward the nice lady in question, whose smile I knew was almost certainly genuine, but to me she looked remarkably like a crocodile. Or a "coco-deal," as Phượng would say.

"Maybe we should come back later. Isn't it lunchtime or something?"

Phượng stopped and gave me a look. "Don't want to go back? Don't go."

"I have to."

"*Tại sao?*"

"*Tại vì.*" I knew how childish it was to answer a Why with a Because, but at that moment, I did not care.

Phượng called me on it. "Lousy reason."

"It's all I've got," I said. But it wasn't.

Aside from the beers and the cigarettes and the suicidal, helmetless motorcycle excursions with Luc up Highway 1 toward Phan Thiết or through the rice paddies west of town over slick wooden and rail-less bridges, there was that guy and his dog, so sweet and so safe, refuge; in a place I might get to go, to pull back and start—what do you call it?—*living.*

I called again. He answered anyway. He was still alone. Or he was alone again. This time I tried to explain what had happened to me, or to us, or hadn't, or ... He said, "Yeah, babe, come on home," and I blithely skipped right over the hesitant part—the part where he was lying— because I didn't recognize it as meaningful, because it was something I had never heard before.

Love is something I do not, obviously, know how to do,

but some recalcitrant tendency keeps driving me to make the attempt. Because sometimes I think what will cure me is to be surrounded, consumed, crushed, forced to feel something besides the all-too-familiar duality of rootless and pointless. Luc was sweet, but he was crazy, and he was going back to Paris. He asked me to go, but I couldn't learn another language. Words I already knew I would never know.

After eighteen months, I had finally done what I'd first gone to Vietnam to do: ridden out to Củ Chi on the back of that Russian motorcycle, roamed the tunnels, the command rooms, the underground hospitals, the reencroaching jungle. Tried to figure out which turn Mick must have taken last and how it could possibly be that he hadn't left me a message. In a Tiger beer bottle. Carved with a sharp stick into a red-mud wall or with a bayonet into a tree.

But there was nothing. It didn't even feel like a war zone. It felt like a museum, or a theme park. It didn't feel real enough for anything important to have been lost there. No heart. No mind. No life. No war.

It had a souvenir stand. That killed me. I wanted to kill something back.

I rented an AK-47. Paid for a handful of bullets. Obliterated the target of an American bomber from fifty yards. The tunnel guides were impressed. "America number one," they said. "American girl số một!"

After a kiss from Luc, American Girl Number One put the gun down and said so long. *Au revoir. Hẹn Gặp Lại.* Sixty kilometers. Three hours. Ten shells. Done and done.

But I could still, too easily, avert my gaze and picture him setting up camp somewhere, living off the land. Maybe in Thailand. From where he could send a postcard. At least.

It came to me how tired I was of pretending I could see any distance at all. I thought maybe if I could find my way back to a clear image I could start over from there, and tried to figure how far back that would be. It turned out to be as far back as Mick, at eighteen, in a cave in Montana, a piece of quartz etched with a dinosaur-feather imprint, shining in his palm. I saw myself on the roof at home, aiming a plain gray rock, hitting him with it, and blood, but no one died; I saw us both in Missoula, hiking into the hills for another geology lesson. Then much blur, with highlights.

The two or so months after Củ Chi were necessarily (I told myself) but still only semi-blurry, and after finally trading all but my last few hundred bucks for thirty-six hours of airports, airplanes, counterfeit Valium, and three or four tiny bottles of bourbon, I was back in San Francisco, trying somewhat desperately to gain traction on slippery pavement in a very steep city. In addition to being jet-lagged and exhausted, I found that Frank was not there, this time, for me. He was done waiting. He tried to let me back in, but he couldn't trust me an inch, and what he was waiting for was for me to go. Now. Not once he'd gotten used to having me around again.

When I was three days back, he got home from work and pulled my duffel bag out of the closet. He set it on the bed and unzipped it. He said, "I hope you find what you're looking for, Riley. I really do. But you need to leave me alone for a while." I started to pack. I took my time. I felt like I was drowning, waiting for the ocean floor to show up under my feet. He didn't help or try to stop me.

He was right to give me the boot, but it still hurt, a lot. I didn't ask him how long a while was but decided all by myself to believe that if I really needed him to, someday he'd let me back in. I don't know why I thought I had to believe this about him. Us. Whatever we were. But I did. It helped a little. Enough to operate.

I had never told him why I went away so far and stayed gone so long. To do that would have required words, turned to sentences, I had no clue how to string together. And something told me it wouldn't matter anyway. I was never meant to be Frank's replacement ballerina, but no one can tell me I didn't try.

Tried for the first time ever to say I was sorry for being so utterly useless when Lucas died. He told me not to worry about it.

"Honey child, it was the eighties," he said. "No one was right." I knew it still hurt him, ten years down the line, and that his studied nonchalance, about love, men, sex, friendship—anything ever meant to be serious—was a front, and one that might never come down. But he took me in, and he made me laugh. I began looking at ads in the paper for a place to settle. Regroup. Sleep. And if the dreams were going to be sad, or scary, quit dreaming them.

Since using telephones in Saigon had run five dollars a minute, I'd braved them only a few times, and they still unnerved me. When I call the number in the ad, though, the welcoming, soft southern accent on the other end of the line gives me the courage to speak. I manage to say hello and to ask if the room is still available.

"Sure, come on over. Can you make it this morning?"

"Yes." I leave it at that, and an almost-whispered "Thank you," so as not to sound too anxious or dazed or unbalanced. His name is Christopher, he says, and he is looking forward to meeting me.

Eddie comes along because he has a car and can give me a ride, but mostly for moral support and as evidence, I tell him, that I am not some sociopathic closet homophobe. When I say the last part, he looks at me so closely and earnestly, I think for a second he might put a hand to my forehead, to check for fever. "You get that you are in San Francisco, right?"

I nod, in what I hope is a convincing manner.

"You know it is not normal for you to imagine people might think that, right?"

"Right," I say.

The place I am going to see is actually on a side street off Potrero Avenue, meaning it is not technically a Potrero *Hill* flat, but I can understand why anyone in search of a renter would advertise it as one. Down here in the flatlands, life is much more industrial, much less picturesque and trendy than it is up higher. But flat land is fine by me: level ground will probably come in handy for the more dissociative times, and those times will surely come around. Despite this new and somewhat disconcerting yen for stability, I know I'll always look forward to—and if necessary find a way to manufacture—the occasional tectonic shift; the feeling of stepping off the curb and for a moment, due to certain smells or sounds or whatever other trigger, not knowing where the hell I am.

The street feels eerily quiet. It is the weekend, but even so, it seems as though there should be more people around, more noise, more traffic. I think about Saigon, the incessant sensory overload, and suppose anything short of an ongoing riot is going to seem strange for a while.

Here there are houses just like on any other block, but also a fair number of businesses, ones that do not cater to the Sunday-afternoon-stroll crowd: auto repair and machine shops, a fenced-in truck rental compound, a Texaco station, a screen printer's studio in a pale-blue building at the corner. It isn't really a neighborhood—is nothing at all like the blocks to the east, on which the coffee shops and florists and boutiques blend right in; they fool you into thinking maybe you aren't in a city at all but in some lovely suburb made to look like one.

I think about trying to relate this bit of insight to Eddie, but don't. I know there is probably something wrong with my reasoning but am unclear as to which parts I should leave out, or what I could add that would change that. It is good enough for now to be able to recognize this place is a little bit *outside*, and even though I can't explain the concept (outside of what?), I can accept this recognition as a small but adequate step toward reentry.

I think of a Rickie Lee Jones song, part of a tape I once played over and over in my car. It is about a gas station, and about love, about running out of possibilities. I haven't heard it in forever. Haven't listened to Rickie Lee Jones since Lu went off the grid.

We ring the bell, and a vision appears. He is wearing cutoff jeans, a pale-yellow sweater vest that sets off beautifully the ornate "Mamma Mia" tattoo covering his left shoulder, fluffy white bunny slippers, and at least a dozen silver rings on each hand. His thick, platinum-blond hair is swept up into a configuration that falls somewhere between pompadour and bouffant. Combined with his shockingly high cheekbones and eyelashes long enough to brush them when he blinks, he looks like the cover girl on some outrageous Norwegian girlie magazine.

A voice from the top of the stairs—the voice from the phone—calls down, "You forgot your boa, baby. I thought you were trying to make an impression."

The door answerer lifts his chin and rolls his eyes. He holds his hand out to each of us in turn, palm down and wrist bent, as if expecting a curtsy and a kiss.

"Max," he says. "At your service."

Eddie simply shakes Max's hand, but I take hold of it with both of mine, because this is apparently one more thing I have forgotten how to do. Max cocks his head and eyes me appraisingly, seeming to decide only now to let us in. He stands back from the door and motions us up the stairs.

"You may ignore the skinny brunette if you'd like. She hasn't had her pill yet this morning."

The "skinny brunette" is indeed both of those things, but with his fine, longish hair and horn-rimmed glasses, he looks, in comparison and just in general, totally unastonishing. Eddie, I'm sure, doesn't differentiate one way or the other. Boys. The more the merrier.

Christopher says, "He made that up, about the pill. In case you were wondering."

"Oh no," I say. "I wasn't wondering."

Eddie says, "Yes she was. I was too. I was wondering if you'd share."

Everyone laughs, except Max, who is only halfway up the stairs. "Don't start the party without me, wenches." He sounds serious.

In the living room are a leather sofa, a huge TV, two brocaded armchairs by the window, a coffee table made of a four-inch-thick slab of what looks to be polished concrete, and the biggest cat I have ever seen. Big and fat. Black and white and enormous.

I say, "That must weigh a ton."

"That is Annabelle," Max says. "Don't hurt her feelings. She has a thyroid problem."

"No. I'm sorry. I didn't mean her. I meant the table."

I bend down and knock on it. It's embedded with hundreds of tiny multicolored pebbles, and is indeed made of cement somehow buffed to glossy smoothness.

"Wow. I've never seen anything like that."

"No one has," Christopher says. "It's Max's only family heirloom. His father made it. Allegedly."

"Nothing alleged about it." Max sits down on the couch, runs his fingers admiringly along one polished edge of the table, and crosses one bunny-slippered foot over his knee. "My father had a very unique sense of style."

Christopher squeezes Max's knee and smiles at Eddie

and me. "Runs in the family," he says. "You may have gathered."

We talk about Montana, as the boys seem fascinated by what little they've heard of it, and have it in their heads that all the sidewalks are still wooden there, and people get from place to place on horseback. I feel strangely at ease, drugged almost, but still able to hold up my side of a conversation. I write it off to jet lag and go with it.

"Some do," I tell them, "But in the cities, they've graduated to buggies. They still need horses to pull them though."

Max slits his eyes at me and cocks his head. "They have *cities*?"

"Oh, yeah. Huge. Four-story buildings and everything."

Max presses a manicured index finger to the hollow below one sharp cheekbone. "You are completely full of shit, aren't you?"

"Sort of," I say. "Sometimes."

Eddie leans in. "Always."

"Not always."

Max says, "I vote for always."

No one is the least bit interested in Vietnam, or why I went there, and that is fine with me.

The boys converse for a while about new bars in the Castro and the Fillmore district, and when that topic is played out, Max offers a proclamation.

"I like this one," he says, motioning toward me but speaking to the cat, who by now is draped upside down over his lap, belly flapping out to either side, love-child composite of cat and manta ray. She peers up at Max and does not protest. Christopher's smile is sweet and guile-less, and I am blown away. Honored. Dizzy as we head for the car.

"Welcome home," Eddie says.

"Home," I repeat after him, as if it is some kind of incan-tation that will eventually take.

The house is a typical, semi-run-down Victorian, ivory white with barely visible traces of rose and turquoise trim. Our flat is on the second level, above the downstairs apart-ment and the garage. The hardwood floors still shine in places, and the ceilings are twelve feet high. In the living room, along with the leather sofa and the huge TV, is a fireplace with two mantels, one below a large mirror and one above it. My bedroom is already fitted out with lace curtains over an entire wall of windows, and through them I can just see a few blocks up the street to the iron picket fence bordering SF General.

The eighties, blessedly, took with them the carnage of boys dying by the thousands on Ward 5B. Some nights, though, I can't help picturing the white coroner's vans mak-ing their way from the hospital to the morgue downtown, past this very block. I imagine processions, van after van, each containing one body only, though back then they could probably have—and maybe sometimes needed to—fit three to a gurney. I see tiny gold hoop earrings, meticu-lously placed and unostentatious in right ears. Hair perfect, streaked, coiffed, still. Things my unruly hair has never been. Of course Christopher and Max are okay, and Eddie, by some miracle. This generation of boys has surely learned how to play it safe, not kill themselves and each other in the name of love, or its likeness.

They have taken me back at the bar, again, so there is that familiarity; something of a comfort. I go in four days a week, on the bus, which lets me off on Bayshore at the bottom of Cortland. From there I can walk, or wait for a different bus, but it hardly ever seems to come. The hill is steep and long, and after I climb it, most days, I am light-headed but clear. A fancy coffee shop has just opened where Ellsworth comes down off the heights, and if I am not running late, I'll stop in for a cup and a bagel or a scone, pretend I am one of those self-possessed San Franciscans not paralyzed by a simple question like "Room for cream?" The first time someone asked me that, I had no idea what she was talking about.

The bar feels both cozy and cavernous before I open, before I turn up all the lights and open the front door, and I like it quite a lot that way. Many days I catch myself wishing there was some way to actually avoid opening, because if I could do that, people wouldn't come in and want things, even though wanting things is fine, but they also want to talk, and that part really isn't. The problem is, I have forgotten how to chat up the clientele. My mouth simply doesn't work that way anymore.

Before I left, I was good at it. Now it is a shock every time my mouth opens to let out something resembling coherent English. I have to believe that eventually I will stop hearing everything I say echo back, strange and brittle, but, for now, it is almost as if someone else is talking, using my voice without permission.

"What can I get you? Anchor Steam? Sure. That'll be three dollars, please."

"I'm sorry, you can't play your guitar in here, but there's a garden out back where you can, if no one objects."

"Nope, no babies allowed. Twenty-one and over. Twenty-one *years.*"

One day a customer drops to the floor after she's had a couple of beers, starts doing push-ups and accompanying herself loudly: "You had a good home, but you left. You're right! Jody was there when you left. You're right! Your baby was there when you left. You're right!"

For a minute I am so stunned I don't know what to do, until a beer glass I'm holding breaks from being held too tightly. I lean over the bar.

"Hey. Hey! Get off the floor. Stop that. Now!" A handful of customers have been standing around staring; they all step back when I raise my voice. The girl pauses, resting on her forearms, and looks up.

"What's your problem?"

"I," I tell her, "do not have a problem. You, on the other hand, have five seconds to sit your ass on a bar stool, quietly, or you're out of here. Got it?" I see her think about arguing. "Now. Time's up."

She removes herself from the floor, drains her beer, scowls briefly at me, and slams out into the cold. I wash the blood off my hand and bandage it. I have to wear gloves, now, to wash glasses. I hate those gloves—that rubbery, confined feeling.

The rest of the day, I replay over and over the tape of me saying "Now" and "Stop" and "Ass on bar stool." It sounds okay, like I actually was the one in control. I suppose there will be more of these moments, and even when I still feel the need to test them for legitimacy, that will be a safer bet for sure than just coming completely unhinged and throwing heavy things at breakable other things. I do not replay the glass shattering in my hand or the stone panic I felt listening to the cadence of that marching song.

At first, at home, I can only rarely bring myself to leave my room. In the evenings when I'm not working, I can hear Max, in his chattering splendor, talking about his clients at Saks and their idiosyncrasies and demands and how utterly gorgeous they look when he is done dressing them.

Christopher's voice is too soft to make out individual words, and sometimes Max will lower his voice as well, so that I imagine they are talking about me, but hope I am not so self-absorbed as to think they don't have other things to discuss. For one thing, they are so obviously in love, and when I do brave a trip to the living room and perch on the edge of the leather sofa, I find them sitting close together, hand in hand, watching *Absolutely Fabulous* or *I Love Lucy* or *The Avengers* and laughing, the cat spread-eagled and still—a great, furry, overstuffed bit of taxidermy, being stroked and petted by one or both of them, her tail wrapped like Cleopatra's snake around a compliant arm.

Mornings, I generally don't come out until both boys have left: Christopher early for his office job downtown and Max, later, for the store. Before Max gets in a taxi at ten or so, he watches game shows on the TV and primps for his customers. With those cheekbones and pale eyes and

incredible eyelashes, he is really more beautiful than handsome, in a totally Greta Garbo sort of way.

I don't mean to avoid him. I want to go out and watch
The Price Is Right with him and listen to him gossip about
the women he waits on, or talk about the silly things people
keep in their pockets and their handbags—hoping Bob
Barker will ask for, say, a hard-boiled egg or dog tags or a
thermometer—but for a long time I just can't do it. I try to
identify the cause and think maybe it is because he is just a
little too vivid for me right now, a little too alive. My head is
still full of Vietnam, in black and white, and I can't change
it. Max, on the other hand, is Technicolor in a big way.

Christopher is much less present, much less daunt-
ing. On Saturdays, when he doesn't have to work and Max
does, I hear him whistling in the kitchen, always something
classical and unthreatening. After a few weeks of sneaking
around the house when the two of them are sleeping or
out, putting my hand on the doorknob when they are here
and awake, but not having the nerve to turn it, and wishing I was more like Eddie—who would have been sitting
on the couch petting Annabelle and eating popcorn with
them the first night—Christopher's whistling lures me out.
He is in the kitchen making tea, Annabelle on the counter
watching him as he stirs it, and they both manage to not
look surprised to see me. I wonder how the cat has gotten
up there—surely she has not jumped—and imagine Christopher giving her a gentle boost, and the image makes me
smile.

"Like some?" Christopher says, motioning to a tin of

Earl Grey. Something barely identifiable but utterly perfect happens: a sudden transfer, another new and unimagined country heard from. I'm not really a tea drinker, but the whole idea seems so civilized, so much like what normal people do somewhere in the real world.

"That would be wonderful."

I sit at the kitchen table while he makes it and brings it to me, along with the little white cow-shaped milk pitcher, sugar and a spoon. The cat watches, metronomically switching her tail across the counter. I pour the milk; watch it spiral cloudy in the cup as I stir it. Christopher leans against the counter and looks out the window. It was raining earlier, but the sky is clearing and the sun is high and bright. Me and the cat watch it streak across the floor.

"Pretty day," Christopher says. "Do you have to work?"

"Not until tonight." I stretch my arms up over my head. "I'm so happy. Seems like forever since we've seen any real blue sky."

The words come out in the right order, in the right language, and I am sure they make sense. Christopher does not seem aware that this is a rather huge accomplishment, and I consider that an achievement in itself. When he asks if I want to go for a walk with him and Annabelle, I do not make up some lame excuse. I go put my sneakers on. Christopher attaches a red-rhinestoned leash to the cat's collar, and we set off up the hill.

"Nice leash," I say.

Christopher smiles. "Max. If I had picked it out, it would have been far less glamorous. Khaki or something. A bit of twine."

"But with a bell."

Christopher says, "Maybe a small one."

I realize that any lingering sense of dislocation may be because of a change in the city itself; it is not all me. It started
before I left but is now kicking in with a vengeance. People
carry pagers around and talk loudly on the pay phone
about very important things like stock options and public
offerings. I do not understand the concepts, and something about "public offerings" makes me thing of human
sacrifices. From there the tangential connections can prove
quite remarkable. I am reminded by those tangents of the
mescaline and acid I took in high school, the pot I smoked,
and all the other substances that in combination probably
rewired my synapses pretty thoroughly. But San Francisco
was the perfect place for someone like me to land, and I
often feel as if I am watching the city I still love grow distant in the rearview mirror.

The interlopers begin to infiltrate the bar, demanding
high-end tequilas and asking questions like "What sorts of
Chardonnays do you have?"

"The kind in the box," I say, and usually, or hopefully,
whatever decked-out lawyer or stockbroker will turn on
his or her pointy toe and depart in a sulk, but something is
definitely wrong.

I try to talk with Eddie about it. "Who are these people?
What do they want?" He is oblivious. To him, it's just a
whole new set of cute boys to ogle at the gym.

One Saturday we go down to Whole Earth Access so I

can buy some new socks and a colander, maybe a cordless drill so I can hang bookshelves. It is a perfectly ordinary thing to be doing on a perfectly ordinary day. Then Eddie heads for the electronics counter and starts playing with the mobile phones. I start to get twitchy but try not to show it. "What are you doing?"

"Just looking." He is playing with the buttons on one, holding it out in front of him like Snow White's mirror. It's the size of a brick.

"You are thinking about buying that thing, aren't you?"

"I think I am."

"Oh Jesus. What on earth for?"

"Talking."

We leave with a new phone for Eddie. No socks, no colander, no drill. All of a sudden the things in my basket looked like debris from a UFO incident: unrecognizable as useful objects. Eddie drops me off at the bar, where I drink beers and play pool with a cute Irish boy until dark. At midnight I leave his place, my shoes in my hand, and hail a cab on Mission Street. Christopher is still up when I get home.

"You okay?" He peers up at me from the couch. His eyes are sleepy, and Annabelle has her head tucked behind him, the rest of her looking for all the world like a decapitated walrus.

I lean down and kiss Christopher on the cheek. "Where did you come from?"

"Oxford, Mississippi," he says. "Proud home of the Rebels." As if he gives a damn about football, or basketball, or bowling, or whoever the Rebels are. He makes me drink water and take aspirin before I go to bed, and in the morning makes me come out of my room and go to breakfast with him and Max. We walk arm in arm to the Castro, with me in the middle. I can picture the three of us clearly from behind: Max aglow with neon highlights, Christopher a lovely pastel, and in between a chalk-drawn outline with a perfect round hole about chest level where the bullet or the spear or the missile has gone clear through but left me otherwise intact. How utterly miraculous that is.

When we get home, Max styles my hair, cajoling it into submission with a round brush, patiently rolling it up in sections and holding the blow-dryer to it as he pulls the brush out. He works in some heavenly smelling waxy substance and then arranges it all piece by piece, just so, around my face and over my shoulders. When he is satisfied with my hair, he applies liner and shadow to my eyes, and lip gloss to my mouth. I am afraid to look, afraid of seeing a kid—someone definitely not me—who's gotten into Mom's makeup bag and gone to town.

Max holds up two mirrors—one in front and one in back—and circles me like a merry-go-round pony. He makes me look, and despite the time he's spent, the effect is subtle but still startling. Each time my face reflects back at me, it seems as though I am looking at someone in an old family photograph, or someone I have not seen in a very long time and never knew very well to begin with, or a person from a movie—maybe Thelma or Louise.

"You are a magician," I say.

"And you, darling, are stunning."

"Or you could be hallucinating. Maybe I'll go up to the bar and see if anyone recognizes me."

Christopher says, "Or asks for your autograph."

"Quit," I tell them, "before I put a hat on and wash my face."

Max pinches my cheeks, sort of hard. "You love it."

"No. I love you."

The next weekend, from the bus, I spot Max and Christopher walking back from the grocery store. Their groceries are in a two-wheeled wire cart, and Max is pulling it behind him with one hand; the other is tucked into the back pocket of Christopher's jeans. Christopher wears a gray cardigan against the afternoon wind, and a long electric-blue scarf, set off against his black leather jacket, drapes elegantly around Max's neck. They look like an old married couple who have already raised the kids, let them go out into the world, and then settled in to ride out the rest of their years tranquilly, as a set. I press my face to the bus window and watch them until they are out of sight.

I fall, fitfully but progressively, into a rhythm: work, pool, outings with the boys and dates with the Boy—the Irish one, who does not seem to mind being referred to as "the Boy"; does not seem to mind much at all, for that matter. He does have a name, which is Dillon, and he tells me it means "flash of lightning." We are not in love, and not likely ever to be, but the feeling I came home with, the need to be suffocated, is all but gone, and closeness and kisses are starting to feel like enough. I feel like I am *in* the world, and not just trying to bring it into focus from another galaxy.

Some days, walking down Valencia Street, holding hands and looking in shop windows, turns me absolutely inside out. It's good. And it's spring, meaning it is warm, and the summer fog banks have not yet begun to slink in every afternoon to remind us what it costs, to live in such a beautiful place.

One night in early June, after a day shift and a few games of pool, I come home to find Christopher and Max, as usual, in the living room in front of the TV. It isn't on, though, and they are sitting too far apart. Feet apart, rather than inches; too many to reach across. I have an almost overwhelming urge to move them closer together, place a flat palm on each of their backs and bring my hands together, like a person might do with a found accordion, simultaneously pressing buttons and keys in the hope of a not-too-discordant noise. Annabelle sits on the back of a chair by the window, looking out or at her reflection, and her tail hangs straight down, motionless.

Christopher looks up at me where I have stopped in the doorway, and pats the couch between him and Max. Max looks away, but not before I see the traces of mascara on his cheeks. All I can think is, *I never knew he wore mascara. I thought he just had the most incredible eyes.* And: *That is not my place. If I sit in that spot, it will mean something is terribly wrong.*

I do sit down, though, and for a long minute, no one moves or speaks. When Max begins to say something, Christopher says, "No. I did this. I should tell."

I have never seen either of them let the other one do anything hard, alone, and this is clearly something hard.

Max sits completely silent and stares straight ahead, his mouth tight and his hands pressed between his knees.

"I infected Max," Christopher says, his voice in pieces.

"I thought you were—"

Max makes a small sound, like a small animal, and puts his head in his hands. I can't remember ever seeing anyone actually do that before. "False negative," he says. Then he says it again. As if he were testing the sounds. As if he could make the words mean something different if he says them enough.

Christopher says, "We—I didn't wait long enough. There was this guy. Just this one guy. This one night. Right before I met Max." The words go wobbly. "There's a window. Six months."

Max laughs, in a way that sounds almost like a real laugh, and it gives me hope for a minute that I have misunderstood something, or that "infected" means the flu.

"Nice round number," Max says, when he is finished with the laugh that only sounded like one. "Where do they come up with this shit?"

I have never heard him swear like that before. Not like he means it to do harm. I want to go to my room, close the door, stuff the last few months in the closet, and wait for the whistling to begin again. I know it isn't going to. And I know I have to say something. They are waiting for me to say something.

I say, "I still want to stay. Here. With you." I know it isn't right. This isn't about what I want or how long I am staying or anything about me at all. But it is all I can think of, and I have to say it. Even if it is the wrong thing entirely. Even if is the dumbest, most oblivious thing I can say. Even even even.

Max looks at me and tries to smile, but it doesn't take. He looks across me at Christopher, shakes his head, and gets up. "Do you think there's any other place that would have us?"

He goes to their room and closes the door, so quietly the click of the lock barely registers. I reach for Christopher's hand, crawling mine hesitantly across the couch; a spider's crawl. He holds onto it for a few seconds, squeezes, and lets go. He stands up and squares his slim shoulders, like a child who has been called to the principal's office for passing notes, and walks resolutely down the hall to the door Max has just closed. *Door number three.* Christopher taps on it, ever so softly, but loud enough for Max to hear. There is no answer.

I watch as Christopher presses his ear to the wood, but I cannot hear what he is hearing, or begin to know what sign of prayer, or absolution, or abdication he is listening for.

Or maybe I can. Maybe I do know.

13. Scablands

know I've heard it somewhere: if in a dream you are falling, and you land, you will never wake up. I've had plenty
of falling dreams but so far have never hit the ground, and
I wonder now if similar rules apply to dreams about trains
crashing into each other or derailing all on their own.

There is, obviously, only one surefire, practical way to
avoid finding out, too late, that the rules do apply, and that
would be to jump from this train before I fall asleep and
begin to dream. I've survived longer drops. Have the scars
to prove it.

I also know that a potential crack-up and the temptation to bail have approximately nothing to do with each
other.

I am on my way—on something called the Coast
Starlight—to Portland, where I will switch to a line that
heads northeast. This train's name is slightly misleading,
as it actually left the coast somewhere around San Luis
Obispo. From Sacramento we traveled up the center of

California, in the dark, though I'm pretty sure I caught the briefest glimpse of Shasta's sun-blasted peak at daybreak.

If I do decide to jump, it would be good if a horse (a real one) were there, galloping alongside. Maybe a blue-eyed paint pony, brown with splashes of white to match his legs. I would leap into the saddle, exactly as if I knew how to do that, and we would ride off into the hills, to a place where there is no past, no lurking future. This train gives me far too much time, to remember and try to process. Everything. All there is or ever was.

The freshest hell has been mostly self-inflicted, sure, but that really is, at this point, beside the point. Because all that matters right now is I am heading back (praying at the very least for a daylong breakdown) to the place where everything I've buried all these years waits, resurrected and suspended in the distance; a collectible set of decapitated, snake-haired Gorgon's heads, hung on my mother's clothesline to dry.

Jesus. Settle the fuck *down*.

After the border we carry on through the western half of Oregon, stopping midmorning at Klamath Falls. I got off another train here, a dozen years ago, and the next morning stood between my mom and dad at Crater Lake, shivering and looking down from the snowy overlook at each other's wavering reflections, dropping pebbles into the arctic-blue water. My folks had driven from Montana, and I had come from California, presumably to celebrate my birthday. I don't know if "neutral ground" applied but think there could possibly be some situational equivalent—if we could even have named the situation—but that would have been asking a lot. In any event, turning thirty had freaked me out, partially because it felt so old, but mostly because I don't suppose I'd ever expected to make it that far. I suspect my parents had been equally astonished and came at least partially to prove to themselves that the birthday girl was no imposter. And because they loved her. Me. That was real.

When they took me back to the train station the next day, my dad helped me with my bag, even though it was small, and there was hardly anything in it.

He said, "Do you ever think about—?"

"Sometimes. Really, Dad. I will. I still know how to get there. Don't worry."

"Okay, then," he said. "I won't." It would never occur to him I didn't mean it, and I have always envied that kind of trust. And I did mean it, for someday, and someday comes whether or not it suits all your well-laid plans, or the ones that were not laid (or plans) at all.

There had been no fighting when I left home, no falling-out—I simply went away. Or not simply so much as quietly, as there hadn't really been anything simple about it. In almost twenty-five years we have met only that once, though contact has grown more frequent, and easier, as we have finally come to our own terms, I suppose, with all the freight of family and love and losing and not exactly telling the truth, to ourselves or to each other. It has become bearable, but only in retrospect. No clear delineation in the arc of time's passing, just the realization that we have all, some-

how, survived (three out of four, anyway, so I guess "all"
really means the ones we know for sure are still standing).
For the standing ones, there has been life. Lives. More than
one each, I reckon. For me? For sure.

In Portland, I find the right track in the huge old station, but no train. I wander the neighborhood for a while,
find myself at the river, and am happy, for this moment, to
be there. It is always good to be near water, and I already
feel the dull ache of missing the ocean. Of all the mind-
and body-altering substances I dipped myself into in San
Francisco, the ocean, as it turns out, finally proved the
most addictive.

I get back to the station to find the train there, get on
and claim a seat. I watch as more passengers arrive on the
platform below, with their duffel bags and backpacks, rolling suitcases large enough to contain one large body or
maybe two small ones. A dark-haired young woman stands
by silently, carrying a black, busting-at-the-seams knapsack, a banjo case tucked awkwardly under her arm, a small
metal box, and a white plastic bag with a red drawstring. A
few minutes later she is standing in the aisle, asking if the
empty seat next to me is taken. She turns out to be more
girl than woman; sixteen, seventeen at the most. Her eyes
are very blue—a cobalt almost black—and reflect more
light than seems possible considering how dark they are.
She's pretty, but not the traffic-stopping kind, not as skinny
and flat-chested as she is, in a gray hoodie, baggy camo
pants, self-administered (it looks like) haircut, a scattering
of piercings, and no makeup save for a smudge of black
liner under her eyes. She reminds me of someone I know

but can't place—probably one of the young, just-coming-out lesbians at the bar.

"Nope," I say. "It's all yours." I tuck my feet under me as far as I can, and pull down the armrest.

She shoots me a timid smile and thanks me. Slides the banjo case and the knapsack into the overhead rack, creeps into her seat, and sets her box and the plastic bag on the floor. After a minute, she picks up the box and holds it in her lap, drawing little X's across the top with her finger, pressing down the corners with her thumbs. She places it carefully on the floor again, and fidgets it between her feet like a kid OD'd on cotton candy. Finally, she pushes it under the seat with her heels, apparently aiming to trap it there.

As the train pulls out of the station, heads across and then up the Columbia, she holds herself tight and still, arms locked to her sides and hands in her lap, as if she is sitting at a school desk, having been scolded once already for accidentally elbowing the teacher as he passed by. I lean away from the armrest and toward the window, hoping she'll eventually relax, or it is going to be a very long trip to wherever she's going. I wait a little while and then ask where that is.

She seems surprised to hear a voice, and for a second appears not to know where it's coming from. She peeks over her shoulder before she answers. "North Dakota?" she says.

I glance behind us too, but don't notice anything suspicious. "Is someone following you?"

"I don't think so."

"You're probably going to want to get comfortable, then."

It's a long way to North Dakota. And I don't bite. I bet none of these folks do."

The girl cocks her head, as if she is trying to determine whether or not the part about biting is actually true. Evidently she decides it is. "That's a relief," she says.

And she does seem to relax then, reaching into her bag for a scratched-up silver CD player and a pair of headphones that look like the cord has been delicately gnawed upon. She paws through a small collection of uncased CDs, settling finally on *Elton John's Greatest Hits*. I am a little bit surprised, having expected something more along the lines of Nirvana, or Alice in Chains.

As she listens to the music, she begins to move all ten of her fingers as if plucking the strings of a phantom instrument. Not wanting to appear nosy, I turn to look at the vast, sage-green, white-capped river as it runs through the gorge and toward the sea.

Ready or not; the words appear vaguely neon tinted across my brain. I try to leave them alone, to not worry them like I would a loose tooth when I was little, until all that remained was a raw, gaping hole, and the prospect of a dime under my pillow to alleviate any residual emptiness. I know if I follow those words—ready or not—to Montana, ghosts will appear, rising up out of the goddamn prairie like those crazy little funnels of dust. A tornado: maybe that's the answer to too damn many people packed into a too-small emotional space. Nothing, nobody really goes away—not once they've infiltrated your life. No matter how many brain cells you drench in rocket fuel and hold your little lit Zippo to.

God, I'm tired.

I fold up my jacket and stuff it between the seat and the window, lean my head against it, and try to think about other things, or to sleep. I've been up a day and a half already but can't seem to keep my eyes closed long enough to nod off. We are headed into evening, but the sun hasn't even come close to setting. We'll follow the river farther and farther east, and it will still be light at nine o'clock, and at ten. I had forgotten, almost, how it goes up here in the summers: twilights lasting hours, skies the deepest, most ridiculous blue, horizons absurdly far off. It is like the ocean, in a sense, except that it really, absolutely, is not like the ocean at all. Not anymore it isn't.

After some in-between time spent simultaneously beckoning and fighting sleep, I give up and turn to the girl next to me, who has been changing CDs every once in a while and is now listening with her eyes closed, fingers still picking away.

"You know," I say to her, "all this used to be underwater."

The girl blinks at me, takes off the headphones. "What?"

"Water," I say again, pointing out the window. "All this used to be underwater."

"No shit?"

"No shit."

"How much water?"

As the girl listens, wide-eyed at the sudden dissertation, I explain about the ancient glacial lake, the one that once covered a whole corner of Montana and then some. Lake Missoula. Every few hundred years, it would fill enough to float the two-thousand-foot-tall ice dam that held it back, in what would someday be (and still is) the northern Idaho panhandle we are heading for—home to old hippies, tweakers, skinheads and wolves, or so the papers say.

"They say that about us too." The girl sounds disappointed, but I can't be sure if it is with the reporters or the people they write about.

"Us?"

"Oregon. The parts that aren't Portland or Ashland or Bend. That leaves a whole lot of spots to park your little meth lab in. Your pot farm. Or your gun rack full of semi-automatics. For Bambi."

"You think they're right?"

"I don't know. Maybe. I never did ever see a wolf, though."

"Maybe we'll see one in Montana."

"When do we get there?"

"Early tomorrow morning. And all day to cross it. I'm supposed to get off about halfway."

"Supposed to?"

"Going to."

She nods, tentatively, but keeps looking at me with something that could be mistaken for attentiveness, so I go on talking about the ice dam. When it started to float, I tell her, it would break down a little bit at a time, and eventually all the water would come crashing through, the whole lake draining in a few days. Billions of gallons, carving out new channels in the land, or widening and deepening old ones, every time it happened.

"Sounds crazy," she says, but there is no detectable disbelief in her voice, just a familiar and painful wonder. Of course it was Mick who told me this story, among a million others, as I sat at his feet with that very expression on my face.

"Yes, ma'am," I say, not missing more than a single beat. "That's where this entire river came from, and this gorge, and smaller canyons, lakes, ponds—everything we can see. They've found pieces of Montana all the way at the Pacific Ocean."

I consider the broken and fused-back-together land-scape. Chunky, ash-colored rock and scrubby brush, more gray than green; buttes and huge potholes that must some-times hold water but are all dried up now, cracked earth the predominant decorating scheme. Evidence of calamity is all around, if you know what to look for.

"Does it have a name?"

"Scablands," I say.

"Like scabs you pick." The girl raises one sermonizing finger. "And make them bleed. And if you do it too many times, you get scars." The words sound ingrained, as if she has been admonished for the very thing on more than one occasion but still has to do it, just to prove to herself that some things will always hold true.

"Exactly."

The train tracks hug the river; they are so close that sometimes I can see only water even if I press my forehead to the glass and look straight down. No more than a few stops between Portland and Spokane, because there isn't much out here to stop for. Unless you want a closer look at the geology—how all the different pieces fit—and I would very much like that, if the train would only stop moving, if only for a little while. It is a place Mick would have loved, and maybe once came to—digging holes and pocketing treasures, dusting off the debris of past lives.

I visited him in Missoula once, in 1967, his sophomore (and last) year in college. He showed me, on the mountains surrounding town, the high-water marks, which in a particular sort of late-afternoon light looked almost drawn there, penciled in by some disembodied hand. I imagined the town and buildings already in place at the bottom of the lake bed, twelve thousand years before. Imagined swimming deep underwater down Railroad Street, Higgins and Front, past the train depot and the Oxford Saloon, Eddie's Stud Club and the old hotels, looking through the windows at the people playing poker and drinking beer, fighting, stomping out chain-smoked cigarettes on sawdust-covered floors. I was eleven and hadn't yet learned how to swim, but nevertheless had no difficulty seeing myself as a fish or some other meandering water creature. Aside from my fascination with all things aquatic, I tended to live an existence not wholly hitched to reality anyway. Mick called me Dolphin Girl sometimes, or Miss Fish Lips.

Aside from the skinny on the lake, the rocks, and the rivers, he filled my malleable young brain with countless other miracles. Then left it to me to figure out how much of it he'd simply made up. The time he told me about water coming from stars, for example, seemed like an easy one—completely not true—but years later I found out it did happen, sometimes, through an intricate, tandem process involving explosions and compression of intergalactic gas and dust. I didn't understand it enough to explain to some-

one else, but was still suitably impressed by the magic of
the process itself, the fact that Mick knew about it, and the
even more astonishing fact that he was not bullshitting me.

The part about coming back, though—that part had
been pure bunk. Dead or alive, he said, like it was some
kind of gangster-movie joke. A joke with the worst punch
line ever. I have still not come to terms with how old old is,
but I know how gone gone is. Dead-end-tunnel gone. No
exit through the gift shop.

And now my father is preparing to slip away too, or so
his letter said. I have no reason not to believe him. If he
had his heart set on something so ordinary as luring his
transient daughter home, he probably would have tried it
a long time ago, and a lot more directly. My mother—in
postcards and letters, during rare phone conversations and
that one time the three of us met in the middle—has deliberately avoided asking, or even hinting. It is as if they have
both always understood that whatever inexplicable trajectory I was on would lead me home in its own good time.
Or wouldn't. And maybe that was not an outcome they'd
ever been waiting for anyway; maybe it was for the best
that I left and stayed gone, since my presence would only
have reminded them every day of their other kid. Maybe
they didn't want to be reminded. There is really no good
way around it, though, except maybe to go and stay gone.
Exhibit A: how well that has worked out. Exhibit B: not so
perfectly, but.

Somewhere between Pasco and Spokane, I finally fall
asleep. Familiar dreams play on a smudgy screen: flying
dreams, where I sail and spin effortlessly on thermals, like

the hawks, or crows just before a storm. And Mick dreams, the two of us riding on his motorcycle, my cheek pressed to the back of his warm, worn leather jacket and my hands in his pockets; leaning with him into the turns, sure he will not let us crash, certain that of his many inglorious traits, unlucky is not one.

In real life, there were a few near misses: one with an elk in the Bearpaw Mountains, a few more with wet roads and gravel, a loopy bird once that caught Mick right in the chest. It was a small one, though, and we didn't go down that time, or any other. I was never even scared enough to take my feet off the pegs, blind faith a waking specialty then.

I open my eyes around two thirty just outside Sandpoint, where the ice dam was, and the just-past-full moon is on the rise, huge and unworldly amber, rolling like Sisyphus's rock up the side of the first real mountain we've come anywhere near. The train rumbles slowly over the long bridge spanning the western end of Lake Pend Oreille, and I can see a few lights on in the town, but not many. The bars have already closed by now and the bartenders given everyone the boot. The only stragglers will likely be the really drunk ones, arguing in the street about things they won't even remember tomorrow, or trying to get lucky, trying to talk some warm human into bed or a skinny-dip in the lake.

At the edge of town, where the train tracks meet up with the land again, I see a wolf, or a big coyote, pull something out of the water, but can't tell what it is. Maybe a fish. Or a goose. Maybe an old mukluk. Some kid's stuffed animal, lost for all time. I remember our conversation about wolves and turn to the girl next to me, but she's sleeping. I sneak a look at the box, which has crept out from under the seat and is now loose on the floor between us. I want to pick it up, shake it, but I don't.

At Sandpoint a few passengers get off, a few board, and we are traveling east again, so nearly in Montana that I can taste it low in my throat. I have begun to feel a clear sense of both anticipation and panic, to fist and unfist my hands, occasionally shaking them in front of me like a little kid performing the corralled equivalent of bouncing off the walls—at the dizzying prospect of something anticipated but more than a little scary and, in a sense, withheld too long. My chest is tight and full—of what, I have no idea, but it feels like tar, or clay, not like oxygen at all. I do understand about heartache, why they call it that, but don't know the anatomy, the chemistry, whatever. It doesn't matter, so long as I don't explode, which every few minutes feels like a real possibility.

By four, I know we have crossed the border, even though there is no sign, like there would be on the highway, saying *Welcome* or *Now Entering the Treasure State*. Something has changed, though: the trees, or the hills, or maybe the moon. My hands are going like hamsters jacked up on Dexedrine, and I leave them to their own recognizance.

I hear the girl next to me say, "Are you okay?" and flinch.

"Yeah, I'm okay. It's just been a long time since I've been back here."

"Back here where?"

"Montana."

"We're in Mon*tana* already?" Like she's saying, "We've already reached Mars?"

I bring my clenched fists up to my face; press them to my cheeks. "I'm almost sure."

"Is this where you came from?"

I repeat the words in my head, but they don't completely make sense. What does "came from" even mean?

"I was born here," I say. "East. The other side of the mountains. Hard telling, however, where I came from." I laugh, but my hands are still fluttering like drunken luna moths, in complete disregard of how others might interpret their behavior. I stare at them briefly, shake my head, and wedge them between my legs.

"I must look totally insane," I say, sort of to myself.

"Maybe a little," the girl says.

I laugh again, feeling less dreadful, and ready to abandon my own spirit-infested memory awhile.

"Where did you come from?" I ask. "And how old are you?"

"I'm seventeen. And I come from Bum Fuck, Oregon."

"Sounds like a fun place. I come from one of those too. I'm Riley."

"Grace." The girl holds out her hand, and I shake it.

"Grace for graceful?"

"Not hardly. *Dis*grace is more like it." She yawns, says, "Sorry, I'm really tired." She leans her head back, tries to keep her eyes open, and fails. Within moments, any remaining tension in her disappears, leaving her face the picture of angel innocence, as some sleeping faces tend to be.

Her mouth is open slightly, and her hands twitch—not like a player's this time so much as the sweet-smelling paws of young dogs, already chasing rabbits in their dreams.

It gets light somewhere around Libby, and the faintly sun-spackled but mostly murky green wildness of it makes me want to set off, hike north, and build myself a little cabin in a deep-woods clearing up by Canada somewhere. Get a dog. Plant a garden. But that would not be going home—that would unmistakably be staying gone.

My hands have finally settled down, but now my legs are starting to ache, so I get up and squeeze past Grace, accidentally kicking her box into the aisle. I stay for a minute, bending over to stretch, and there it is, right there, begging to be investigated. I fight the temptation to pick it up, and lose.

It's not light, not heavy, copper colored, slightly dented, and hand-etched with an array of wild creatures: moose, coyote, bear, rabbit. I straighten up to examine it further in the dim light. Not to actually open it. Because that would be snooping. But the lid comes off so easily, with barely a tug.

Those are not cigarette ashes. I can make out specks of bone, something that might have been a tooth. I sneak a look at Grace, but she is still sleeping. I reach in, scoop out a small handful, rub a bit between my fingers before separating them to let the grainy gray dust filter through. One shard, maybe a half inch long, stays in my hand. The fire apparently didn't burn long or hot enough to take the sharp bits off, though I don't know how that could be. I press it lengthwise between my thumb and forefinger until I feel it poke through skin with a slight pop. I put the box back, close the lid, crouch to slip it under Grace's seat. I keep the one little fragment, though, tucking it into the small hip pocket of my jeans.

Behind my breastbone, in place of my heart, I feel a fish flopping madly, trying to dash its own brains out on the beach before it suffocates. I make myself take a deep breath and set off to find the dining car, but it is still dark, and the sign says there will be no dining until seven. I know there is a snack bar too, somewhere, but do not need caffeine desperately enough to go searching for it. I head back toward our car but stop between two others before I reach it. The metal floor pitches and shifts beneath my feet, keeping me a bit off balance as I stand at the small window. It takes me a minute to realize it has a latch, which I test, wondering if I am doing something that could get me in trouble, knowing I am too old to be thinking like that but still feeling, especially now, pretty much seventeen all over again. Or still. Like that sleeping girl.

Being in trouble at seventeen, for me, had among other things meant becoming another statistic for the state to file under "stupid teenager tricks." Early pregnancies were big in Montana, as were suicides, drunk-driving fatalities, hunting accidents, and domestic violence. I don't think any of it, save the pregnancy, would have applied to me and Darrell, though; don't believe that if he had stayed either of us would have been so inclined. At least from what I remember, all those bright images still occupying their own crowded and dust-covered corner of my mind.

It makes me crazy, even—or maybe especially—after

so many years, that Darrell was kidnapped, as far as I am concerned, by the same folks who spirited my brother off, and sent to do something about the Viet Cong, who were similarly dark but not nearly as tall. Surely he knew he was going to hate it, maybe have to kill someone, maybe have to die. But some people had a way of surviving these things. People who didn't *not* survive them. I have always thought I knew, could feel in my bones, that Darrell survived. If this is true, I would like very much to be able to ask him how.

I open the window, and the smell of the outdoors nearly knocks me over. I did not by any means spend all of my California years stuck in the city; I searched out forests, spent time and hiked and camped in them, climbed their trees, lived a few stretches at Golden Gate Park and Muir Woods. But this is different: it is what a Montana forest smells like, this particular arrangement of growing things. Mick tried like hell to teach me how to identify the different trees, how to *see* the woods, how to tell all the different elements apart. Some trees were easier to pick out than others, but the pines were especially hard, since there were so many different kinds, and I still didn't have them down by the time he went away.

I am still trying, or trying again, when the train enters a tunnel and the trees disappear. It stays dark, and not at home in tunnels of any length, I lose my sense of direction, don't know for a minute which door to go through to get back to my seat. I feel my pulse speeding up and have to keep wiping the sweat from my hands onto my jeans as I make myself start moving toward any hint of light. When

I find the right car, and Grace, I see that she has folded her skinny body into thirds like a lawn chair, and is now wedged between the two armrests, arms around her knees and head tucked into her shoulder as if it were a wing. I am amazed anyone can sleep so long sitting up, let alone execute the contortionist act. I reach out and set my damp hand lightly on her head, feel her thick, tangled hair. She murmurs something I can't catch, but she doesn't wake up. The box is right where I left it.

We get to Whitefish around seven, a little early. It is a long stop, so we have time to get off the train to find and drink a cup of coffee in the fresh air and sunlight. I leave everything behind, but Grace brings along her box, tucking it under her arm while she puts about half a cup of sugar and two inches of cream into her coffee.

"Wow," I say. "What do you call that concoction?"

"Coffee. Why?"

"Do you always drink it like that?"

"Yeah. It's free nutrients. Calcium and protein. Whatever sugar is. Carbs, I guess. Calories. It's sort of like a meal in a go-cup."

"You want something real to eat?" I ask.

"Nah. This is good."

"No it isn't. Come on."

She doesn't argue; she follows me into a café near the station, where I buy bagels and pastries and fruit. We traipse across the soggy grass to sit on top of a picnic table, where Grace wolfs down a plate-size bear claw and a bagel, and I drink coffee and nibble chunks of cantaloupe and an entire bunch of grapes.

The next table over has a neatly axed beer can pinned to it by the hatchet (abandoned) that obviously committed the crime. I wonder what the motivation was, but it isn't a far stretch to come up with a variety of possible scenarios. I know there have been times, and probably will be again, that axing an innocent beer can will seem like the very thing.

A huge, jacked-up pickup in the parking lot has a bumper sticker that says, "Keep Montana wild. Gutshoot subdividers and wolves." Another one on the same truck: "Honk if you've bitchslapped an environmentalist today."

"Wow," Grace says. "Someone's angry."

"Home, sweet home." I feel like an interloper, as if by going to California I have abdicated any claim I might ever have had to this place. Because I have.

I wish, for the first time in months, for a cigarette, despite the fact that smoking is the reason my father's lungs are, as he puts it, closing down shop. I know the first drags would taste terrible, make me sick and dizzy, but after that, I bet I'd remember why I loved it so much. I managed to quit a while back, and somehow, with the help of nicotine patches, paced half shots of Jim Beam, and a bottle of Valium, managed also not to kill any of my customers at the bar. After a few weeks I began to notice how keen my sense of smell was becoming, and spent hours walking around the city, no particular destination in mind, sniffing the ether like a bird dog after quail. Something similar happened as so many altered states became less appealing, less necessary, or both: I'd be driving, noticing only what I needed to, to get from one block to the next, and suddenly, at a light or in a traffic jam, lean forward and look up through the windshield to see the sky, and it would be a revelation: *it had been there all along.*

I lie back on the picnic table, realizing I have not looked at the sky yet—that famous Montana one; the one they brag on in all the brochures. I know they've also taken to talking about the state as the "Last, Best Place," whatever that means. Last place for what?

Grace lies down next to me, pastry crumbs coating her lips and drifting into her hair, tin box next to her on the table. "So that's it, huh?"

"What?" I ask, though I pretty well know.

"The big sky."

"Yup."

"Why do they call it that?"

"Because it's bigger."

"Than what?"

"Other skies."

Grace turns her head, eyebrows raised. "How does that work?"

"Just does," I say. "It's magic."

"You," Grace announces, "are full of shit."

I nod. "You are not the first one to point that out, but thank you for noticing."

"Mmm-hmm," she says.

When the conductor hollers "All aboard!" Grace jumps up, grabs her coffee, and runs for the train. I know I have to go too, but I am busy cleaning up after our breakfast. I throw away the trash, save the leftovers, and pick Grace's box up off the table. It is warm from the sun.

I think about the woods again, about that cabin near the border. Some horse. Some pony. Think maybe if I loiter long enough, the train will leave without me, but it seems to be taking its sweet time too. Any more messing around will make missing it a deliberate act, and I have to draw the line somewhere. Don't I.

I hear Grace's voice calling to me from the doorway of the train, where she and the conductor stand together. "Riley! Get my box! It's right there. Hurry up! They're going to leave you!" I rub one eye with the heel of my hand. Look around. Begin to lope toward the train as if it is what I have meant to be doing all along.

Grace takes the box, and when we get to our seats presses it to her forehead, panting a little, eyes closed, knees jiggling like my hands were earlier. "Thank you," she whispers, and I almost answer, but stop before the words come out, thinking maybe she is not talking to me after all, but to the box. I sit down and throw my head back against the seat, wishing it were harder; a slab of something. I do not touch the hard bit of stolen bone in my pocket. I leave it, and ask Grace where in North Dakota she is going.

"Turtle Mountain," she says matter-of-factly, like she is saying "Fargo."

"Really? Where's that?"

"The west, I think. Close to Montana."

"Is it pretty?" I have to ask, but know I sound doubtful, having been indoctrinated early in life to believe that North Dakota was nothing but one big wasteland.

"I think so," Grace says. "I don't remember anything about it. I left when I was three."

"So why now?"

She shakes the box; the ashes rustle inside.

"Grandma," she says.

"Grandma."

"Yeah. Some of her. Is that weird?"

"I don't think I am qualified to say," I say.

"Did you know?"

"Know what?"

But Grace doesn't answer, and I don't look to see her expression. Instead, I take a page from Mick's book. And lie. "I thought it might be a bunch of those little airplane bottles of whiskey. I was hoping. I could use a drink."

"There probably would have been clinking," Grace says.

Her story comes out in chapters: a messy family one ending with Grace being raised by her grandma while her mother found sanctuary in a pipe. "And not any peace pipe, either."

She was raised in a little logging town near the Oregon coast. "It went belly-up in the eighties," she says. "That spotted owl thing. It hasn't exactly found its new calling yet. Only so much chain-saw art one town can support."

Her grandma sent her to school and fed her when she came home, taught her to play the banjo and think for herself, and is now in a cookie tin in her lap, heading for her final destination. "There's a spot in the hills where two streams come out of the same spring. She wants me to leave her there. She drew me a map."

Wants. I say, "Is someone meeting you?"

"My grandpa."

"Her husband?"

"Ex. I don't know what happened, but she still loved him."

"They stayed in touch?"

"Some years, but he got a whole new family."

"She ever remarry?"

"Nope, but she didn't let any grass grow under her, neither. She was kind of a wild one."

"Not like you, I bet."

Grace shakes her head, cocks it at me, and raises her eyebrows. "Maybe more like you," she says. Sweetly.

I shrug. "Maybe." I am hardly surprised. Shit shows. In the aftermath of a shit show.

After Essex, as we cross the old trestle bridge high over the river and roll through the south edge of Glacier, Grace brings down her banjo and quietly plucks the strings, curved metal picks on the fingers of her right hand. I think I recognize a slowish version of "Foggy Mountain Breakdown" that somehow morphs into "Tiny Dancer," and suddenly realize I am listening to "Up on Cripple Creek."

When Grace stops picking for a minute, I say, "How the hell did you do that?"

"Do what?" she says, stretching out the "what" so she sounds like she's just come down from ole Rocky Top. She's smiling wide, though, proud. She plays some more songs, most of which I know but have never heard them played like that before, or maybe I just wasn't really listening.

When Grace stops playing and puts the banjo away, I say, "Damn. That was amazing. I wish I'd had the patience, or any talent, to learn how to do something like that."

"You ever try?"

"A couple of times, but I never stuck with it. I have my

brother's guitar back in San Francisco, though, so it's not like I couldn't have." Except I never did. But I did keep it. That guitar is the only thing left—the only thing I didn't lose, hock, or break—from the trunkful of Mick I'd taken with me to California.

"Your brother play?" Grace says.

"He did. He taught me some chords, but I keep forgetting them."

"My grandma taught me every song I know."

"You miss her?"

"Yeah, I do." She sucks in the corners of her sweet mouth. "Not sure it's sunk in yet. That she's gone gone."

I do not say, "It may never." I say, "You thinking about staying in North Dakota?"

"I doubt it. I was thinking New York. Or New Orleans. New something."

"I've never been to New Something. Always wanted to go."

"I'll send you a postcard. When I hit the big time." Grace grins again. "Would that be okay?"

"Sure," I say. "I'd like that."

Nearly a whole day has gone by, and my stop is less than an hour away. Grace finds a timetable, stuffed deep in the seat pocket, to write on, and I give her the address, the one I've sent some letters to, when I found the time.

"You going to be there for a while?"

"No idea, really," I say.

"Does your brother still live around here?"

"No." I swallow. "He left a long time ago."

"Where is he now?"

"Dead," I say, for the first time ever, knowing full well I have not answered "Where?" but also knowing that once you said "dead," where doesn't really matter all that much anymore. I wait for the ache, for the tears I have never once cried sober or stoned, but they do not appear, again. Maybe someday I'll send out a posse. Put out an APB.

Grace asks, so I tell her they never found his body. There was nothing to bury, nothing to put my hands on, kiss good-bye, say, "This was my brother. This was my best friend."

Grace holds up the box and looks at me, eyes shining more than usual. "You knew, didn't you?" she says. "You looked."

I bite my lip, nod. Busted.

"These are my grandma's ashes," Grace says. "They can't help you. I can't give them to you."

"I know." I thank her, silently, for something I'm sure neither of us could put a name to. We are in cow country now. Probably not much prayer of that horse anymore either.

Grace gets her banjo back down and starts to play, messing around for a minute, trying to find the right key, or whatever it is that banjo players do. I have no idea how it works; I just know the song when I hear it, like I heard it so many times from behind his bedroom door, or from inside his room—"Rave On"—when he'd let that little girl in, grab her, and twirl her like a little top, like a little gyroscope set to spin across the floor, careening into shoes, bed legs, the bookcase, and back into the middle of the room, until it finally fell over, like someone had shot it.

Her. Like someone had shot her.

14. Gone So Gone

The letter my father sent did not say Mom had taken to wandering off, or that her head sometimes trembled uncontrollably in a regal, Katharine Hepburn *On Golden Pond* sort of way.

"I can't go after her," he says, shrugging, slinging a hitchhiker's thumb over his shoulder at the small oxygen tank that trails him everywhere now, strapped to its little wheeled cart: tentacled, shiny, ferociously present. "I thought if I told you, it would make it hard for you to come back." I think he must mean hard*er*, but I do not say so. He tries to meet my eyes with his own matching turtle-green ones. Tries. Nearly succeeds. "I thought it would scare you. I thought you might not come." I might not have—might have gone ahead and jumped off that train and onto that pony, somewhere on the forested side of Glacier Park. Or not gotten on the train at all. Probably? Most certainly probably. Most probably certainly.

Sometimes she'll bum a ride back with the neighbors.

People we don't know, who have bought up small parcels of subdivided land (some of it once ours), out here on the still mostly empty prairie. Still mostly still. In the scope of things, at one time a half section—320 acres—did not seem a lot, certainly not enough to share with strangers, in a place where the cattle ranches run to a thousand square miles or more. But a world gets smaller, doesn't it? All of a sudden my father has a range of about a thousand square *yards*. It's like someone came when he wasn't looking and installed one of those underground electric fences, the kind that shocks when a dog (presumably a dog) gets too close. But this is my most-human dad, forced into retreat by invisible barriers, driven inside or to the porch, where it doesn't cost him so much just to breathe.

We play Scrabble; sometimes the three of us, sometimes just us two. Mom goes in and out: lucid some days but often drifty, flirting intermittently with pure loopy, or gone. She always leaves on foot, can't get too far walking, and seems generally to be a happier version of herself when she gets back, so Dad and I leave it to the neighbors to decide how they feel about it. They don't tell us. Typically.

I am amazed at how easily those two words—Mom and Dad—have again become a part of my vocabulary. For so many years now, they have been Rose and Henry to me, as if removing the familial tags would make it all right to stay away. On the loose, out on my own recognizance—that has been my MO. I had my reasons. Who knows if they were good ones? Who the hell even knows what they were? Other than us, there are only two, maybe three other people on the planet who could possibly care.

Mom adds her letters to an existing word, making "fun-house" for thirty-four points. She's kicking our asses. She's always been good at this game.

"Nice one, Rosie," Dad says. Her expression softens as she looks up at him. I wonder when he started calling her Rosie, and not just plain Rose. I wonder if it was when she started going away. Or maybe he always called her that when me and Mick weren't around. Maybe it was part of a dialect they spoke only with each other. I feel an intense and alien longing, somewhere in the vicinity of my stutter-stepping heart, and it takes me completely by surprise. I know I once had, at least with that long-haired boy out at Cherry Gulch, the slightest taste of a similar, if less evolved, kind of love. I have been invited in but had no idea what to do about it, save for leave it in the rearview as quickly as possible. Do I regret that? Something fierce I do.

I watch them when I think they won't notice. Signs of age—the usual—overlay faces that were once a full half of my entire solar system, two of the three planets that would always be visible in the night sky. Then, of course, I thought it would be that way forever, and even if the third planet's orbit sometimes kept him out of sight a bit too long for my liking, he would still keep coming around. That's what planets are supposed to do. They are not supposed to jump the track, fly off into an alternate universe, leave a gaping black hole in space. We don't talk about my flight path. Not here we don't. Except to say I think I was not meant to be that fourth planet necessarily. I think I was meant to be a moon, or a satellite. Gravity was meant to be my friend. I don't know how any of this happened.

Dad's thick, dark hair is only now beginning to turn gray. Absently, he runs his fingers through it, clutches it in his bony fist, as if making certain he is really still here. The backs of his hands, and his forearms, are darkly bruised. Sarcomas. A constellation of blazing black stars. I ask if they are painful.

"Only to look at," he says, tugging the sleeves of his flannel shirt down as far as they will go. He smiles. I see exactly now what they mean when they say "ruefully."

I have the letters to spell most of it, hunt down an opening and spell "rufely." To make my mother laugh. She cuts her eyes at me, sly.

"What did you study out there, Riley?"

"Boys," I say. I don't mention the other things I studied, or my frequent sightings of nothingness. Though I know the evidence is visible, and not only to me.

She turns her head, tilts her chin down, and looks into my eyes. "Books?" she says, and I nod. She knows. There is no point in pretending, about train wrecks, holding patterns, or reconstruction. My mother is no dummy, even when the synapses misfire, and throw sparks.

A few minutes later: "Remember that time I fell off the roof?"

"Roof?" my mother says. "What?" Meaning, I suspect, *Don't be an idiot, Riley. Of course I do.* Or could it be that she really doesn't remember? I don't believe it. How effortless, though, for me to be clueless and seven, nine, ten again. As if I could take us all back to that picture-perfect existence. And by "all," I do mean all four of us. This is a trick I have been working on since I was a teenager, a poster child for the seventies. It's amazing I remember anything. But I did, goddamn it, have a brother. He was not one of my frequent hallucinations or one of the flashbacks I was promised. And, no, I don't have those anymore. They too have passed their expiration date.

My feet reach for Cash under the table, but of course he is not here. I feel an imprint though. An outline. Some residual dog warmth. "Roof roof," I say. My parents look at me. My mother nods. I see the corners of her mouth think about smiling. Dad just goes ahead and does it. Rufely.

Mom's hair is straight and long and pure white. It is lovely, as she is. She bites the ends sometimes; it is a signal that she is flighty, as in liable to fly. I see just the smallest, moon-sliver curve of ear peeking out. I reach over slowly and touch it. I can't help it. She stays perfectly still, a bit taken aback, frightened even, at having been snuck up on like that; then relieved, or released, when I pull my hand away.

They have already restarted my father's heart once, brought him back to the land of the living, so he can play Scrabble with us in the kitchen. One night after a game he pulls letters from the board, and on the red-faded-to-pink Formica table spells, "D-o n-o-t r-e-s-u-" and then hesitates, his long, battered fingers spidering between an *s* and a *c*. Mom helps him finish it, and with letters of her own, and a few she steals from Dad, spells "gone so gone." I try not to wonder what it means, and do not enter into this braille-like conversation, as I have clearly not been invited in. It is almost as if I am not here.

I recognize that they are trying to make a place for me,

for my actual body, but there will be times it will not seem worth the effort, and my role will be to witness. Whatever comes next. I do realize I've had my chances.

If I had been listening, and reading her letters more carefully, I might have at least sensed something coming. One letter told about waves crashing against the front door. In another, she was trying out names for all the itinerant ground squirrels and gophers, voles, mice, and wood rats: Smokey, Clarence, Ophelia, Sparky (Smokey's evil twin), George. And on the phone, when the conversation faltered, or strayed into dangerous territory (disappearing acts, family), she would tell me who was at the bird feeder, or in the horse trough turned birdbath.

"Magpie," she would say. "Drowning feathers." "Baptismal finch." Lone geese worry her, up there honking like sonar, waiting for that twin sound, that echo in another's voice, to return to them. They worry me too. I remember daily the source of my echo, in every cell. And I remember, as if I had actually been there, Leonard on a wild-goose rescue, going through the river ice. The current grabbing his boots and pulling him in, where he skimmed the undersurface like a shadow. Like a big sturgeon, Darrell said, even though he had never seen one of those.

I asked him, not right away, but later: a recalcitrant challenge. I was like that then.

"How do you know?" I demanded.

"I can imagine," he said, not wanting to argue, obviously, but knowing I did. I often wonder what he could have loved about me, or wonder if maybe, after all, he only wanted to take care of me, a mission I would not have wished on anyone at the time. I wonder how we would find each other now. If our boy has been given a real name. I really ought to know. No one needs to tell me that.

Mick's motorcycle is in the barn. Exactly where he left it, up on blocks, though the canvas tarp looks suspiciously new. I wonder how many of those my father has replaced, laid over the bike and pinned down with the same water-smoothed, calf-skull-size stones my brother chose so carefully and hauled back from the river in 1966. The wheels still hang on the walls, the tires completely dried out, brittle as shed snakeskin.

I remember enough about motors to get it started, take the wheels to town for new rubber. Mick taught me to ride a long time ago, so long now that I stall her once or twice before we are out on the road, and then it is all I can do not to twist the throttle full on and just wait for the road to turn. But I know I have to baby her, or she'll die, and my brother's reincarnation, in whatever form, will have my ass if that happens.

When I get back after the first ride, I see that my mother has fastened a helmet to the porch rail. I undo its strap, hold it up to inspect it, thinking for a second it might be my old one, but then remember mine was red, and smaller. This one is black, with an American flag decal, upside down, on the back. Clearly Mick's. I am not putting it on my head. I will get a new one. I forgot I had promised him to never ride without one.

I had also promised to never drink more than I could handle, not to do drugs other than smoke pot, never sleep with anyone I didn't at least think I was in love with. Since I was too young at the time to even be able to imagine doing any of those things, it was easy to say yes. I promise. Swear on the moon. The helmet, at least, I can do something about.

Every night after my parents have gone to bed, I get a beer and go outside, stretch out on my back in the prickly grass, and wait for full dark. It takes a long time, but it is worth it. Even with the new houses, there is almost no ambient light here, and I can clearly distinguish so many individual stars it makes my head spin. The Milky Way appears painted on. It is as sharp, as delineated, as the stripe on a skunk. It is harder to pick out the constellations, with so many minor players swarming the stage. But I do at least still remember where to look for a lot of them, as I had two authorities to teach me: first Mick and then Darrell. Between the two of them, I got several versions each of the same arrangements. My eyes stray habitually to where the Pleiades will appear when they come back around in the fall. Darrell called this group the Seven Sisters, or Dancing Girls, but he told me, too, that in tribal legend they are orphan boys, abandoned at birth. Blue stars—there are thousands of them in just the one cluster, but only six are clearly distinguishable to the naked eye from this little planet. One of the sisters is missing, and there are various theories as to her whereabouts. These stars might also, as far as some ancient Greek poet was concerned, be a flock of doves. This, according to Mick. There is another group nearby, the Hyades, meaning "piglets." I love that. But I keep thinking about those boys and hating that word, "abandoned." It seems so judgmental, as if someone did it on purpose. As if she had a real choice.

The last time I looked, his eyes were blue, but they told me all babies' eyes are blue at first, and that if they are going to change color, they do it over time. Aside from his eyes, whatever color they turned or stayed, he did not really resemble a white person—certainly not me—very much at all. He was a burnt-umber baby, with a little *Where the Wild Things Are* nose, and his hair was amazing: thick and black when he came to us, six weeks early and small enough to hold, like a drink of cold creek water, in two cupped hands. Darrell was gone by then, of course, so I couldn't introduce them.

There are no farm animals anymore, save a whole new generation of frenetic and mangy barn cats. I want to remember to ask if they still call the cats Slick and Slim, interchangeably, just for the hell of it. I have to believe that calling the baby Slim started with me, although it could very well have been my dad, clumsily and chivalrously trying to take some of the pressure off. Even for the few weeks I tried to convince myself I could keep and raise him, I was afraid to give him a real name, afraid of what that would mean. Or afraid I would give him the wrong one. I knew that Darrell should be the one to do it, but I couldn't even tell him. I probably wrote the letter six or seven times, but it didn't seem right. It seemed cruel, where he was going, and it also seemed like he might ask me to at least try. I couldn't chance it. I think I must have known all along.

I find my old helmet, and it still fits; the bike, after a bit

of tinkering, runs fine, smooth, strong. I don't usually stay
gone more than an hour or two, and Dad mostly sleeps
now anyway. For a while, he tried to do things the living do,
like go out to the mailbox for the paper, rehang a picture
that has fallen off the wall, cook eggs, play a whole Scrabble
game. But it is all too much, too hard, and only deepens the
lines in his face, exaggerates the curve in his back.

His frustration—with himself, with his lungs—shows in
every movement, but he never says a word about it. He gets
up in the morning for coffee and cornflakes and then goes
back to bed. We, or I, if Mom is off wandering, generally see
him again for supper, but except for rare occasions, that's
the extent of it. Unless I go and watch him sleep, which
sometimes I do just to make sure he's still breathing. It's not
always easy to tell. I catch myself trying to do it for him.

Mom has carved out a trail of sorts: a circuit that sometimes does lead to her lying on the railroad tracks, but the
train stopped running on our spur before I was even born,
and I hardly think that's the point anyway.

There is an almost infinite number of back roads I can
travel around here, to places where humans almost never
go. The land is much flatter than it is west of here, but not
as flat as people imagine when they think of the plains, and
the roads do turn, and they do rise, and they do fall. There
are mountains, even, scattered ranges disconnected from
each other, and massive buttes like altars.

Sometimes I drive through the towns—deliberately,
slowly, to see the people, maybe to feel some connection to
them. It is summer, so there is no school, and small cadres
of young men, both Indian and white, roam the streets,

maybe in search of—like I once was—something to keep them here. I tell myself I am not looking for a certain face, for the father or the son, but of course I am, and sometimes I will circle a block two or three times to make sure. The white boys eye me suspiciously, but the other ones don't give anything away. Nothing at all. In the towns, I do not find what I am not looking for.

I haven't yet had the nerve to go onto the rez, so I get as close as I can, circling it on the boundary roads, seeing ghosts and real evidence of all the too-slow or terminally indecisive animals flattened on this stretch of highway. Fence posts that once cast a fairly regular pattern of shadow across the road are mostly down now, or lean into each other at crazy angles. I hear there has been some kind of economic upswing in this country over the past few years. The news does not seem to have reached this place yet.

One night, while I am outside lying in the grass, Mom comes with her own beer to join me. She sits cross-legged, making moustaches with her hair as her head bobbles like one of those baseball dolls, like it's on a spring. She's humming something that sounds like "I'm an Old Cowhand," the shaking of her head adding a just-perceptible vibrato.

After a while she says, "Your brother—" and then she stops. But she has said it in such a way—or I have heard it in such a way—that for a second I think the rest of the sentence is going to create an entirely new reality; that she is going to tell me he really has been holed up in a cave in the mountains all this time—emulating Ho Chi Minh, writing his memoirs, collecting fossils and painting hieroglyphs—and that now he is ready to come home.

What she says, though, is, "When he was a baby, I could make him stop crying by singing that song. Just that one. He'd watch my mouth like it was some magical animal, making a sound only he could decipher. It worked every time."

"What about me?" I say. "Did it make me stop crying too?"

"You never cried," she says. "Never."

I don't believe it. No one doesn't cry.

Then she tells me it worked on Slim too.

"Slim," I say, as if I am trying to place the name. I say, "I did this all wrong, didn't I? I fucked everything up."

She goes back inside. She doesn't have time for this.

I start a new letter to Darrell, even though I haven't a clue where to send it.

They say tourists are flocking to Vietnam now. It is the new
Thailand, or Bali; take your pick. Cheap hotel rooms and
beer, the utter cachet of it all. Củ Chi has gotten so busy
they have had to expand. They've opened up and widened
tunnels the B-52s caved in. They find bones, dog tags,
rotted scraps of green fatigues. DNA. They send letters
that read something along the lines of: "We think we may
have found someone you knew a long time ago. In another
lifetime." (That part, truthfully, they do not come right out
and say.) Our letter is in the kitchen. It moves from table
to counter to windowsill, apparently of its own accord. The
dog tags will come soon. The bones after. Where are you?

Both our rooms are pretty much the way we left them. The dust is thick, but not twenty-five years' thick. My mother has written her name in it, on the bookshelf in Mick's room. "Rose," it plainly says, with an arrow through it, but no heart. I pick up an old notebook, from a geology class Mick took in college. In his angled and rambling script, I read, "One section = one square mile = 640 acres. Sections are not always nice and square. Due to the geology and uneven surface of the earth, its curvature and the failure of neighboring sections to 'butt up' perfectly, there may be variations." At the bottom of the page he has written, "Failure to butt up = Withholding of affections. Refusal to spoon. Spooning leads to forking, etc., etc., etc."

No wonder he left. He must have been bored out of his skull. He probably knew more about rocks, and what's under them, than the teacher did. All those books. All that digging.

It is late afternoon. I have circled the reservation twice. I am blindingly sad but afraid to explore, to even locate, all the precise causes. That is so me. I have always been so good at this.

A rise comes; I clear it, it flattens out, and there is a boy—no, a young man—standing in the dust and rocks beside the road. He is tall, lanky, and he has a bird. He is not actively hitchhiking but looks instead like he is waiting for a prearranged pickup. *I'll meet you at four, at the corner of nowhere and nowhere else.* I slow the bike down, ease her onto the dirt. Take off my helmet. I see that the bird is a falcon, hooded, talons clamped to a piece of leather around the young man's forearm, which he holds at an angle slightly away from his body, as if it is set in an invisible cast, held by an invisible sling.

I am afraid to look at his face, but I don't have to. Something about the way he stands, slouchy but graceful, entirely comfortable in his skin. And his hands are identical to Darrell's. Once I know, I can look up to see he looks like both our fathers, his and mine. That I did not expect. His eyes did not stay blue, but they are not completely green, either. They are nearly the color of the Flathead River in spring, when the glaciers begin to melt and turn the water turquoise. I wait to see how this is going to feel, and think it will be bad, but it is more a sense of déjà vu, a sense that I am dreaming, or that I am watching myself dream. Here he is. He was born. He survived. He grew up.

My voice, incredibly, works. "Can I give you a ride somewhere?"

He nods once, so slowly it is almost a bow, and mumbles something about "grateful," something about "ma'am."

Even though on the outside I am perfectly calm, on the inside I feel that bird's wings flapping frantically in my chest. I imagine my heart could stop any second now. There is, you know, always the possibility.

So much this time of year is the color of mountain lions. Everything is dry, dry, dry, and grasshoppers appear in great hordes out of nowhere, smacking me in the face and arms and knees. I can sort of feel Slim (which is how he introduced himself, and to which I said, stupidly, "It certainly suits you") trying to duck behind me, but since he is

probably four or five inches taller than I am, I bet it's difficult, especially since he also has to keep track of a bird. He
directs me onto the rez, up a draw, toward the mountains,
but not quite into them. The bottomland unrolls to either
side of us, tall lion-colored grasses bending almost parallel
to the ground in the constant wind.

The house is small and looks as if it has been painted
not so long ago. It is a kind of orangey yellow and reminds
me of the walls in Mexican restaurants in San Francisco,
and the kitchen in Primo's apartment in the Mission, where
I lived only for a short time—nine months or so—but it
seemed like so much longer.

I think about Primo adopting me when I was down to
close to nothing, and who tried cold turkey first, and then
treatment, and then God, and finally drove his newspaper
truck into the ocean at Baker Beach. He was the second one
to go, if my brother was the first. Lu kind of surprised me,
tenacious as she was about living, but still the while trying to
kill herself as indirectly as possible. I heard somewhere that
Max had spent some time on the AIDS ward at General—
Christopher at his side daily—and then made it back into the
world. Cole got a new heart and Eddie finally got infected,
needing to prove he was not immune, but the drugs have
taken, and San Francisco takes care of her own. So some do
make it out alive. Yay for people who can fix other people.
Yay for the retrovirals. Yay for hanging in there.

After about fifteen lost years ending in exactly six
excruciating church-basement meetings, I did finally realize I could save only myself. And as much as it goes
against every reality I have ever created or lived through,

those meetings—that passively but persistently annoying prodding—ultimately did make things about half as hard, more or less. I took Levon Helm's word for it and took what I needed. The rest, I left. He also said (in a song about war) it was wrong to take the best ones. But aren't they the easiest picking somehow? Standing there all bright and shiny and good, waving their stupid hands and calling attention to themselves, like they do. Did. *Pick me. Pick me.* How thoughtless. How fucking ill-advised.

Slim backs off the bike, arm still held aloft, talking softly now to the restless falcon. He doesn't move away right away, and I can tell he is waiting for me to give some indication of what I am going to do. Maybe he thinks my instinct—paleface on the rez—is to say good-bye and go, but for right now, I am pretty much rooted to this spot.

The door opens, and an old man is standing there, too old to mistake for even one fleeting second for someone who would still be decades younger. He has a walking stick in one hand and shades his eyes with the other, even though the sun is behind the house—high still but heading for the horizon.

"Where'd you find this one?" he asks, but it is impossible to tell which one of us he is talking to. Slim tilts his head forward and raises his eyebrows at me. When I don't say anything, he shrugs.

"She was out on the highway, Uncle. West side."

"Does she want to come in? For coffee?"

Slim starts to open his mouth, probably to say, "Hard telling what she wants," but I say, "No, I have to get back home. But thank you for asking."

"Well, then," the old man says, "if you're sure. Thanks for bringing the kid back." He salutes and disappears into the house. I turn the key in the ignition, put my foot on the kick-starter. The kid nods, as if this makes sense, and I stomp down once, but it is not hard enough, and the motor doesn't catch.

"Crap," I say. Then, "I'm sorry."

He cocks his head, just like that bird, narrows his eyes, and pulls his eyebrows together. "Do I know you?"

I say, "I don't think so. Why?"

"I don't know," he says. "Just—I don't know."

"I only got back to town a few months ago," I say.

"From where?"

"California."

"Why'd you come back here?"

"Family stuff."

"Yeah," he says, "I get that." He offers the hand that doesn't have a bird attached, and I reach for it, squeeze, and let go. "Anyway," he says, "thanks for the ride."

I say, "No problem," and give the bike another stomp. This time it starts. Slim backs away, waves, and turns to head for the house. I look past him at the still-open door, but since the sun is directly in my eyes now, I can't see anything behind it—can't see if anyone else is in there, watching me watch my son walk, for the first time.

15. All That Water. All Those Bridges.

M y father dies. Peacefully, as they say, in his sleep. They
also say dying like he did feels like drowning. Right
now I wonder if there is anything that doesn't.

We were never, that I can recall, very close to many of the
neighbors or the folks in town, though we did know some
well enough to call them friends. My mom and dad went
to PTA meetings, gatherings at the grange hall, to dances
sometimes. But we lived a long way out, and it never seemed
to matter that we just had each other to hang around with.
When it comes time to plan a memorial, or a wake, or whatever, then we are sort of at a loss. And by "we," I guess I mean
"I," since my mother wants no part of it.

The second night, after he has been gone for one full
day, she comes outside at midnight to meet me on the
grass. She leans back on her hands, legs stretched straight
out in front of her, face to the sky, hair loose and brushing
the ground behind her.

"What if," she says, "you only ever got to see this once."

"What?" I say, but it is only a reflex. I am not blind.

"All these stars," she says, pretending my question really does require an answer, like I'm sure she did at least a million times when I was a kid. "The doves and the piglets." It has never occurred to me that maybe she was the one who taught a lot of these things to Mick in the first place. Or to me, and I just gave all the credit to Mick. Is that possible, as clearly as I think I remember it all?

"I don't know," I say. "I bet it would kind of blow your mind."

"You'd never stop talking about it," she says. "Not ever."

I close my eyes for a minute and reopen them to watch the sky explode. I do this over and over. Every time it is different. Every time it is the most miraculous thing.

I feel her lie down beside me, and she slides her hand toward mine so just the outer edges of our little fingers are touching. "Thank you for coming home," she says.

I can't believe she's thanking me. Now. I think, *All that water. All those bridges.* "Mom—" I say, quietly, instead of hollering.

She says, "I know, Riley. We were never meant to be perfect. Especially you and me. Maybe we didn't do it right, but we did it."

Whatever it is. I am happy for her. For getting to that place. And I can do this thing: meet her halfway. "Thank goodness we weren't meant to be perfect."

She laughs. It is like seeing the night sky for the first, and only, time.

· · ·

I pull it together long enough to put a notice in the paper saying if anyone wants to drop by the house on Saturday, that would be really nice. We've already had him cremated, so there is no casket or cemetery to deal with. Mom says he would have hated that part anyway; would have preferred instead to be buried in the backyard, or chucked into the river. She was all for either of those options, but for some reason I decided it would be better to leave at least a couple of laws unbroken.

People come, a lot of people. They tell me about times my father helped out, with a calf, a tractor in the ditch, a truck off the road in a blizzard. A few even mention his first wife, delicately, in the context of how lucky he was to have found my mother after the accident. And how fine a young man Mick had been turning out to be. They were sorry, they said after all these years, for our loss. Losses.

Gail comes. She is with her husband, and she keeps staring at me. She looks old and sad. I tell her I'm sorry I didn't write back after the last letter. It was more than I could deal with. I hope she understands. I can see she doesn't, but I can't do anything about that now.

No one stays very long, but they leave enough food to last the two of us at least a month. I fit it all into the fridge and the freezer somehow, and we head outside to drink a beer. Before we go, I find a pack of cigarettes my father had stashed in a cupboard, not really hidden, just out of sight. I put them in my pocket, take them with me. I don't think I want a cigarette; think instead I just want the temptation so I can resist it, so I can congratulate myself for some damn thing.

I was supposed to come back sooner. I have known this, in some not-as-hard-as-I-made-it-to-get-to place, forever. Known that these people, *my* people, were not exactly en cased in amber, waiting for me to come along with my little rock hammer.

I took too long. I barely had time to say hello. Among other things. *I missed you, Dad. I'm sorry I missed you, Dad. But, hey, can you still help me get this boulder off my chest? I don't know who else to ask.*

"Do you think," I say to my mother, "some people are too good for this world?"

"Your father and your brother," she says, as if she is agreeing with me.

"Yes."

"Maybe," she says. "Those two were certainly good enough."

"I lost everything," I say. "Everything of Mick's."

She says, "No, you didn't. Go look."

She is biting her hair. I can feel her body vibrating. She reaches for my hand and squeezes. Then she's gone, like a cat burglar, through an opening in the fence where a gate used to be. I am on my own to see what's left, which is as it should be. Certainly she already knows. I could understand if she was sick and tired of knowing.

I drink her beer after I have finished mine, stare at the house for a while, go on a ghost hunt. It's not hard to find them; they haven't left the premises.

There are still a few boxes in Mick's closet—stuff I didn't take when I left, even though my name is still written on a lot of it. I didn't take it because there was only so much room in the trunk of my car, and I didn't know, really, where I was going, as the West Coast is a very long one. And maybe I knew enough to keep something in reserve. Maybe I at least knew that, but I had forgotten.

I find drawings of animals, birds, the river, the mountains, wildflowers, me. In a small, obviously handmade wooden box is a photo of a young man, maybe eighteen or nineteen, I have never seen before. It is quite old, cracked around the corners and overexposed, a little bit out of focus but still somehow recognizable, as is the shadow of the person who took it. There is a drawing of this boy's face too, and next to it a self-portrait. They are not identical, but there is no mistaking the resemblance.

I make a ring of the drawings, lie on the floor in the middle of it. I reach out and put my hands on every piece of paper I can touch, waiting for one, any one, to touch back. The cool floor holds me there while I follow the cracks in the ceiling to the cobwebs in the corners. I flop my head to one side and look under the bed. Dust bunnies and his other guitar. The classical one. If I tried to tune it, I know it would just piss me off, but I am almost tempted to try. Almost.

In my parents' room it is evident Mom has been sleeping on top of the covers, as there is a slight depression in the comforter on her side, and a blanket kicked down to the bottom of the bed. Medicine bottles and his inhaler still sit on Dad's night table, and a book: *To Kill a Mockingbird*. I pick it up, and the bookmark is one of my school photos, from the second or third grade. He has just gotten to the part where Scout is stumbling through the woods dressed up like a ham. *Had.* He *had* just gotten to the part. I can't read any more of the words, can't make my way through to where it all works out in the end, so I put the picture back, put the book down.

I pull open my mom's slip drawer, from where I used to nick the goods to play dress-up, before the tomboy in me kicked in and took hold. I find a stack of letterss tied up with a shoestring. The two oldest ones are postmarked 1948 and '49, from Fargo. They look like they have never been opened. Others are from Mick: from Missoula, from basic, from Vietnam. I will save those for later, for when there is enough time, space, beer, whatever. A few are from my father, not stamped or addressed; simply, I imagine, handed over or left on the table or her pillow. They say he loves her. Mick. Me. They say clearly this is the life we were meant for, after all was said and done. It was just a matter of getting here. And staying.

One letter is from my father to me. It begins, "Dearest Wanderer." It talks about the animals. About my mother. About rain. It is in an envelope with my name on it, but no address. Another, quite a long one from my mom, mailed to an old address in San Francisco, is marked "Return to Sender" by an unknown hand. I try to think back to where I was then. Figure she missed me by six months or so. Around the middle of the worst years. This one I open to read. She was trying to tell me something. A few some-things. One, she didn't know what M-O-T-H-E-R stood for. I want to tell her she's not alone. But I also want to tell her I think she's wrong. She knew. She just didn't know she did. Two, Mick is my half brother. I don't know where to go to begin to process the actual words, the pronouncement. The thing is, I knew. I don't know what good any more processing would do now. Or ever. Because it doesn't matter.

I wonder why she never sent the letter again after I resurfaced. A change of heart, I suppose. Or she forgot about it. Or maybe it was never really meant for me. I put it back. I wonder if all homes are so full of surprises. I want there to be someone here to ask, Where have I been all your life? But there are letters from me as well, so I was somewhere. I was real.

A stack of postcards from Slim. "Dear Miss Rose," they say, "Thank you for the birthday card. Thank you for the check." The handwriting on the most recent ones is an adult's. I wonder when she stopped. I wonder if.

I look out the window of my parents' room. It faces away from the road to pure, open, absolute nothingness. I think I see my mother in the distance, tacking across what used to be a wheat field, a small one, compared with what surrounds us. But it was enough. I remember her kneading dough; I remember bread straight out of the oven. I decide to make some—tomorrow, maybe—though I have not tried since I lived with the Cajun shape-shifter; tried the patently impossible trick of making him happy, a very, very long time ago on a hill in San Francisco, from where I could almost see the bay.

My room is the same, though the paint around the windows is peeling some, and the fish seem in places to have lost their way. My stuffed rabbit is still on the bed. Both eyes are missing, and still just the one ear. If I didn't know what it was supposed to be, it would take some doing to figure it out. A few remnants of my kid life hang from hooks in the closet: a nearly disintegrated pair of overalls, a red scarf, a beaded belt. Ancient T-shirts lie crumpled on the floor like a pile of sleeping kittens.

Mick's motorcycle jacket hangs from the door handle. I wonder why Mom would put it here, and then I remember: she didn't; I did. Spirited it out of his room just before he went away. He would have taken it, but I had it too well hidden. He knew it was me, but I wasn't giving it up. He left anyway. Without it. I pick it up and press my face to it. It smells old. It smells like Mick. It smells like when I was a little kid, just learning how to cuss, and everything, *everything*, was right with the world. I put it on and go for a ride.

16. The Given World

The school has been shut down now for decades, though I guess sometimes they still use it for stuff like meetings or bake sales, so it doesn't feel completely abandoned. The solstice is two months past, the days noticeably shorter now. It is late afternoon, maybe five, and the sun is a few degrees farther south than it would have been when I came back here. This century is only a few years, now, from becoming a collective memory.

The fence around the playground is still standing in most places, though the equipment is largely useless. I have taken off my boots and Mick's jacket and am dribbling a ball down the court, barely managing to avoid the most gaping craters in the asphalt. The first shots I miss by miles, but I keep getting closer, so I keep trying. Something else I never told Darrell (something far less critical, but still) was that I had played a fair game of basketball in school too, but had given it up for volleyball, a game I could play when I was high on mescaline and could watch the trails crisscross the net like shooting stars.

Darrell is watching me from the other side of the fence, hands grasping the metal bar at the top. We rode here together after I found him parked at the foot of our driveway, leaning against his truck, bouncing this basketball off the hard-packed dirt.

"You are one sneaky Indian," I said, because I couldn't think of one single other thing to say.

He said, "That's redundant," and threw me the ball. "Let's see what you got."

I threw it back. "Okay, let's. Get on." It would be a little while before I could put more words together. I didn't have to ask for time.

What I've got isn't much, but once he comes around the fence to join me, it looks like we're a little more evenly matched than we once were, since his one leg seems to want to buckle if he doesn't plant it just right. He's still almost impenetrable, though, and there's no way I can shoot over him, especially not once he gets those long arms up in the air. All I can do is try to get around him somehow, and to my basket before he has a chance to catch me. Even when I do, I miss most of my shots. And there's no point in even trying to block him. He can shoot pretty much from midcourt, without really looking. But he's getting tired, and the limp is getting worse, so I take the ball, go up to the school, and sit on the steps. He follows, sits by me.

"Come here often?"

Like we're in a bar, and probably a whole lot younger. And totally different people.

"Not too."

We're both winded. We breathe in tandem, empty our lungs slowly.

I ask if he saw the obituary. He says yes, but he was afraid to come all the way in.

"Afraid?"

"Something like that. Nervous, maybe." He shrugs. "Does it matter?"

"Nope."

He says he's sorry about my dad, and I say it's okay, and that I am not any more prepared to process death than I have ever been, so I will be going at it slowly. We can talk about something else. Pretty much anything.

He studies the basketball court for a few minutes, yanks the cuff of his jeans up to pull a burr off his sock. He says, without looking at me, "Slim told me he met a lady on a motorcycle. He thought he might know you. He thought maybe you were one of his teachers when he was little."

"I didn't tell him."

"I know."

I feel a little sick, but I suppose that's to be expected. I can't tell if he's mad at me. I have spent well over half my life thinking he would be mad.

"Do you think—?" It's a dumb question, so I don't finish it.

"Yes," he says. And in case I have any more dumb questions: "I'm not going to do it, Ginger."

"Tell him?"

"Yes. Tell him."

"As soon as—"

"Possible."

Of course I had not thought this through; had thought, if anything, Darrell would tell him, if it came to that, and then we could all just go on and do whatever it was we were going to do, whatever it was.

While I am busy thinking about what I had not thought through, Darrell is busy getting ready to say, "I'm not the one who left."

I almost say, "The hell you weren't," but I don't have to, because he hears me thinking it.

So this is the part where he is angry. As angry as Darrell gets, which isn't very, or maybe it's very, but it doesn't hold. "That was different. And, yes, I should have told you. Do you want to play who should have told who what?"

"No," I say. Because he did not say, "I'm not the one who left *him*."

"Good. I don't either."

"Okay."

He picks up the basketball, does that finger-spin thing with it, palms it back to earth, to the concrete space next to him. I ask what happened to his leg.

Multiple fractures, he says, while he was still in Texas. A bunch of white guys jumped him at a bar. Army guys, from the same base. "One of them stomped my leg with his shitkickers. No one even called the cops or the MPs." He pulls up his pants leg and shows me the scar where the bone came through. I want to touch it, but I don't. He spent six weeks in traction while it healed, which it did just in time to ship out.

"Except they were done shipping us out. They'd stopped the deployment. Just like that."

"They what?"

"They stopped sending guys over there."

"Enlisted guys? Or drafted?"

"Both."

How could I not have known that? Because I had pretty much stopped paying attention, is why. For some years. For some reasons.

"So—"

"I was never going anywhere. Or I wouldn't have been. Or, you know."

Well, I'll be damned. "So none of this—"

"Ginger. Don't." He's saying we can't go back, but that's easy for him—I'm sure he's already done it.

"Didn't you?"

"Oh yeah." He pauses. He drops his head backward and frowns up at the sky. "And you can if you want to, but it won't change anything. It'll just keep you up at night."

I have two choices: believe him, or make myself crazy. Seems so simple. Flip a coin. Pick one.

I ask him if he wants to hear something funny. He brings his chin back down and turns toward me, raises one eyebrow. "Funny weird? Or ha ha funny?"

I say, "The first one, I guess." I say I did end up going to Vietnam, looking for . . . things.

"Your brother?"

"For starters."

"What did you find?"

"Not sure, but something." I look down at my hands,

thinking maybe it will appear there, like whatever the opposite of stigmata is. Are.

"Name it?"

"Not hardly."

"Yeah." He gets it. Me. He still gets me. Like when I was seventeen. I believe this.

But I still have to scout the territory, do some recon. Start at the beginning and creep up, or it will bury me. "Who was I then?"

"Ginger," he says.

"I wasn't really."

"To me you were."

"Exactly."

He nods. Because, again, he knows. This is not something so easily sorted.

Ginger. Cupcake. Punk. Tinker Bell. Cookie. Stolen identities. Or borrowed. Some kept. Maybe all.

"Tell me the rest," I say.

"I thought we were talking about Ginger."

"Not yet. Tell me the rest."

"After Texas?"

"Yes."

They didn't send him to Vietnam, but they held on to him and his bum leg anyway; he still owed them some time. So he went AWOL: came home for a week and then headed, finally, for Alberta. Lived on the rez up there and started back after the amnesty in 1977. Somehow he was included in the all clear.

"Good timing, I guess. Or they just didn't know what the hell they were doing."

"I'm glad." Without planning to, I reach for the braid that still goes halfway down his back. His hair is shot through with a few streaks of silver. I tug on it. Lightly.

"You're a pal," he says. "Thanks."

The years come together, not crashing, more like a folding paper fan I brought back from Saigon and forgot to take with me when Annabelle and the boys didn't have room for me anymore. I am too dumbfounded to even wonder how such a thing could happen, with the years; how it could seem, if only for a moment, as though I have, after all, taken the most practical route (if scenic was a consideration) from point A to point B. It makes no sense.

"When did you find out?"

"About Slim?"

"Yes. That."

"My uncle wrote me in Canada," he says. "And then when I got home, there he was, for real, like magic. You always were a clever girl."

"Not so clever," I say.

He says something about camouflage, something about pain ponies.

"Pain? Or paint?"

"Whatever," he says, smiling, and I don't know why, but also know I don't need to. "Ponies is ponies," he says.

He pulls a loose thread from the hem of his shirt, wraps it tight around his finger. "I didn't go home right away," he says. "Slim was four already, by the time I got there."

What? If he was four, that means at one, two, three, he didn't have his mother *or* father. But here we both are, so how is that even possible? I try to picture him. It's easy. I know just what he looked like. How long his hair was. How he never wanted to wear shoes. I can't imagine a world without him, even though we've hardly met.

"Why?"

"They arrested me at the border for some pain pills a buddy gave me. For my leg. One bottle, but they gave me all the time they could get away with."

"Where did they send you?"

"Leavenworth. Always keep track of your drugs, girl. And you can skip Kansas altogether. It's as flat as they say."

"I'll try to remember that."

I get around—before long is too long—to asking about our son. He tells me Slim has been jumping out of planes about five years now, since he graduated. Smoke jumping. I smell sage, sweetgrass, tinder for the fires that come every other summer, like clockwork.

Now he wants to go to college.

"Away from here," Darrell says.

I wonder if my mother has anything to do with this. Encouraging him to go away, but to something legitimate. Not to war. Not to the coast to try all the different ways of forgetting. My mother, as I have already said, is no dummy, and maybe Slim is her second chance. Maybe he is all our second chances, and maybe, more likely, I am the only one who really needs one, and including a cast of others just makes me feel less like the Lone Ranger after Tonto has had the good sense to ride off into the sunset.

"College," I say. "That's good. That's—"

"Yeah," Darrell says. "It's good. It's great. But he wants to join the Guard to pay for it." He clearly hates the idea. The army. "But I can't tell him what to do. He's not a kid."

I think, but not aloud because I know he won't want to hear it, *It's only weekends, right?* I've seen the commercials. Weekends and a month in the summer. Something like that. It's not like he's *joining up.* Not like he has to go fight real enemies. It's not even like we have those anymore. It's just practice. Killing practice, but no one actually dies.

I think we must all have had enough of war by now, that from now on it will be there—always but only peripherally—like a shadow, to keep us expectant, keep us on our toes. But not real war. Not boys putting on uniforms to go away and not come back. It makes me feel better, to know this.

"Maybe it'll work out, or there'll be some other way."

"Maybe," he says. This time what he does not say is "He's yours too, you know," for which I am grateful, and I imagine it is because he knows I am not planning to fall off the face of the earth again. Like before. Once was enough. I know that. I don't know what I'm going to do, but it won't be that.

He looks at me for, it feels like, the first time. "How have you been?" he says.

I have to smile. "Not bad. Getting by."

"Sure?"

"Sure."

He leans into me, and I have to lean back, hard, or fall over.

"So now what?"

"I don't know. I miss California. The ocean."

"Just the ocean?"

"And a whole gang of dead folks. Some live ones too, though."

"Ghosts," he says.

"All of them?"

"In a way."

"Are you a ghost?"

"I am." His shoulder feels so necessary, next to mine. Like a limb I didn't know I was missing. I don't know which limb, or what kind of necessary, and it's okay. He tells me we need our ghosts; we are *made* of our ghosts.

"I could be starting to figure that out," I say. "I could be starting any day now."

"Don't wait too long," he says.

I say I won't.

Something else to figure out, and soon, is what, on earth, I want. And to know if this trip has been worth . . . all I let slip away. Maybe if I knew the final destination. Or not. Could be that's the whole point of this exercise, to not really *know* much of anything, but to feel it, finally, and to live with that.

We wait, still leaning but not quite so hard, not so much like there's something we're trying to prove.

Eventually he says, "The ocean isn't going anywhere."

I look beyond the sagging fence, the precarious confusion of swings and slides and monkey bars taken finally down by the weather, and the years. I see no hawk, no rabbit, no horse—just that one small mountain range in the distance, still holding its own out there, a reminder that there is such a thing as permanence, or something close to it.

Darrell reaches his long arms out, palms up, toward those mountains. I know what he is doing. He is present-ing to me this landlocked, bone-covered, rock-strewn, river-crossed country—and that ridiculous sky. These are extravagant gifts I really do not deserve. But it is just like him, always trying to give me things I don't deserve.

"What about this?" he says.

"This is good," I say, and stay where I am, for now. I try as hard as I can to concentrate, to see what he is seeing. What is out there. What is left. What is possible. Still. Or again.

ACKNOWLEDGMENTS

This book would never have been realized or even dreamt of without the benevolence of the Creative Writing Program at the University of Wisconsin at Madison. I am eternally and deliriously grateful to my teachers, my cohort, and the ones who wandered in, for generous teaching, reading and thoughtful criticism; for believing in me and for making me believe; and for setting the bar so damn high. Special thanks to Yuko Sakata Burtless, Lydia Conklin, Jesse Lee Kercheval, Judith Mitchell, Chris Mohar, Lorrie Moore, Rob Nixon, Jonis Agee, Meghan O'Gieblyn, Hannah Oberman Breindel, Barrett Swanson, Jacques Rancourt, Josh Kalscheur, Vicente M. López Abad and Seth Abramson.

I am also indebted to the John Steinbeck Center at San Jose State University, Nick Taylor in particular, and to the Elizabeth George Foundation, for generous support while I wrestled these sentences. And to Jon Peede at the *Virginia Quarterly Review*, for invaluable assistance in wrestling a critical mass of them; I learned a lot from you.

Thank you to the Squaw Valley, Napa, and Mendocino writers' conferences for support and community, and especially to Jim Houston, in memory, for his indelible warmth and good heart; to Gary Short for many reasons, but mostly just because; and to Peter Orner, for his generosity of spirit and for the final chapter.

Friends, family and fellow writers who have read this book for me in all its messy iterations, bless and thank you: Constance Palaia, Terese Palaia, Lee Doyle, Al Perrin (in memory), Raoul Biggins, Coco O'Connor, Frances Scott, judy b, Margaret Sofio, Sallie Greene, and Emily Nelson.

Bless and thank you, too, Dick Jones, for giving me Asia (and free rent for life at 1 Nga Kau Wan), but not for leaving us so soon.

For the others we lost before I had a chance to say in just the right words what a huge part of my life you were: Tenley Galbraith, Shery Longest, Pat Ramseyer, Bill Owen, Jeffrey Kirk, and Anthony Holliday, you are dearly missed. And for the ones still kicking (too many to name) at the Wild Side West and Teamsters Local 921, I hope you know who you are. I bet you do.

Finally, a million thanks to my agent, Emma Sweeney, for her many talents and her guidance; to her assistants, Suzanne Rindell and Noah Ballard, for all the not-at-all-little things: and to my editor, Trish Todd, for hawk-eyed and insightful editing, and for taking a chance on an old dog and her tricks.

ABOUT THE AUTHOR

Marian Palaia was born in Riverside, California, and grew up there and in Kensington, Maryland. She spent two of her college undergraduate years on a ranch in Montana and studied creative writing in Missoula with Richard Hugo, Rick DeMarinis, and Barry Hannah. She received her BA from The Evergreen State College, moved to San Francisco in 1985, and received her MA in creative writing from San Francisco State University. In 2001 she moved back to Missoula, where she received her master's in public administration. At the University of Wisconsin—Madison, she studied with Lorrie Moore, Judith Mitchell, Jesse Lee Kercheval, and Rob Nixon, receiving her MFA in 2012. In 2012–2013, she was a John Steinbeck Fellow at San Jose State University. She currently lives in San Francisco, and has lived in, among other places, Hong Kong, Ho Chi Minh City, and Nepal, where she was a Peace Corps volunteer. She has also worked as a bartender, a landscaper, a truck driver, and as the littlest logger in Lincoln, Montana.